THE
WILLARD

THE
WILLARD

LeAnne Burnett Morse

Bluestocking Books

Published by Bluestocking Books. Bluestocking Books is an imprint of Bluestocking Media, LLC.

Library of Congress Control Number 2016901173
ISBN 978-0-99664-15-0-0
ISBN 978-0-9966415-1-7 (ebook)

For Kelly—in this or any other time.
44.

PROLOGUE

In another place and another time he would have been a proper English butler. Like Mr. Carson from *Downton Abbey*, doing things the "right" way because that's what one does. Knowing where the scandal lies and how to keep it under wraps. And always presenting an immaculate façade to the world. Just watching him walk up 14th Street there's an obvious air of the dandy about him. Perfectly coiffed, every seam pressed, and just the right break of the trousers over his freshly polished wingtips. But it's the tilt of his head and the purpose in his stride that makes him look like he belongs. It would be hard to imagine a place in the world where a man with his confident demeanor would be out of place and that's no accident. Even his standing out makes him blend in because no one would think to question his presence.

Not a single person noticed him standing on the sidewalk that day as President Kennedy's funeral procession marched by. How touched he had been when little John had saluted his father. And why would anyone pay attention to another well-dressed white man in the gallery of the Supreme Court during final arguments in the Brown v. Board of Education hearings? Even as crowds had swarmed the White House the night of Andrew Jackson's inauguration, he wasn't noticed as he tried in vain to keep the raucous crowd from tearing off souvenir pieces of the East Room drapes.

But today he doesn't seem to have anywhere pressing to be. At the crosswalk, he waits patiently for the walk sign among tourists in fanny packs and fourth graders in matching t-shirts and their exhausted chaperones. When the light changes, he crosses Pennsylvania Avenue and takes a sharp left along with the touring masses. But he's not going the two blocks to see the most famous house in the world. Under the leaded glass awning, up the granite stairs, and through the brass-laden revolving doors, he walks into an elaborate lobby and crosses with his purposeful stride to an imposing wall of mahogany behind a desk of carved wood and marble. From this vantage point, he has been going about his work diligently all of his adult life. The antique clock above the cubbies tells him he's right on time, naturally. Below the clock in elegant brass letters is one word. One word that sums up his life's work. CONCIERGE. Yes, he belongs here and fits in so well that in a busy lobby no one has seen his entrance. No one notices him settling in behind the massive desk. No one except the elegantly dressed lady with the rolling Louis Vuitton luggage and the slightly travel-worn look about her. Her name is Catherine Parker and she is the reason he has come to work today. He gives her his best smile and sets into motion a series of events that should have happened 151 years ago. Better late than never.

"Good morning," he says to the businesswoman. "Welcome to the Willard."

CHAPTER 1
CATHERINE PARKER

Sixteen dollars plus tip for a cab from the airport to the hotel. It could have been worse, but really it was *ten times* more than the buck sixty she would have spent taking the blue line from Reagan to Metro Center and hoofing it the three blocks to the front door. Normally that's exactly how she would have done it, but *normally* she wouldn't be checking into a hotel of this caliber and frankly, nobody cared how you arrived at the Best Western. But this trip was different and that's why she had sprung for the pricey luggage (secondhand of course, Craigslist) and the designer heels she had regretted by the time she got to her departure gate in Dayton. *Now I understand why office workers wear running shoes with their business suits on the way to work. Who cares how you look on your way somewhere if it keeps the blisters away?*

It's not that she wasn't a fashion-conscious woman. She loved designer clothes and fancy hotels as much as the next girl, but for all the stretching she had done to it, her wallet refused to support more than TJ Maxx and seasonal sales at the mall. This trip could change all that and that's why Catherine Parker was determined she would not set foot in Washington, D.C. without the full benefit of an upgraded wardrobe, fresh highlights, and professionally-tamed brows no matter how painful it was to her bank account. Here she would look the part. *Fake it until you make it.* How many times had she heard that? This time she would try out the old maxim and see if it worked. All she had to do now was get the job, but before she could do that she needed to ditch the luggage and freshen up. She thanked the doorman and casually waved off the bellman who offered to help with her bags. The "LV" bags were part of her carefully crafted new look and, besides, that was just another tip she could keep in her pocket. But for all her attempts at nonchalance, her first steps inside the lobby of the Willard Hotel left her a bit stunned. The expanse of marble and the fine French furniture. The chandeliers hanging from a ceiling that looked like a work of art. And the smell. *Is that lilies? Or is it money?* The Best Western this was not. *Don't act like a bumpkin, Parker. You've checked into hundreds of hotels.* Snapping out of her reverie she strode purposefully across the massive lobby to an ornate concierge desk.

"Good morning. Welcome to the Willard," said the man behind the desk. He was exactly the type of person she expected to find working in a place like this. *They probably recruit them right out of boarding school,* she thought. "Are you checking in, madam?"

"Yes. Catherine Parker. I'm here for one night."

"Excellent, Ms. Parker. Let me see to your reservation."

The concierge quietly typed in a few words and responded in his velvety patrician English. "Everything has been taken care of by the ambassador. There's no need for you to go to the front desk. I have your room key here." He retrieved a small envelope from a wall of cubbies that looked like old-fashioned mail slots. As he reached to hand her the envelope she noticed his nametag. "Edward Chase" it said in deeply engraved brass.

"Your room number is 414 and our staff will be happy to assist you with anything you need during your stay. I understand you have an important meeting this afternoon. I'd be happy to arrange for a car to take you to your appointment."

"Oh, that's really not necessary," said Catherine. "I'm very comfortable with a cab."

"It's no trouble at all, Miss. The ambassador is a very good friend of the hotel and it would be our pleasure to offer you this service. It will give you more time to rest before your meeting. I believe you need to leave at 2 o'clock. Would that be acceptable?"

"That would be fine," she found herself answering. *How does he know I have an appointment and that it's at 2:30?* She chalked it up to the ambassador's office making very detailed arrangements. *I guess this is how business gets done in these rarified circles.* "Yes, that would be excellent. Thank you, Mr. Chase."

"It's my pleasure, Ms. Parker. Michael will see to your bags." Yet another bellman appeared and this time she let the luggage go with him.

No cab equals extra tip money. It's a wash. Oh, for the love of Pete, I can't nickel and dime everything I do if I'm going to fit in with one of the biggest international business firms in D.C. And with that, she turned on her expensive heel and made her way to the elevator, aiming for a bit more confidence with each step.

Once Michael had deposited her bag on the luggage stand and she had rewarded him with a generous tip, Catherine surveyed her surroundings. She had a beautiful cherry bed and a velvet chair and ottoman that practically begged her to sit back with a good book. But it was the view of the National Mall and the Washington Monument that sealed the deal. At that moment she decided she would get the job, no matter the obstacles. This was the world she wanted to live in. Not the extravagance necessarily, but the feeling of being at the center of things and having a purpose. No, she wouldn't let this opportunity slip by. Especially not when it had come in such an unexpected way.

After law school in Cincinnati, Catherine had passed the bar exam and taken a job with a small firm in her hometown of

Dayton, Ohio. She hadn't planned to return to Dayton or even to take the Ohio bar. Her sights were set on digging into cases where she could help people in a big city prosecutor's office, preferably New York. Dayton was too small, too familiar. It was even too "brown." She had always thought the buildings of downtown Dayton looked like they were clad in mud. Catherine wanted the bright lights and soaring glass skyscrapers of New York and the plethora of criminal cases that came along with the city. The altruism bug had bitten her early and helping others had become her mantra. Becoming a doctor was out because she nearly fainted every time at the sight of blood so the law was the next best thing. She would use her brains and ability to argue for a good cause and help put bad guys behind bars. She even toyed with the idea of a future in politics and was itching to get in the game.

Three weeks before her graduation, the call came from Dayton. Her father was in intensive care after a massive heart attack. Though they were never especially close, she raced home to be at his bedside. After four long days, the decision was made to discontinue life support and her father passed away. Then there was the funeral to plan and details to manage. She made it back to school just in time to take her final exams. Years of devotion to her studies paid off and she graduated with her class. Graduation was a celebration for most, but Catherine walked the platform with no family or friends in attendance. They were still grieving in Dayton. That afternoon she packed up the last of her belongings and left the tiny apartment she had shared with two other students. No fanfare, no reminiscing. Her mother was a mess. Her father hadn't done much with the family finances and there was a mortgage to pay, not to mention her own school loans. Her brother lived nearby and had a wife and two kids with another on the way. His wife wasn't shy about telling him that his duty was to her and to the kids.

"Your sister's a big-time lawyer now and doesn't have a husband to deal with, so this is her problem." At least that's how Catherine's aunt had relayed the story to her.

So five boxes, a coffee maker, and a stack of textbooks went into her Honda Accord and she made the one-hour drive to the house on Fisher Lane where she had grown up. One week after the bar exam, she took a job with a small firm in Dayton that handled mostly bankruptcies, divorces, and small property claims. There would be no saving the world here—just trying to save the family home and keep her mother together. And that's what she did, day in and day out for four years until her mother joined her father in Magnolia cemetery and she and her brother split the meager proceeds from the sale of the house.

"You should get a bigger share," said his wife, Amy. "You're the oldest and she's a lawyer. She probably makes a couple hundred thousand a year. Why should she get the same as you?"

"She makes $62,000 a year and she's spent most of it taking care of Mom. Leave it alone, Amy."

It was the one and only recorded appearance of a backbone her brother Chris had ever shown with regard to his wife. The money was split evenly between Catherine and Chris. Amy used Chris's half to put an above-ground pool in their back yard. Catherine used hers to finance a week-long mission trip to help build wells in Africa. She wanted time to think about her future and to do some good at the same time. It was in one of the poorest places on earth that she met one of its richest men, and eventually found herself sitting in a five-star hotel two blocks from the White House.

Robert Tombac wouldn't have thought twice about staying at the Willard. He'd likely stay in the largest suite they had and he wouldn't have turned down the bellman when he came for the bags at the curb. Where he should have looked out of place was in a muddy field in Sierra Leone. Even in this unlikely place and wearing a t-shirt and cargo trousers he looked like he exuded money. But when Catherine first spotted him he was elbow-deep in a ditch securing the last pipe in the run. He bounded up out of the ditch and jogged with a gaggle of shirtless children to the pump handle a few yards away and with a huge smile, he began to work the handle until the water was running fast and clear. After much cheering and dancing, the adults shooed the children away from the pump and began filling their containers. Tombac made his way over to the group that had just arrived, which included Catherine.

"Eight down, two to go! Ready to work?"

He almost seemed to bellow at the new arrivals, but his enthusiasm was contagious. Over the next two weeks, the group worked hand in hand with Tombac and his team and built out the remaining two wells and a bonus well in a nearby village. While they worked, he talked with each of the volunteers and everyone noticed right away that he had a special affinity for Catherine.

"Dirty old man," some twittered out of earshot.

But nothing untoward was happening with Tombac and Catherine. In a couple of days he had learned she was a bright woman with a good heart. She was also a twenty-nine-year-old attorney at a crossroads in her life. She wanted to do something important and felt that getting down in the mud in a third world country was a good way to start. It almost seemed to him that she was doing penance for the fact that she'd been unable to do anything outside of her family circle over the past four years. Robert Tombac had made billions spotting talent and opportunity and when he saw both in one place he knew lightning could strike. When they returned to the States, he contacted Catherine and told her about a chance to do good for others on a global scale and he introduced her to the world of international business law.

Catherine thought she had a pretty good idea of what that meant.

International business law. Sounds like a bunch of overpaid lawyers raping and pillaging the people and resources of the globe. No thanks.

It took a few months but Robert, as he insisted she call him, finally was able to show her the big picture.

"More and more governments around the world are concerned with the impact energy development, manufacturing, and most other types of industry have on the planet as a whole. To combat this, they're enacting laws to control everything from resource management to air pollution to fair wages. The bigger the company, the more they need to put a good face on what they're doing and that means getting ahead of the laws with new technology to show they're not only following the rules but actually developing new ways to go above and beyond them. That means technology, and who is willing to invest in new technology by way of tax incentives and trade agreements? Foreign governments. Therefore, international business law has a hand in how workers, property owners, businesspeople, and the kids down the street from the plant drinking the local water supply benefit or suffer from development." It was a pitch he made to her daily until she started to see the potential.

What's more, one of the largest and most effective (read: prosperous) firms in the country was looking for someone with Catherine's skill and passion. Could he make the introductions for her, he asked? Two days later she was Robert's guest at a reception for the ambassador of a Middle Eastern country known for soliciting western business. He, too, was impressed with Catherine, so much so that he picked up his cell phone on the spot and called one of the partners at Cameron, Hanson and Smith. That was one week ago and this afternoon she would meet with Lawrence Cameron IV and try and convince him that a small-firm lawyer from Dayton with four years of experience and only three court appearances to her credit would be the best possible new associate for their international firm. Word on the street was that nobody at the firm brought in less than $350,000 a year plus perks including international travel and a reported seven figure expense account for wining and dining billionaire investors.

It's not selling out. To have a big impact you have to play with the big boys and this is how they play, she reassured herself.

It was a lot to take in. For the past few days Catherine had tried on and rejected outfit after outfit and styled her hair up, down, straight, and "business wavy." She'd polished her resume and practiced her answers to the most common interview questions including where she saw herself in five years and what "Who Packs Your Parachute?" means to the philosophy of business. She was as ready as she was going to get. She glanced at the clock on the bedside table. It read 12:02 p.m. The crack-of-dawn flight she'd taken had gotten her here with time to spare. Lunch was out of the question because her stomach was a ball of nerves. Maybe the concierge was onto something with his suggestion that she rest before her appointment. *Just a power nap.*

After setting the alarm on the bedside table and two on her iPhone, she wanted one more backup so she called the desk and asked Edward Chase for a wake-up phone call at 12:45 p.m.

"It will be my pleasure, Ms. Parker. Do enjoy your rest," he said.

I believe I will do just that, Mr. Chase, she thought to herself. She took off her heels and suit, hung them on a hook in the bathroom, and wrapped herself in the luxurious hotel robe. She also unpacked the suit she had brought for the interview, still in its dry cleaning plastic. On the lapel she had pinned the one item she owned that wasn't a knock-off or found in the clearance bin, though it was secondhand. Her grandmother's diamond brooch sparkled against the dark blue of her best Ann Taylor suit (45% off last season). Even though the diamonds might be a little flashy for daytime wear, it was very elegant and she felt like her grandmother was with her when she wore it. It was a one-of-a-kind piece her grandfather had had made for her grandmother when their oldest daughter had gotten married. Gramma Aida would know how to handle these bigwigs and Catherine was glad she had brought it. She pulled off the plastic protector and hung the suit in the closet. Then she slipped between the sumptuous sheets and, with one last glance at the Washington Monument through the window, she drifted off to sleep.

She awoke suddenly at 12:43 before any alarms went off. Her room was hazy, like the afternoon sun was playing tricks with shadows, but it was barely after noon. She stood up and crossed the room trying to shake the sleep from her mind.

Midday naps can really be disorienting.

She yawned and started toward the window but stopped in her tracks. She rubbed her eyes and was shocked that at second glance it still appeared the Washington Monument was gone. Well, not gone exactly but only the bottom portion was there. A good two-thirds of it was missing! What had happened over the past forty-one minutes? She hadn't felt an earthquake. Then it hit her. It had to be terrorism. It was 9/11 all over again. Her heart caught in her throat and she pulled back the drapes to see what kind of panic must have ensued below, but what she saw was even more confusing. There was no panic, just the regular slow procession of traffic on Pennsylvania Avenue. Only these weren't cars or SUVs. They were carriages and solitary horses with riders. And when she turned again to look at her room, Catherine knew something was very wrong. Her suitcase was gone and in its place was an antique valise. The furnishings in the room were different, even the doors.

Where is the phone? She couldn't find it and she felt like her head was full of cobwebs.

Boy, I'm having some dream. At least I hope it's a dream.

She located the phone, an ancient-looking contraption, and she lifted the receiver to her ear. After an unfamiliar ringing noise on the line she heard the reassuring sound of Edward Chase's voice come back to her.

"Mr. Chase! What's happening? I woke up and the monument has been destroyed!"

"There is no problem, Ms. Parker. Your carriage will be here to take you to your appointment precisely at 2 o'clock. It's a lovely spring afternoon although I would recommend you bring your wrap. The winds tend to change here without warning," he responded, with no hint of sarcasm. "Is there anything else I can do for you, Ms. Parker?"

Had this man even looked outside in the past hour? Had she slept longer than she thought? Maybe it wasn't even Wednesday anymore. Something wasn't right.

"Yes! What is the date and time that you were given for my appointment?" She was practically screaming at the man by this point.

"You needn't worry about being late, madam. I assure you we have all the right information. The gentleman's office was very specific. It says here two-thirty today, April 12," he calmly told her.

She could hardly believe the next words out of her own mouth.

"April 12 . . . of what year?"

"I beg your pardon, Ms. Parker?"

"What is the *year*, Mr. Chase?" The tension in her voice was mounting.

"Madam, it is 1865 of course. Are you feeling unwell? Would you like me to send up a lady's maid to assist you, Ms. Parker?"

Catherine sank to the bed and noticed the sounds the old springs made.

"No," she answered. "I don't think the maid can help me."

And with that, she started for the closet to see what she could find to wear. There was an answer to what was happening to her, but she wasn't going to find it in this room. Catherine Parker was going out.

CHAPTER 2
THE GRANDE DAME

The Willard Hotel stands at the corner of 14th Street and Pennsylvania Avenue, two blocks from the White House. The grand Beaux-Arts structure has stood sentinel at this corner since 1847 when Henry Willard combined a number of existing hotel structures dating to 1816, expanded them, and put his own name on his creation. From this vantage point, more than 165 of years of history has marched through, and past its front doors.

For decades the Willard family built, tore down, acquired, and repurposed the property, bringing to life the magnificent hotel that exists today. Though it was shuttered for almost twenty years beginning in the late 1960s, the Willard re-emerged as the grande dame of upper class hospitality in 1986.

Legends abound regarding the Willard and while some are documented fact, others are open for debate. One such story has it that President Ulysses S. Grant would walk the two blocks from the White House to the Willard to sit in its expansive lobby and enjoy his evening cigars because his wife didn't like for him to smoke in the White House. When word got out that the president could be found there, people began to converge on the Willard in the evenings to bend his ear about all kinds of plans and schemes for which they hoped to solicit his support. Thus the term "lobbyist" was born. It makes for a good story, but likely isn't true since the word "lobbying" appeared in print more than forty years earlier. While the word may not have originated at the hotel, it *is* true that Grant frequented the Willard to enjoy his cigars and brandy and some visitors today claim they can still smell his cigar smoke. Stories like these have given the Willard the kind of insider status other hotels can't claim.

It is absolutely true that Abraham Lincoln stayed at the Willard when he arrived in Washington before his inauguration. He stayed there on the advice of security chief Alan Pinkerton, who feared for his safety with threats of continued secession and war abounding. Pinkerton sneaked Lincoln into the hotel in the early morning hours, frustrating thousands of people who had gathered at the train station to catch a glimpse of the man from the frontier. After a nine-day stay, newly inaugurated President Lincoln paid his $773.75 bill with his first chief executive paycheck. It's no wonder the hotel came to be known as the "Residence of the Presidents."

This period of history is rife with Willard importance. Shortly before the inauguration, delegates from both North and South gathered in Willard's Hall to form the Peace Commission. There they undertook the task, unsuccessfully, of trying to find a way to keep the Union from fracturing.

From her room at the Willard, Julia Ward Howe wrote the stirring lyrics to "The Battle Hymn of the Republic" and Martin Luther King, Jr. finished his "I Have A Dream" speech here before the March on Washington.

Mark Twain wrote not one, but two of his famous stories while staying at the Willard. It is said that he liked to enter Peacock Alley from the back stairs and saunter down the lane drawing as much attention to himself as possible. Other famous guests included P.T. Barnum, Buffalo Bill Cody, and a long list of presidents and politicians. In fact, some regarded the Willard as both the social and political center of the city. It was such a popular place that, despite space limits, the proprietors packed in more than 1,500 guests on occasion during its pre-Civil War heyday. This meant strangers weren't just sharing rooms, but also the beds themselves. But not every patron could be paired with just anyone.

Before the outbreak of the Civil War, the Willard went to great lengths to accommodate those of both Northern and Southern loyalties. Northerners entered through the F Street entrance on the north side of the hotel; Southerners made their entry on the Pennsylvania Avenue side, the south entrance. They were assigned to different floors in an effort to keep the peace.

From the marble, crystal, and mahogany of the ornate lobby, to the intimate alcoves of Peacock Alley, the Willard Hotel is a Washington character all by itself. It seems to breathe stories and at the same time attract the kind of modern traveler who enjoys a grand, almost European experience.

Since the first night a hotel bed was sold on this corner of real estate, things of importance have happened in connection with the Willard. There's something almost mythical about the place. Edward Chase knows the feeling well; he was here before Henry Willard acquired the property and turned it into the place to see and to be seen. Sometimes he misses the days of the presidents leisurely strolling over to enjoy a glass of brandy, but the Secret Service would never allow that now. He doesn't miss the days of packing in the people three-to-a-bed, though. His sensibilities are much too refined for that. No, the modern Willard is a place he is proud of. If only he wasn't so busy taking care of details. Perhaps one day he won't have to spend his days looking back.

CHAPTER 3
TOM KELLY

"Honestly, if this traffic jam is caused by another motorcade I'm going to start thinking there's a conspiracy with the oil companies to ensure more fuel consumption. I don't know how you tolerate this traffic," remarked the frustrated passenger in Baahir Anand's taxi.

Tom Kelly wasn't usually so impatient but he had landed at Dulles after a whirlwind eight-day business trip that had taken him from Los Angeles to London, to Geneva, to Abu Dhabi and now here to Washington. He wasn't even sure what time zone he was in or what day it was. On top of that, his production coordinator, Lily, had booked him into Dulles instead of Reagan so he had just endured an hour and a half of stop and go traffic on top of the delay he had in Boston for his layover on the flight back. Now the sun was going down and all Kelly could think about was a hot shower and a warm bed. At least he'd be staying in style in Washington. This part of the trip was all about the investors. It's the part of independent filmmaking he dislikes the most but after seeing the extraordinary locations he wants to use for shooting over the past eight days he's willing to grip and grin if it gets the money in the bank. The photos he took, especially in Abu Dhabi, should definitely seal the deal. And he needs this deal.

At forty-two, Tom Kelly has long since given up the dream of being one of those producers who makes it rain. He's not Jerry Bruckheimer or Brian Grazer or any of the big names who can get a studio to green light a project over the phone. At thirty, he thought he was on his way. By thirty-five, he thought he'd missed the boat entirely. At thirty-eight, he made his first indie film, *By Way of War*, and it made him the toast of Sundance that year. He rode that wave to Hollywood and the hype lasted all of three weeks. Sure, the critics loved it and so did the audiences in Park City, but with no big names in the credits he couldn't get wide distribution. Still, it got decent play in arthouse theatres and in limited release in large markets and he made enough money to try again. The second time around he knew a big name would help get him onto more screens so he bet the farm on a deal with one of the industry's hottest properties. The actor was young, universally referred to as "hot" by women, and reasonably talented. He had more magazine covers and Twitter followers than pretty much anyone else and his appeal was extremely wide. The audience's appetite for him was insatiable. As it turned out, his appetite for underage girls and heroin was equally insatiable. When word reached Tom Kelly that his star was not only in rehab but also planning to avoid charges by "concentrating on his recovery out of the country for the next year," Kelly frantically searched his contract for the one thing that had been left out by his cut-rate lawyer: a morals clause. The star was gone, the money was gone, and Kelly decided his career had gone with them.

That was until one day while visiting friends in North Carolina when he met three men on a deep sea fishing trip off the Outer Banks. They caught few fish that day but the three guys knew they had an even bigger catch—someone who could tell their story. They were retired military guys and each was still wearing the high and tight cut well into his 60s. Vietnam had been the war of their youth but they were career men who had spent time commanding troops in the sandbox during Desert Storm as well. Their trip from the jungle to the desert was the kind of thing little boys dream of when they play with little green army men.   Scott Langdon and Marcus Green had been members of the Army's elite Delta Force, and Joe Chamberlain was one of the Navy's fabled SEALs. Chamberlain, "Salt," as his buddies called him, was the reason they were on the fishing trip that day. Apparently a golf wager had gone his way and saved him from having to attend a University of Tennessee home football game with both Delta men who were diehard fans. Since Neyland Stadium is no place for a Georgia Bulldog, he had insisted they spend a day on the water instead. He was secretly hoping the two of them might get a little seasick along the way. That would have been a bonus for the Navy man.

Instead, the bonus that day was meeting Tom Kelly. Chamberlain had spotted him right away—green around the gills and not very handy with the equipment. He could always tell when there were newbies on a boat. Kelly had listened intently to all the instructions but once the boat started rocking on the swells he seemed to be less interested in fishing and more interested in hanging on to the rail. Chamberlain struck up a conversation with him to try and get his mind off his stomach. That's how Tom Kelly, the struggling movie producer, and Joe Chamberlain, the former Navy SEAL, came to know one another. Six hours later and back on dry land, Kelly and his three new friends sat around a battered pub table at one of the ubiquitous seafood shacks that line the coast of OBX, as the locals call the Outer Banks. Kelly was feeling much better on his land legs and was enjoying the tales they were telling about their military exploits. He took everything they said with a grain of salt, especially the later it got and the longer the beer flowed. As it turned out, they weren't spinning yarns. All three men had joined the military as grunts, not one of them ROTC or "college boys," as they called them. And none were drafted either. That was a point of pride among them. All went willingly to the jungle, swore they'd get their asses of out the military if they were blessed enough to get said asses safely out of Vietnam, then found that when the time came to hang it up what they really wanted was to go deeper in. And these weren't just war stories. These men had families and knew the heartache of leaving a wife and children behind, sometimes for more than a year at a time, and not knowing if they'd ever see them again. They had lost buddies on the battlefield and in training, and they'd lost parents and friends back home when they were deployed and couldn't be there to offer comfort in the last days or say a proper bedside goodbye. Two knew the pain of divorce and one the extreme agony of burying not just a wife, but a child as well. A child who had followed his father into the service and paid with his life in a dusty desert halfway across the world. The more they talked, the more Kelly realized he was picturing their stories vividly in his mind's eye. He knew he could transfer those images to the screen and that, big names or not, this movie would find its audience. He had some experience working with military topics in his only success thus far, *By Way of War*. He decided this story, these men, would be his last run at the golden ring. Before they parted company that night, plans were being made to put something on paper and see if they could find investors to pay for it. Chamberlain, Langdon and Green were as good as their word and they brought some heavy hitters to the plate with excellent military contacts and decently deep pockets. That was fourteen months ago and Kelly had lived and breathed this project non-stop since then. He had a strong script and some solid, if little-known, talent loosely attached to the project. All he needed now was one or two more benefactors willing to pony up $500,000 each and production could get underway.

Kelly had come to Washington for a meeting that was arranged by Langdon with two potential investors who had all but said they wanted to be part of the film if they felt Kelly could deliver what he promised. They were stalwart D.C. types and skeptical of what they viewed as the liberal Hollywood crowd. This wasn't going to be some "apologize for America's strength" film, not if their money was involved. Kelly knew he had to reassure them he was onboard with his three veterans and that he intended to tell their story in such a way that both the Army and the Navy would likely see a spike in enlistments after its release. This was an American story at heart and he didn't have any intention of saying otherwise.

Anand finally pulled his taxi to the curb beside the leaded-glass entry to the Willard. *Definitely nicer digs than in Abu Dhabi*, thought Kelly. Lily chose the hotel in an effort to impress the investors with traditional good taste minus any "Hollywood-like" flash. Kelly guessed upon entering the lobby that Lily had chosen well. The bellman retrieved his luggage from the cab and pointed him to the front desk, which was actually in the far corner of the lobby. Before he could get there a distinguished looking gentleman in a well-cut suit stopped him.

"Mr. Kelly?" the man inquired.

"Yes, I'm Tom Kelly."

"I've been expecting you, Mr. Kelly. It is my pleasure to welcome you to the Willard. I'm Edward Chase, your concierge. I spoke with your charming assistant and your registration has been taken care of. I understand you've had a long journey and I'm sure you are looking forward to a relaxing evening."

"I haven't had service like this where I've been these last few days. Thank you, Mr. Chase." Kelly made a mental note to e-mail Lily and thank her for arranging a quick check-in.

"This is your room key. I'll send your bellman right up with your bags. You'll be in suite 1022. I've arranged lunch for you and your guests tomorrow at the Occidental Grill next to the hotel at noon. Is there anything else you require this evening?"

"I believe you've covered it."

"Very well, sir." Chase summoned the elevator and reached inside to press "10" when Kelly entered. "If there is anything else I can do for you please don't hesitate to call," said Chase.

I wonder if he'll come to my room and put a mint on my pillow? "Thank you Mr. Chase. I think a shower and bed is everything I need tonight."

"Have a very pleasant rest. Good evening, sir," Chase responded and stepped out of the way of the elevator door.

Kelly made his way to the suite Lily had reserved. *A suite? I understand showing off a little for the moneybags but a suite might be going a little too far. I'll never get this film made if I spend all my money on suites.*

It shouldn't have been a surprise to find his bed had been turned down and there was a chocolate on his pillow.

It's not a mint, but I suppose it'll do, Kelly mumbled. *I guess a suite isn't that extravagant just this once. I've been flying coach for thousands of miles. And that bathtub looks like it could probably work out the kinks those airline seats put into my back somewhere over the Atlantic.*

After his bags were delivered, Kelly filled up the bathtub and tossed in some of the complimentary salts that indicated by their very proper label that they were designed for "relaxation and rejuvenation." He wasn't normally a bath kind of guy but . . . when in Rome. When the tub was full and frothy with relaxing and rejuvenating lavender scents he stepped in and sank down until his chin was touching the surface of the water. Immediately his mind went to the meeting scheduled for noon the next day and he began rehearsing his pitch to make sure he hit all the right notes as Langdon had instructed him. He also wanted to share some of the photos he'd taken on his scouting trip over the past few days. He knew that once the investors could see the physical locations for themselves they could get the vision. He was still running through how he would answer any questions they might pose and he even started imagining what he could do with an extra $100,000 on top of what he planned to ask for. Everything about tomorrow's meeting was feeling good to him. He knew it had the potential to salvage or sink his career and everything had to go well. He didn't taste the delicious chocolate that had been left for him because before Tom Kelly could try out his sumptuous bed, he drifted off to sleep in a lavender-scented bath.

He had no idea what time it was when he awoke but the water was no longer warm. In fact, he was freezing. Standing up he reached for the robe on the back of the bathroom door. His prune-like skin reminded him of when he was a little boy and liked to see how wrinkly he could get in the pool. He was anticipating hitting the sack (could you call a Queen Anne style, four poster bed with six pillows a "sack?"), but before he could finish drying off he heard the phone ringing beside the bed. As he crossed the room to answer it he noticed the early morning light coming in through the window. *Had he slept all night in the bathtub?*

"Hello?"

"Where are you?   I've been calling you for an hour!" yelled the voice on the other end of the line.

"Who is this?"

"Are you hungover or still asleep? You have to be the only person in Washington, if not the whole country sleeping!" the voice continued to yell.

"Look pal, I think you've got the wrong room," Kelly responded.

"Front desk says this is Tom Kelly's room so I'm going out on a limb that you're Tom Kelly, right? You weren't invited here for a vacation. I wanted you here last night when your plane got in but the boss said you needed your beauty sleep. Well, you'd better be good and beautiful because you've gotta get over here right now and I don't know when you'll sleep again. Hell, I don't know when any of us will sleep again. Most of us have been manning the phones since the announcement last night. Just throw on something nearly respectable and get over here."

"Where is 'here'?'"

"They kicked us out of the Oval for the president to take a call. Meet me in the Cabinet room. The guards are expecting you. You've got twenty minutes and if you're not here you can explain to the attorney general why a possible nuclear war isn't important enough for you to get out of bed!" Kelly heard the phone slam down.

"What the hell?"

As he was asking this question out loud he heard a sound at his door and saw that a newspaper had been slipped under it. He picked up the morning's "Washington Post" and saw a picture of President Kennedy.

"Kennedy Orders Blockade of Cuba As Reds Build Nuclear Bases There; U.S. Will Sink Defiant Arms Ships" read the bold headline.

Why had someone slipped a fifty-year-old newspaper under his door?

Just then the phone on the table rang again. For the first time, Kelly noticed it was a rotary phone. He hadn't seen one of those in ages. He picked it up.

"Mr. Kelly, this is Edward Chase from the concierge desk. I understand you have an important meeting today."

"Yes, I have a meeting at noon with some important men and something strange seems to be happening. I just—"

Chase cut him off before he could continue. "Mr. Kelly, your meeting is quite important, yes sir. But it's not at noon. The attorney general's office has been calling for you since 4 a.m. Since the president's address to the nation last night, the panic level has risen and you are needed right away. I have a car waiting to take you to the West Wing entrance. Please hurry down sir. I'm told the president is waiting to see you."

Without another word Tom Kelly dressed in the black suit that was only slightly wrinkled in his suitcase. The tie that was with it wasn't his style but Lily had chosen it and it was still in the bag from the store. He hadn't even looked at it before but now he thought it looked vaguely retro.

I don't know what these guys are up to. Maybe it's another one of their friendly wagers. I knew they had contacts high up in the government but if they've gotten me in to the White House this morning I'll be really impressed. A VIP tour, maybe? Something to do with their Vietnam days, since they're going all out with this Kennedy thing?

Whatever it was, Tom Kelly was sure it was a practical joke and he was willing to go along if it moved the project down the road. Yes, he was sure it was a practical joke, right up until he stepped outside to meet the hotel's car that would take him to the White House. The Willard only used the newest and best of course.

The car was a 1962 Cadillac Sedan de Ville.

CHAPTER 4
CALVIN WALKER

"I double-pinkie promise I'll bring you a Redskins jersey, pal."

"Not just any number, Dad. It has to be number ten and it has to have his name on the back," instructed eight-year-old Will Walker.

"Number ten, 'Griffin III' on the back. Check," assured his exhausted father. Calvin Walker never missed a night telling his kids goodnight, but he couldn't help eyeing the pile of work on the desk and wondering when he'd be able to get some shut-eye himself. "Here comes your goodnight kiss, ready?"

"Ready!"

Calvin made an exaggerated "mmmwwwwaahhh" sound with a proper lip smack at the end and sent the kiss flying through space to his home in Chattanooga, Tennessee. Little Will received it with a grunt.

"That one nearly knocked me over!"

"That's great. Now kiss your mother and hit those sheets, bud."

"Night, Dad. Love you."

"Love you too, pal." Calvin waited until he heard the click of the phone. He had already said goodnight to his wife and his two daughters. Will always insisted he had to be the last one to talk to Dad whenever he was traveling. His older sisters teased him about it but he didn't care. It was their thing and if

Dad had to travel, and he often did, this was just how it had to be done.

Calvin Walker didn't relish the time he spent away from home but it was the price of the success he had achieved with his company, Diagnosis Digital. "DD," as he called it, had started as a simple software program back when guys with names like Gates and Jobs had just started to make a name for themselves and the field was still wide open. While he hadn't built a Microsoft or an Apple in his garage, he had developed a program that could be found in virtually every doctor's office and hospital in the country. Over the next twenty years, Diagnosis Digital would create software, hardware, and integrated strategies for medical practices that could give a one or two-doctor office the tools that were normally out of reach because of cost. DD had helped level the playing field and the newest offering on the table was designed to help small offices manage the extensive red tape and paperwork related to insurance. Walker was in Washington for a conference at George Washington University to get the word out to the medical community and he had spent the past four days pressing the flesh and demonstrating his product. He had made a good impression, as always, and now he could turn it over to his sales team. It had been a productive week so far.

Before he could go home he had to tie up some loose ends with regard to a new product the company had in development. For some reason there were issues with the patent application and he and his attorney planned to meet with a representative at the U.S. Patent Office the following day. His engineers had been sending him e-mails with reams of proprietary data and he had to familiarize himself with the case they needed to make. It was the kind of reading that could be counted on to cross a few eyes, and Walker was already worn out, but coffee was out of the question. He knew he wouldn't settle down for hours if he succumbed to the coffee crutch.

Just an hour on the summary page Dan sent this afternoon and I should be good to go. Two, tops. Still in bed at a decent hour.

Three hours later Walker was craving coffee more than ever, but it was after midnight and way too late now for a pick-me-up. He jotted a few notes and settled back in the chair by the bed to knock out the last few pages. The last thing he read was a mind-numbing technical explanation of an online database management component.

The sound of a siren at seven-thirty in the morning jolted Walker from his sleep and he jumped up from the chair only to quickly realize his back hadn't fared well during the night. Sleeping in a chair all night is for college students cramming for finals. Forty-seven-year-old men are better off sticking to high-quality mattresses.

Fortunately, he wasn't late. After a hot shower he dressed in his last clean suit, packed his briefcase, and headed for the elevator. He planned to stop in the hotel's café downstairs and pick up some chocolate biscotti he had discovered the morning after he arrived at the Willard. And, finally, he could have that cup of coffee he'd been wanting all night.

He stepped out of room number 828 and started down the hall. There was a man in a dark suit already waiting for the elevator. He was reading the morning paper and a section of it fell out and fluttered to the floor, separating some of the pages when it landed. Calvin instinctively reached down to assist in putting it back together. He picked up a couple of pages and the man who had dropped it reached for the others. Calvin stood and folded his pages neatly and waited for the man to stand so he could hand them over. As the man stood Calvin heard a deep, resonant voice say "thank you."

He was about to answer that it was his pleasure to help but he was struck speechless when he got a look at the man's face. For the life of him he couldn't explain how it was happening, but Calvin Walker knew with absolute certainty he was staring into the face of Dr. Martin Luther King, Jr.

CHAPTER 5
OLIVIA FORDHAM

The limo pulled up to the end of the carpet that led to the Willard's revolving door. By the time the bellman reached for the car door, Edward Chase was striding down the carpet to meet the guest. The woman stepped out of the car with the regal air of a queen. She was dressed exquisitely in a designer dress and jacket of lavender silk and she carried a Hermes Kelly bag on her arm. She had never gone for the illustrious Birkin that all the celebrities in Hollywood toted around. It was too big for her taste and she found it unbecoming that so many women carried it because they thought it conveyed status. The Kelly was smaller and classic and she was nothing if not a classic lady. She came to Washington often for her business and had only sold her townhouse in Georgetown a few years before. She loved the house and had wonderful memories there but at her age the stairs were getting to be too much. She could have put in an elevator like some of her neighbors had done but the thought of doing that to the venerable structure went against her notions of historic preservation. *This old beauty has aged gracefully, like I hope to do,* she thought. She sold the house to a young family who would love it as much as she and her husband had. Since the sale, she had made the Willard Hotel her home in Washington whenever she was in town. Edward Chase always took excellent care of her and she looked forward to the time she spent there.

Chase reached to shake her hand as she exited the car and, as usual, she bypassed his outstretched hand and enveloped him in a warm hug.

"Hello, Edward."

"Welcome to the Willard, Mrs. Fordham."

"Edward, are we doing this again?" she sounded stern but smiled when she spoke.

"Welcome to the Willard, *Olivia*," he said. "You know I don't feel right calling you that."

He offered her his arm and they walked to the door.

"That's because you have excellent breeding, my dear Edward, but I insist. We're a couple of old birds in this town and if old birds can't call each other by their given names then who can?"

It was fine to talk about old birds but Chase knew even the President of the United States had not been asked to call her by her given name. "Because he's a Democrat, darling Edward," she had once told him with a smile. "And I refuse to give a *Democrat* the satisfaction!"

Olivia Fordham was a legend in Washington and in New York where she lived full time. Her late husband had been one of the country's richest men, having made his fortune in the 1950s in land development. A decade before, he had bought up thousands of acres in Texas, Oklahoma, Illinois, and New York. After the war he started selling them off one at a time, each with an affordable home on top where returning GIs could raise a family. He developed hundreds of planned subdivisions and bought more land with the money. It was making him a rich man, but it was nothing compared to the windfall when large portions of his Texas and Oklahoma land were found to be sitting on top of generous oil reserves. Eventually he dabbled in mutual funds and his keen business sense served him well in all his endeavors. He'd had a hand in dozens of businesses by the time he met Olivia Asher in 1964. She was a brilliant coed with plans to become a lawyer. He saw her for the first time walking down Fifth Avenue in New York. She had long, raven hair that shone in the midday sun, and she walked with an air of confidence about her. Their two-year courtship was a struggle because she believed marrying him would mean giving up her own dreams. He finally convinced her they could dream together and they married in 1966. He was forty-seven. She was twenty-four.

Before long, it became apparent to both Robert and Olivia that she had a head for business and instead of practicing law she eventually became his most trusted executive. She bought new businesses and grew them all over the world. They bought the house in Georgetown in 1970 and kept Robert's Park Avenue apartment where she still lived. For thirty-two years they were happy, even though they had no children, a disappointment to both of them. Their fairy tale came to an end when Robert died suddenly in 1998. Olivia had been a youthful woman of fifty-six when she became a widow, but the idea of marrying again was a nonstarter. Within a year she had turned the day-to-day operation of their global business over to a trusted CEO and opened the Robert L. Fordham Institute, which was devoted to charitable causes around the world. The institute had become her passion and while she had gentlemen callers, as she referred to them, she took her role as Mrs. Robert Fordham very seriously and let nothing interfere with the work they both held dear. Robert had always talked of spending his last years giving away a great deal of the money he had made. Olivia was committed to seeing that happen.

The staff was handling her luggage as they always did as she and Chase proceeded to her accommodations. Olivia was a frequent and very high-profile guest of the hotel and her billing was always handled between her assistant and the front desk. Only a few steps from the elevator, Chase stopped with her outside the double doors to her usual suite.

"It's so wonderful to have you back with us, Olivia. Please do call upon me if there is anything at all that I can do for you," he said as he opened the door and held it for her to walk through.

"It's so good to be back, Edward. It feels like home," Olivia said as she took the key from him. There was no exchange of tip at that point. Olivia was extremely generous with all the staff who served her at the hotel and she quietly arranged for their gratuity when she checked out each time. It was a pet peeve of hers to see people in service treated like servants and she felt that passing a few dollars from hand to hand was demeaning. Her way was better, she was sure of it. And the staff seemed to love it. They were all happy to see her in the hotel.

Edward let himself out of the grand suite and walked to the elevator. Without a doubt he was always glad to see Mrs. Fordham, but he couldn't shake the guilty feeling in the pit of his stomach. He knew something she didn't, that this trip would be different than the others. But it had to be her. He had wrestled with the decision and determined it simply had to be her. She could do the job. And she, maybe more than anyone, would appreciate the opportunity, once it was all over of course. Sometimes he really disliked his job. Edward stepped into the elevator still telling himself she would appreciate the opportunity.

It wasn't home but it had really grown on her over the past few years. Olivia always stayed in the Jefferson Suite when she was at the Willard. It was easy to forget one was in a hotel in this suite. It was really more like an apartment and much bigger than many New York apartments she had seen. From the double door entrance she stepped across the black and white checked marble floor of the sunlight-flooded foyer to the hall table where she laid her purse and checked her makeup in the mirror. *You could use a touch-up old girl,* she said to herself. A lovely powder room was behind her in the foyer but she didn't go in. It would be used by her guests during her stay. Taking a right off the foyer brought her to the bedroom with its cherry bed and separate sitting area. The wall of windows faced out onto Pennsylvania Avenue, the National Mall, and the Washington Monument. The bedroom had an elegantly appointed bath and dressing room and she knew the staff would have her things expertly arranged shortly. Crossing back though the foyer she entered the first parlor. This was the room she would use the most. It had ample seating, all in reproductions of furnishings found in the White House in shades of red and gold, and a flat screen television centered on a wall of built-in cabinetry. There was also a desk conveniently placed near the windows with the same view as the bedroom. Further into the suite was the second parlor, this one slightly smaller and more formal. She would host her highest profile guests here for tea as it was nearest to the dining room. A second marble-floored area led to the exquisite oval dining room, which faced 14th street at an angle that allowed for a view all the way to the Capitol. The room seated 8–10 for dinner in total elegance. Beyond the dining room was a butler's pantry with a separate entrance and a second bedroom that could be included if needed. All in all, it was more than 3,000 square feet of supreme luxury and the staff's impeccable service made it even more special because anything Olivia or her guests could possibly need was only a phone call away.

The bellman and two maids arrived to unpack her things. They were familiar to her as they normally worked exclusively for Mrs. Fordham when she was in residence. She asked them about their families and told them how happy she was to see them before taking some papers from her bag and sitting down at the desk in the first parlor.

She had several invitations that were awaiting responses. In her youth, Olivia had loved to attend parties. Now it was more of a chore with her beloved Robert gone. He had kept her entertained by whispering in her ear all the juicy gossip surrounding the biggest names in business and government as they endured the long evenings. He had told her who had skeletons in the closet, who was sleeping with whom, and who was just plain in the closet altogether. He had a gift for finding the humor in every situation and she missed having him with her. But the parties were important to her work. All were benefits for causes she supported. Only rarely did she attend a party that didn't have a cause attached to it. While she was in town for the week she would attend four galas where she would be presenting checks totaling nearly thirty million dollars. But that wasn't the main reason she had come. Beginning first thing in the morning she would host representatives of the Smithsonian Institute and diplomats from around the world here in her suite to put the final touches on the ceremony planned for the end of the week. At the event, an announcement would be made that the Robert L. Fordham Institute would be making a donation of $500 million to open a new museum under the auspices of the Smithsonian. The Fordham Museum of Philanthropy would be a combination exhibition and working center for charitable giving. It would showcase not only the work of large-scale philanthropists like the Fordhams, the Astors and the Gateses, but also the impact of grassroots fundraising and charity by everyone from children to church groups to corporations. Olivia dreamed it would stand as a beacon to the importance of voluntary giving with a global reach.

She finished her RSVPs and handed them off to a hotel courier to be hand delivered. The staff had finished unpacking her belongings and one of her regular maids had left a silk dressing gown on the bed for her. She knew Mrs. Fordham liked to relax when she arrived. Olivia changed clothes and hung her lavender suit in the closet. On cue, room service delivered her afternoon tea and she settled onto the sofa with a cup of Earl Grey and her datebook. She had a leather appointment book, also Hermes, that had been a gift from Robert years before. She carried it everywhere with her even though she used a smartphone for everything else. Her appointments, like her thank you notes, were handwritten. She liked paging through to see where she was going and where she had been. She checked the date, March 1. She had a great deal to do before the event on the fifth. In years past, she would have booked appointments for the afternoon of her arrival but at age seventy-one she simply didn't have the stamina for it. She finished her tea and went to the bedroom for the afternoon power nap that had become a regular habit for her the year before. She found that it gave her the energy she would need for the long evenings of charity events and it helped keep her mind sharp.

As she drew the drapes she thought for the millionth time what a beautiful view the room had. She never tired of looking at it. Olivia approached her naps as temporary stops so she never turned down the linens. She reclined on top of the white duvet and pulled the throw blanket over her. She let her mind wander over the details she still needed to arrange, but before long sleep claimed her as it did every afternoon, no matter how busy she was.

When she awoke half an hour later she didn't feel as refreshed as she would have liked. Traveling was beginning to take more of a toll on her, but she wouldn't allow herself the indulgence of any more time in bed.

She got up and went back to the windows to open the drapes. As she reached for the pull cord she heard a loud noise that was so out of place it startled her. It reminded her of the sound of old car horns from the early 1900s. *Ahruuuuuuga!* That thought had just crossed her mind when she pulled back the blackout drape and looked down onto Pennsylvania Avenue. The honking continued as a traffic jam had developed at the corner of 14th Street. Traffic jams in Washington were as common as lobbyists, but Olivia Fordham had never seen one made up entirely of Model Ts.

CHAPTER 6
CATHERINE PARKER
1865

The carriage Mr. Chase had arranged for Catherine didn't take her to the offices of an international business law firm. It was apparent right away that the only business that seemed to matter in this town was the kind that got worked out on the battlefield. Soldiers were everywhere in their blue wool uniforms. As they marched she could see the weariness in their steps. The carriage stopped in front of a lovely three-story townhouse and the driver helped her down.

"Whose house is this?"

"I'm sorry, ma'am, I don't know the answer to your question. I was given this address and told to drop you off here." He held out a piece of paper and when she saw the address written on it she was confused. It was the address of the law firm she was supposed to visit. She had researched the firm well and had seen photos of their posh, modern offices with stunning views of the Capitol. Looking toward the Capitol she could tell it was the same basic view, but this was no office building. She told the driver to wait and walked to the front door. Reaching up, she knocked loudly with the brass doorknocker that was shaped like a lion with a giant ring in his mouth. When no one answered she started to turn back toward the driver and that's when she saw it. There was a name on a placard beside the door.

Lawrence Cameron, read the name. Catherine's head swam as she tried to make sense of that name, at that address, and the realization that she was supposed to meet with Lawrence Cameron IV at that very same address this morning before the whole world had gone topsy-turvy. The carriage driver looked concerned as his passenger walked slowly out of the gate with a glazed look on her face.

"Miss, would you like to go back to the hotel?"

Catherine didn't answer. She turned without a word and began walking down the street, leaving the driver to wonder if the young lady had seen a ghost.

The rutted streets made for a difficult crossing. As if it hadn't been hard enough maneuvering into the old-fashioned clothes and fastening the tiny buttons on the shoes that were in the closet of her hotel room, now Catherine had to dodge the tripping hazards of the dirt roads while trying to keep her skirt out of the muddy pits that seemed to be everywhere. It was too much for her mind to take in to figure out how all this was happening. One thing she had been sure of right away: the corset hanging in the closet wasn't going to get any use if she had her way.

After reading the name on the house she had taken off walking aimlessly. She'd been walking for some time and just taking in what she saw. She walked to the White House and was surprised at how small it looked without the east and west wing additions. Even more shocking was the casual way people came and went from the mansion with no discernible security to stop them. She got a closer look at the Washington Monument and found that her eyes had not deceived her when she had looked out her hotel window. It was short and stubby and there were hundreds, if not thousands, of cattle grazing in the field around it. The smell was terribly unpleasant and Catherine used the white handkerchief she had found in the tiny purse that had also been in her closet. She vaguely remembered that purses like this were called reticules.

What a random and utterly useless fact to recall. I have no idea what's going on with the world or my own life but I know this thing is called a reticule. Perfect.

Catherine walked and walked until her feet were sore and she was no closer to understanding anything that was happening. She thought perhaps she'd had a medical crisis and was in a coma. Maybe it was a long and detailed dream like Bobby Ewing had on *Dallas*. There weren't any good explanations and she was about to give up and head back to the hotel when she heard a commotion coming from an alley.

"Well, I don't care for your attitude either, missy, and I was just doing this as a favor for Minnie Maxwell anyway. I can't for the life of me figure what she sees in you, but she got it in her head that you were somebody worth knowing. Well, Minnie can just find something else to brag about to those gossipy, bandage-rolling biddies!"

The screaming woman laid the whip on her horse's back and her carriage raced out of the alley and nearly over the top of Catherine, splashing her with muddy water.

The woman who had been on the receiving end of the screaming diatribe saw what happened and disappeared into a doorway in the alley. A moment later she came running out with towels and did her best to clean up the mess that Catherine had become.

"I'm awfully sorry you were caught up in our little drama." The woman spoke with a lilting voice. It was a captivating sound. She was dressed in a fine gown of heavy emerald green fabric that might be better suited for evening, but she carried off the look with ease.

She looks a little like Scarlett O'Hara after she made a dress of her mother's drapes. Excellent, another useless recollection. Reticules and drapes.

Catherine could see faint lines around the woman's eyes, which were deep pools of amber-flecked brown. There was a quiet maturity about her that was strangely soothing. She looked at Catherine and saw the tears that threatened to spill from her eyes. "There, there dear; it's just a little dirt and grime. A girl can't spend time in a city like this and not get her pantaloons a little muddy, now can she?"

Catherine was taken with her kindness, but the ordeal of the afternoon had caught up with her and she was at a loss for words. The woman seemed to take her silence as proof that some delicate female sensibilities must have been offended because she led Catherine to a stoop and told the skinny girl who had followed her from the alley to run and get her salts.

"I'm not going to faint," Catherine finally managed to say. "I'm just a little overwhelmed."

"Yes, I can see that. Is your husband nearby?"

"My husband? I don't have a husband."

"Your driver, then?"

Catherine stared blankly at the woman.

"Ma'am, I can tell from your appearance that you're a lady so I'm sure you aren't here in this part of town by yourself. You must be in shock. Where is your carriage?"

"I walked here from the hotel," Catherine said.

"What is the name of your hotel?" the woman asked.

"I'm staying at the Willard."

"Ah, the Willard brothers run a fine establishment. I'm staying there myself. Shall I see you home, then? Edward can help us sort everything out," the woman assured her.

"Edward?"

"Yes my dear, Edward Chase. He's the concierge. I'm sure you met him when you checked in."

"You know Mr. Chase?"

"Of course." The girl returned with the smelling salts and the woman said to her, "Go and tell Desmond to bring the carriage. We'll be going to Mr. Willard's for the evening. And bring my bag and green wrap."

For the first time since she woke up from her nap, Catherine began to hope that everything was about to get straightened out.

This woman knows the concierge! I don't have the slightest clue how that can be, but finally I can get some answers.

"I've been so rude," the woman said. "I haven't inquired of your name or introduced myself. I'm Laura."

"My name is Catherine Parker."

"It's a pleasure to meet you, Miss Parker. Here is my driver now. Let's get you back to the hotel and into some clean clothes. I believe you'll feel much better when you've had a chance to freshen up."

Laura, you have no idea how much I hope you're right.

CHAPTER 7
TOM KELLY
1962

The driver opened the door for Tom after a ride of about a minute. There was no traffic jam this morning and as he stepped onto the sidewalk he found he was indeed looking at a guard station just outside the White House. The guard seemed to expect him and after a few cursory security checks he was handed off to a harried-looking staffer who had either slept in his clothes or not slept at all.

He was rushing Tom down a hallway and into the West Wing. Before he could catch his breath he heard his escort speak.

"This is Tom Kelly, Mrs. Lincoln."

The dark-haired woman barely glanced up as she worked the blinking phone lines, but he noticed she gave a barely perceptible nod toward a door Tom had seen in photos. He knew that door led to the Oval Office. His escort opened the door a crack and after a short pause said, "He's here." The door opened wider and Tom Kelly found himself looking into the world's most famous office space. A file folder was passed from a man seated with his back to the door to another man who ran it over to Tom's escort and as quickly as the door had opened, it closed and once again they were walking quickly down a hallway.

"Read this," the escort said, handing Tom the file. "Talk to no one in this room about it. He doesn't want you to be influenced by anyone else's thinking until he can hear from you directly."

Tom entered a room with a long conference table surrounded by chairs, one of which was taller than the others. The Cabinet Room.

Around the table was an array of tired-looking men in shirtsleeves devouring reports and filling ashtrays with nubs sucked clean of their nicotine loads. There was little talking, but the frenetic atmosphere of the room was electric. There was volatility in this room. And anxiety. And fear.

Tom pulled out a chair and started to read.

CHAPTER 8
CALVIN WALKER
1963

"Dr. King?" Calvin asked, scarcely believing the words were coming out of his mouth.

"Yes, I'm Dr. King," the man said, extending his hand. Calvin shook his hand but said nothing. He was too stunned to speak. "And you are?" the reverend asked.

"I'm sorry. I'm Calvin Walker." He kept examining the man before him. "It's extraordinary, the likeness," Calvin said. "You really do look just like all the photos I've seen."

"Well, I've been told the camera doesn't lie although I wouldn't mind a fib or two from time to time," Dr. King said with a smile. The elevator doors opened and he stepped inside. "Are you going down?" he asked Calvin.

"Um, no. I forgot something in my room," Calvin answered.

"Well it was nice meeting you, Mr. Walker. I hope to see you at the march tomorrow."

Calvin said nothing further and the doors closed, taking the best Martin Luther King, Jr. impersonator he had ever seen down to the lobby. He went back to his room to call his wife and tell her about the experience he'd just had. It had literally shaken him up because it felt so real.

Why didn't I pull out my phone and ask for a picture? Nobody will believe how much this guy looked like the real thing.

Calvin reached in his pocket for his cell phone but couldn't find it. He didn't remember picking it up this morning at all so he walked over to the nightstand to get it and noticed the rotary phone on the table, but no cell phone. *This phone is a little old school for such a fancy hotel.*

Outside there was a commotion of some sort at street level and he could hear raised voices and an intermittent siren. He went to the window and everything looked surreal. The cars were all old and everyone was dressed in what looked like vintage-wear. The women on the street had little hats on their heads and proper pocketbooks on their arms. It looked like a Hollywood back lot for a period film. Maybe that was it. They must be shooting a film outside today and the man he met is an actor playing the part of MLK. Now he really wanted to find his phone so he could snap some photos on his way out. Who knew what big-name actors might be out there? His son would be really impressed if he came home with a football jersey AND a photo of Will Smith, or maybe Denzel Washington would be there. That shot would win him points with his wife for sure. He was still looking for the phone when he heard a knock at his door. He opened it to find an impeccably dressed man standing there.

"I'm sorry to disturb you, Mr. Walker. My name is Edward Chase and I'm the hotel concierge. I understand you made the acquaintance of Dr. King this morning."

Calvin smiled. "Yes, I met the illustrious 'Dr. King.' It looks like they're shooting a movie outside. It must have been a no-brainer to hire that actor. He could be the man's twin. What can I do for you, Mr. Chase?"

"Mr. Walker, I'm afraid you have misunderstood what you've seen this morning. That man was not an actor and this is not a film location. The man you met is Dr. Martin Luther King, Jr., the famous civil rights leader."

Calvin stood there waiting for Chase to say something else but nothing was forthcoming. "What's the punch line, Mr. Chase? Is this a reality show or something?" He looked into the hallway, both left and right, but there was no crew there and no cameras.

"Mr. Walker, if I could come in for a moment I can explain everything."

Calvin stepped aside and let the concierge enter.

"First, let me start by giving you this morning's paper."

Chase handed him a newspaper and Calvin saw the date on the masthead. *August 27, 1963.*

Calvin looked at Chase questioningly. "What the hell is going on?" he asked.

"Mr. Walker, most of what I'm about to say you'll have to take on faith because we don't have much time. Today is August 27, 1963. There is a march scheduled for here in the city tomorrow. I believe you know it as the March on Washington. Dr. King is one of several prominent civil rights leaders heading up the event. As you know, the march is historically known as one of the great moments in the quest for equal rights."

"I'm very well-versed on the March on Washington, Mr. Chase. What I'm less sure of is why you seem to think we're fifty years in the past here."

"There has been a disturbance in the fabric of history, Mr. Walker. You are not here at this time and place by accident. You possess a unique ability to interact with the people of this time to see that history is preserved. For reasons we don't understand, there are, from time to time, disturbances or "tears" in the fabric of our history. Across the centuries there have been people like you who have been tasked with extraordinary opportunities to travel back to these places in time and see things with your own eyes that most people will only ever read about. At the same time, you have a responsibility to every person who comes after you to make certain that things happen as they are recorded in history." Calvin sat down and invited Chase to join him as the concierge continued his story.

"You may notice I didn't say 'as they should happen' and there's a very good reason for that. History is made up of both the sublime and the tragic, the glorious and the horrendous, the good and the bad. With benefit of hindsight we can look back and say 'Why didn't someone put a bullet in Adolf Hitler before he could take power?' or 'Why don't we tell Bobby Kennedy's security detail not to go through the kitchen?' And we want to do those things, to right the wrongs when we have this chance. But we cannot. History must play itself out in the way that it happened, no matter how much we wish it could be different. Good or bad, it's up to you to make sure it doesn't change from the original."

Calvin vacillated between thinking Chase was out of his mind and thinking he was playing a practical joke on him. Either way, he didn't have the time or the patience for it. "I think you'd better leave if you don't mind, Mr. Chase. I'm not sure what kind of game this is but I've had enough of it. This isn't funny and I have places I need to be," Calvin said as he urged Chase toward the door.

"With all due respect sir, where you need to be is up for debate right now, but I have a couple of leads for you."

"Seriously man, you need to go."

"Mr. Walker, I realize this is very hard for you to believe so I'll cut to the heart of the matter. In twenty-four hours, without your intervention, the peaceful March on Washington that is best known for the eloquent 'I Have A Dream' speech Dr. King is currently working on in this very hotel will be known for something much different and it will likely set the course of civil rights back a hundred years." He could tell he had Calvin's attention now.

"Everyone in America knows about that speech. It was a brilliant moment in American history. What could possibly overshadow what happened that day?" Calvin asked.

"Bloodshed, Mr. Walker. Tremendous bloodshed."

CHAPTER 9
EDWARD CHASE

It wasn't surprising that Calvin Walker was having trouble believing what he was hearing. Chase remembered so clearly how he had felt when he sat in Walker's shoes all those years ago. As a twenty-two-year-old student at Cambridge University, he'd been burning the midnight oil in the library preparing a presentation for a notoriously difficult professor of philosophy. He had read and read until his eyes burned and his brain threatened to overflow with complicated theories when he decided to just close his eyes for a few minutes. He had a short, but deep nap and awoke to find himself in a most undignified state of drooling on his journal. Straightening up, he noticed a change around him. He still felt groggy and decided a quick walk in the brisk night air might revive him. When he exited the library that's when his odyssey really began. His whole world had changed. When he had closed his eyes for that brief rest it was 1812 and when he awoke the year was 1587. Over the next five days he found himself involved in an unbelievable adventure, a date in the past reborn for a second run.

Upon his return to the library to gather his things, he found the old librarian was still at his post. Nothing about the situation seemed strange to this man and he watched as Edward slowly packed his belongings into his knapsack and then he approached him. What the librarian told him boggled the mind.

He was sending him out into the night on a grand adventure, one that was too impossible to be believed. But Edward followed the librarian's instructions and made his way to London where he became involved in the intrigue surrounding the conviction of Mary, Queen of Scots, for treason. Edward found himself in the court of Elizabeth I as the countdown to execution made its macabre march. His role was to get a message from the court to Mary's son, James VI, King of Scotland. Should this message not get through in time there was thought the army that had been raised by Mary would launch an attack on the English court. Mary was guilty of many offenses in her life and in her time she brought terrible repute to her people, but her son was no better in his own way. He was an arrogant and proud young man who had no real relationship with his mother. She had abdicated the Scottish throne to him under duress and now she believed that he could possibly sit on the throne of England one day as she, herself, had plotted to do for so long. No one is sure of what was in the message or even if it had come from Elizabeth herself or had been an attempt by the court to prevent an uprising. Most believe it was a simple barter, urging James to keep his mother's supporters in line in exchange for something he himself wanted. For whatever reason, Edward was tasked with delivering the message into the hands of the king's liaison in the English countryside. On February 8, the execution order was carried out with no interference from Mary's loyal subjects or from her son. While it is impossible to say what could have happened, all Edward knew was that everything went as history had recorded it. He didn't know if he had made a difference or not. Had he prevented bloodshed in the defense of a traitor? Or had he been a pawn stopping the resistance and allowing a woman's death when it might have been prevented, even by war? He struggled with the questions that were circling in his mind and when he returned to find the librarian he sat down to wait for him, determined to get answers. The librarian didn't appear right away and as the shadows of evening grew longer Edward grew more tired. He settled into a comfortable chair to wait and once again the peaceful library lulled him to sleep. When he awoke he found the librarian standing over him holding a stack of books about the great philosophers.

"Sorry to disturb you, young man, but I found the volumes you were interested in," the old librarian said with a chuckle.

"Volumes?"

"For your paper. Before your catnap you told me you needed the most complete works I could find on Aristotle and Plato. Here they are," responded the librarian.

After more back and forth it became apparent the old man either didn't know or wouldn't admit that he knew what Edward was talking about with regard to Mary and Elizabeth. He'd just been digging in the stacks for these books, he told him. Edward jotted some notes from the books and tucked them into his bag so he could finish the paper later. He wasn't ready to work on it just yet. He assumed he'd been asleep longer than he thought and that he'd had a very vivid dream.

I wish I had a history paper to write tonight instead of philosophy. I feel like I could write that just from the memory of my dream.

He bid the librarian goodnight and walked out into the misty night. As he walked he began to get a chill and he reached into his knapsack for his sweater. That's when he felt it. A small, waxy disc was stuck to his finger and when he pulled it out of the bag he stopped in his tracks. It was the wax seal from the message and it bore the imprint of Queen Elizabeth I. There, in his hand, he held the blood-red wax he had seen the sovereign seal just before she handed the message to her courtier who then handed it to Edward. It could not be. And yet it was. Thus began Edward's journey to find the truth and ultimately, to become the concierge. He had learned about portals—places rich with history that opened up to times in their own past. The

Willard was one such portal. There were many hotel portals in various cities around the world, but there were also libraries, like the one he had found at Cambridge. There were also museums, historic homes, government buildings, trains, ships and just about anywhere else where people had gathered in times gone by. Through these portals, other guides like Chase came and went with their travelers, all of them looking for the tears in the fabric of the past.

CHAPTER 10
OLIVIA FORDHAM
1913

Very little ever rattled Olivia Fordham. Having spent nearly five decades navigating the worlds of both high society and high finance she could be counted on to react to almost anything with aplomb. That's why she didn't jump to any conclusions when she first saw the traffic jam of classic automobiles. She pulled a chair over to the window and watched the scene unfold on the street below her for some time. She saw the angry drivers get out of their cars and shake their fists at one another but even that anger seemed tempered. The men were dressed in dapper suits with hats and the women wore tailored dresses with wool coats and gloves. Most wore large hats with embellishments like flowers and feathers, much like what one would see today at the Kentucky Derby. Before long, the police showed up to untangle the mess and send everyone on their way. The officer looked like a character from a Charlie Chaplin movie, but he did his job effectively and traffic began to flow again, all of it cars and a few trucks of a bygone era. Olivia turned her attention to the pedestrians strolling the sidewalks and crossing the streets. There were more well-dressed patrons like those she had seen in the cars but there were also young boys that brought to mind the term *street urchins*. They were wearing ragged pants and overcoats and had flat, wool caps on their heads and dirt on their faces. Olivia didn't know why but she found herself thinking they must be up to no good. There were governesses walking their young charges and shooing away the urchins when they got too close to the young ladies in their lace finery. Some of the women had dresses that went all the way to the ground but many ladies had hemlines that ended at their ankles revealing delicate slipper heels.

Olivia watched for a while and noticed there were a few horse-drawn carriages mingling with the automobiles. When she had seen enough she went to straighten her bed and get dressed. She went to the closet where the maids had unpacked her things and was only slightly surprised to see that the clothes hanging in the closet were not the ones her New York maids had packed. Hanging there she saw long dresses like those on the street outside, some long enough to touch the floor when she walked and not a single pair of trousers. There were shoes with tiny buttons across the bridge and slippers with demure heels. She also noticed several hat boxes stacked on the shelf and when she examined their contents she found a collection of large, extravagant hats in a variety of colors. There were even a couple of fascinators with radiating plumes and simple combs for placing in the hair. These would look right at home at a royal wedding. There were beaded clutches and a couple of sensible pocketbooks and on the dressing vanity she noticed several pairs of white gloves in different lengths. She was delighted with the items she found.

Considering the clothing, the vintage automobiles, and the mannerisms of the people she had observed, she imagined herself to be somewhere around the early 1900s, likely the Edwardian period. This was a new one for her. She had always been fascinated by the era but never had a chance to "visit" it. The timing on this episode was terrible with everything she had to do this week but it couldn't be helped. Part of her secretly hoped she would stay in the era long enough to really enjoy it. She wanted a chance to wear everything in the closet. She would place a call to her friend, Jane, who had checked into the hotel and was staying in the adjacent second bedroom. Olivia had begun reserving the second bedroom about a year before and made sure it was always included when she stayed at the Willard. Jane had been given a key to the adjoining door so she could come and go as Mrs. Fordham needed.

Yes, Olivia would call Jane soon, but not just yet. She went back to the chair by the window and opened it a few inches so she could hear the sounds of the city. She didn't know how long she would be in this time and she wanted to enjoy every minute.

✑

Half an hour later Edward Chase rang the doorbell of the suite. Olivia greeted him still wearing her dressing gown.

"Come in, Edward."

"Did you enjoy your rest, Olivia?"

"Yes, very much. I feel very refreshed."

Chase noticed she did indeed seem alert and calm. He walked to the window and looked out. Traffic was flowing nicely on Pennsylvania Avenue, the classic cars blowing their horns at the boys who darted between them. He wondered if she had looked out the window or noticed anything different. She was still wearing her dressing gown so maybe she hadn't gone to her closet and seen the period clothing he knew was now hanging there. He was going to have to be very careful how he broke the news to her.

"Would you like some tea, Edward? The water has gone cold but I could order up a new pot."

"No, thank you. Olivia, I thought you might like your maid to come and help you dress for this evening but I wanted to speak with you first."

"I don't require any assistance this evening but it's good of you to be concerned. I'm afraid I may need to stay in tonight. I was going to call Jane and spend the evening with her. Has she checked in?"

"Yes, she's all taken care of but she's not, um, *available* right now."

"That's no problem. I'll call her in a bit." Chase glanced at the circa 1910 telephone on the desk. If Olivia hadn't noticed it, she would when she got ready to make the call. He had to tell her what was going on.

"Olivia, would you please come with me? I need to show you something."

She followed him into the dining room where he drew back the drapes on the corner window with its Juliet balcony overlooking the intersection. He pointed to the street.

She looked down but didn't make any remark.

"Do you see anything unusual?" he asked.

Olivia saw the old cars and the pedestrians dressed in their vintage finery but she didn't want Edward to know what she was seeing. He wouldn't understand. In fact, he would likely think her crazy.

"Whatever do you mean, Edward? The fact that traffic is actually moving well this time of day in Washington?" she said jokingly. "I'm sure you've seen that a few times at least."

"No, Olivia. I mean the Model Ts and the people in vintage clothing."

Olivia stepped back from the window like she'd been slapped. Her mind was spinning and she couldn't figure out what was happening. Chase thought she might faint and stepped toward her as she put her head down. He supported her arm and she looked up into his eyes with fear in her own.

"You can see those too?" she asked. Then she collapsed on the floor and started to seize.

CHAPTER 11
CATHERINE PARKER
1865

The doorman offered his hand to the ladies as they stepped down from the rented carriage. Laura kept a steadying hand at Catherine's elbow just in case the younger woman felt faint. Edward Chase saw the two as they came through the revolving door. He rushed to their side and, in spite of Catherine's protests, ushered them up the steps to Peacock Alley and seated them in an alcove between two enormous potted palms. He insisted on fetching a carafe of cool water and some salts. When it was clear Catherine was not in danger of collapsing, Laura excused herself to check her messages. She approached the large concierge desk and was handed the slips of paper that continued to arrive in her room's cubby every day. Granted, a few years ago there would have been too many messages to contain in the small cubby. There would have been calling cards and invitations as well as letters of introduction and outright adoration. At thirty-eight years of age, it was undeniable she wasn't at her prime anymore. Her long hair was not as lustrous as it once was and her gowns had been let out in recent years to accommodate her more matronly figure. But she was still a beauty by most standards and the years had been fairly kind to her in reputation. At least as kind as they could be for a woman of her profession. She knew that even in her heyday the invitations had not been to the most fashionable addresses. They didn't come from the grande dames of society. She found herself more the toast of the nouveau riche crowd, those with a tendency toward ostentatiousness and attention. Their drawing rooms were filled with Sheraton and Chippendale reproductions, not the real thing. Their crystal chandeliers came from France, but their provenance was bought, not inherited. But the evenings were lively and gay and the wine and spirits flowed freely. If the hosts thought they were anything less than the crème de la crème they were determined not to show it. Entertaining on a grand scale in their new mansions was de rigueur and their guest lists had to glitter with beautiful and interesting women and influential men. Though Laura wouldn't be welcome in the homes of the old-moneyed set, she was a sought-after guest at these soirees.

Today's mail was decidedly short on invitations and completely devoid of letters of adoration. She slipped the messages into her reticule. She could go through them later and decide which ones to accept. She crossed the lobby and was about to rejoin her new charge, but she noticed Catherine was sitting with her head against the rear of the sofa and her eyes closed so she decided to give her some privacy. As she watched her sitting there she began to wonder about the young woman. Who was she and why was she traveling without a chaperone in a part of town known for its boarding houses and theatres? She said she had no husband and seemed very confused almost like she was suffering the effects of strong drink. And Laura was fairly sure the young lady was not wearing a corset although her gown was certainly new and fashionable.

Surely, it can't be, Laura thought. *She doesn't seem the type at all.*

All evidence seemed to indicate young Catherine might be plying the streets of the nation's capital engaging in the world's oldest profession.

But how many prostitutes can afford to stay at the Willard on their own? And Mr. Chase seems to know her well. I seriously doubt he would allow such goings on under this roof.

The more she considered the possibility, the more convinced she became there had to be another explanation. She started up the stairs to find out for herself who this mysterious woman was and why she seemed to need help. At that moment she determined she would lend a helping hand because Laura knew well how it felt to be looked down on for her profession. The society ladies thought the same of her. Too vulgar. Unrefined. Loose. Except she was none of those things. In their eyes she was worse. Because Laura Keene was an actress.

CHAPTER 12
TOM KELLY
1962

The images were familiar in some ways. The U2 high-altitude reconnaissance photos marked with missile sites. The maps showing strategic points and civilian population numbers. Photos of Fidel Castro and Nikita Khrushchev and a host of lesser-known, but clearly Russian military types. These were the kind of images Kelly had seen while studying American history in high school and later in college. He'd been fascinated by the idea that Americans, his own parents included, had sat paralyzed with fear for days as the threat of nuclear war drew closer. Now he was sitting in the Cabinet Room of the White House looking over these documents and others that were marked "Top Secret" in what must be some kind of dream. He had been led to believe he had just caught a glimpse inside the Oval Office of John F. Kennedy, and that Robert Kennedy was in the office as well. But Tom knew this was impossible because both brothers had fallen at the hands of assassins just a few years apart. His own mother had remarked on it one day when he was working on a history paper in high school about the Kennedy years.

"That poor Rose Kennedy," his mother had said. "She buried a son and a daughter years earlier and then had two sons shot to death by madmen in the 60s. I don't know how she endured it," she said as she pulled then 15-year-old Tom to her for a mama bear hug. "I would have gone out of my mind," she remarked as she perused the black and white photos of the Kennedy state funeral in Tom's textbook.

The memory was bittersweet because Tom's mother had died his senior year. She had wanted him to go to college and become a lawyer. In her mind that was a steady career with potential. She knew he loved writing stories and talked of making movies, but she would have none of it. Writing and moviemaking weren't real careers in her mind. She wanted Tom to hang out his shingle and then push paperwork through a crowded legal system all day before coming home to a wife, kids, a dog and a reasonably mortgaged house on a cul-de-sac in a good school zone. It was the life his older brother, Jason, had chosen to pursue and by the time of their mother's death Jason had received his acceptance letter to the esteemed school of law at Florida Coastal. All these years later Jason, at forty-seven, had the law degree his mother had so wanted. He also had an ex-wife, a minor gambling problem, one kid who cost him a fortune in private violin lessons and one who was costing him a fortune in rehab. The ex-wife got the house and the cul-de-sac, but Jason kept the dog. That bitch could have the McMansion, but there was no way she was getting Jake, his beloved golden retriever. What kind of lawyer was he anyway if he couldn't hang on to his dog?

Tom never had to disappoint his mother by letting her know he had chosen to pursue a writing degree. He thought writing sounded better on a resume than filmmaking so that was his one concession to his mother's practical nature. So now here he was at forty-two, never married, no children, no dog, and one last chance to prove, posthumously, to his mother that he hadn't made a mistake in choosing this path. She might not be here physically, but Tom was convinced she somehow knew and one day when he finally "made it" he planned to go to her grave and tell her all about it; as if he had been keeping her from resting in peace all these years.

"Son of a bitch! We missed one, right here! It's four, maybe five miles from a school! Mother. . ." the excited man was interrupted before he could complete his expletive.

"It's on the newest grid, Stan. They know about it. Simons found it last night," the man across the table explained.

Stan was not to be pacified. "Why am I looking at outdated maps?" He slammed the papers down on the table and grabbed the nearest intern who cowered under his grip. "Go get me the updated maps and then you stand your ass outside the Oval and make sure I have new information the SECOND it comes down! If some Commie bastard breaks wind on this island you'd better be in a dead run down here to tell me about it! Understand?"

The chastised intern scurried from the room as Stan ripped off the tie that had been loosely hanging from his neck. His bulging veins and red face indicated he might keel over in the chair normally reserved for the Secretary of the Interior, but the outburst seemed to relieve some of the pressure and he settled down and buried his head back in the reports.

Tom had been observing everything around him, like being aware that you're dreaming during the actual dream. Everything felt so real and he wanted to remember it. He almost didn't recognize his name being called from the doorway. Yet another terrified intern was beckoning him to come to the door. The boy looked like he was afraid he might be in for some of the same kind of wrath Stan had been handing out and he was visibly relieved when Tom picked up his paperwork and came to the door without a fuss.

"They're ready for you now," the intern said. The badge around his neck proclaimed his name to be Ethan York. He looked to be about 18 years old. He turned to walk away and Tom stopped him.

"Hold on a minute, Ethan," he said. The young man turned, certain now that he was about to have his head handed to him for some unseen slight. Earlier today he had failed to recognize the rank on a Colonel's uniform and referred to him simply as "sir."

"*Sir?*" the man had asked condescendingly. "Do I look like a man who would spend years slogging through France getting shot at for pipsqueaks like you so I could be called '*Sir*'? You will address me as 'Colonel' if you must speak to me at all young man!"

Where Ethan came from, "sir" and "ma'am" would open any door and get you a pat on the back for being a polite young man with good manners. But here, "sir" could get you dismissed from the White House intern program and he wasn't looking forward to telling his mother he'd gotten booted his first week on the job. He vowed to study the symbols of military rank as soon as he got a break, but there had been no breaks for the last forty-eight hours and nobody seemed to know when there might be again. At least they got fed in the White House mess. They were handing out free sandwiches down there, which was good for Ethan's budget. Speaking of sandwiches, he was getting hungry again. As soon as this guy, whoever he was, was finished yelling at him he thought he'd go down and see if there were any left.

"Yes. . .um. . .*he's not wearing a uniform*. . .sir?"

"I was wondering where we're going, Ethan. Where are you taking me?" Tom asked.

"To the Oval Office, sir."

"Do you know why I'm being summoned?"

"Sir, I don't know anything about anything. I just learned which wing was the west one two days ago and I've been running around ever since. I was just told to get Tom Kelly and bring him to the Oval. One of the guys at the door back there pointed you out," Ethan said.

"Are you alright? You look scared, Ethan," Tom said.

"To be honest, sir, I am scared. I was supposed to come here for orientation for the intern program and about an hour after I got here all Hades, excuse my language, sir, broke loose. Nobody has gone home and I heard that last night the president went on TV talking about the Russians getting ready to nuke us. They don't let us watch TV here but that's what everybody's saying. I'm nobody important, sir, but I would think if the Russians were wanting to nuke us, the White House would be a bad place to be sitting when it happens. I'm beginning to think I'd rather be back in South Carolina, but my mother worked hard for me to be able to do this and I don't want to let her down," Ethan was obviously relieved to be able to talk to someone. It seemed this Tom Kelly wasn't going to yell at him like the colonel had so he breathed deeply and took a chance.

"Sir, you're obviously somebody important here. Do you think you could tell me if it would be a good idea for me to bug out and head south? I know you can't tell me top secret stuff and all that, but maybe you could just give me a sign if the shit, sorry for my language, sir, is about to hit the fan."

Tom wasn't sure whether to laugh or give the kid a hug. The young man was obviously terrified. He wanted to tell him it was all just a dream, but they had arrived at the outer office and Mrs. Lincoln was saying something to Tom about the president being ready to see him now. Everything happened quickly after that, and the idea of all this being only a dream gave way when John F. Kennedy reached out and shook Tom's hand and thanked him for coming in that distinctive Boston accent. Tom felt the weight of the world descend on him as an aide went to close the door to the Oval Office.

The last thing Tom saw was Ethan York standing in the hall, waiting for a sign.

CHAPTER 13
CALVIN WALKER
1963

All over the city, the March on Washington for Jobs and Freedom was the main topic of conversation. Public opinion was divided between those who predicted an important event with the potential to bring about real change for those being persecuted on the basis of race and those who believed the event was likely to bring trouble. They thought the trouble could come during the actual march or as a result of the changes the advocates wanted to see. There were plenty of people in Washington that week who believed the status quo was just fine and that people should know their place. In lesser hands the planned march could have been a powder keg, but the top civil rights organizers in the country, those who advocated non-violence and peaceful demonstration, had worked hard to ensure a positive and safe event.

The program read like a Who's Who of leaders in the black community. They had chosen to use the march to mark the anniversary of the enactment of President Abraham Lincoln's Emancipation Proclamation. One hundred years earlier the document had given their ancestors freedom from their slave masters, but today they still fought for equal rights and protections. A. Philip Randolph, James Farmer, John Lewis, Roy Wilkins, Whitney Young and Martin Luther King, Jr. all had a hand in the planning. They represented an alphabet soup of the most noted organizations including SNCC, SCLS, National Urban League and the NAACP. Marian Anderson was scheduled to sing the national anthem. She had gained fame after the Daughters of the American Revolution organization refused to allow her to perform at their venue in the late 1930s. Eleanor Roosevelt had been so incensed by the action she arranged for Anderson to sing at a special Easter concert on the steps of the Lincoln Memorial. March participants were already talking excitedly about hearing the famous singer along with another favorite, Mahalia Jackson. Christian and Jewish leaders would be on hand to help bring the group together along religious, as well as racial lines.

Everything was falling into place for a once-in-a-lifetime event. There would be no fire hoses or attack dogs. No grandstanding sheriff or local politician would be permitted to interfere with the program. Though they may have had different ideas about the specific call to action, all the organizers had worked hand in hand to make this march a showpiece for civil action. The emphasis was on the word "civil."

It wouldn't be just black marchers on the mall. White citizens in large numbers were also planning to attend to stand shoulder to shoulder with their fellow Americans. The march would reach across the lines of race, religion, and class and for one extraordinary day the voices of the masses could not be ignored.

From all indications it looked like a glorious day was set to dawn. Would the promise the organizers imagined echo the promise felt by those who first heard about the Emancipation Proclamation one hundred years ago? Or were they setting themselves up to be equally disappointed by the reality?

CHAPTER 14
OLIVIA FORDHAM
1913

Dr. Mabry Mitchell was a frequent guest of the Willard and happened to be in residence when Olivia had her seizure. Chase sent for him at once and by the time he arrived at the suite Olivia was sitting on the floor against the wall of the dining room. She looked dazed, but was breathing normally. Chase and the doctor helped get her to her feet and tried to usher her to her bedroom, but she wouldn't hear of it. The doctor settled for seating her in the first parlor and insisted on a cursory exam. Chase gave them privacy and waited in the hallway for the doctor to finish.

You can see it too? Chase mulled over what Olivia had said to him. He noticed she had not seemed at all surprised to see a different world outside her window than the one she was used to seeing. She did seem surprised that *he* could see it. In all the years since his own traveling experience he had never known anyone to react that way. Most were uncertain of what they were seeing at first, believing it to be a dream. Once he talked with them some accepted it more readily than others, but all of them, without exception, had required extensive explanations. Olivia had not. She had simply looked upon her present reality without any discernable concern. Chase didn't know what to make of it, but before he could dwell too long on it the suite door opened and Dr. Mitchell came out.

"How is she?" Chase asked.

"She's weak, but completely coherent. She has some muscle stiffness and a slight bump on the head from the fall, but overall she seems fine. I couldn't get much medical history from her. She tried to pass it off like she'd had a case of the vapors."

"Trust me, Dr. Mitchell. Olivia Fordham has *never* had a case of the vapors. She probably just didn't want to be a bother. What should we do?"

"I'd like to check in on her this evening. I've given her a sleeping draught for later, but I doubt if she'll use it. She seems quite headstrong. Do you know if she's had episodes like this before?"

"I'm not certain. I've always known Mrs. Fordham to be in excellent health. Is there anything I can do for her to make her more comfortable?"

"Have some mint tea and a light dinner sent up. Her stomach may be a bit upset, but it will be good for her to have something to eat if she can. As I said, I'll come back to check on her when I return to the hotel for the evening. I'll be at the National for a performance this evening, but please do send for me if she should have any problems in the interim."

"Very good. Thank you, Dr. Mitchell. Good evening."

"Good evening to you, Mr. Chase."

Chase knocked gently instead of ringing the bell and as he knocked he used his passkey to open the door while calling out her name. He didn't want her to have to come to the door if she wasn't up to it. She heard him and asked him to come to the parlor where she was standing at the window and looking distressed. Chase was immediately concerned.

"Olivia, are you alright? Shall I get Dr. Mitchell?"

"Edward, tell me what you see outside this window."

"Olivia, let me explain."

"Explain? Please, Edward, tell me what you see."

Chase crossed to the window where she was holding back the drape. He looked down. "I see a variety of cars from the early twentieth century, several horses and many pedestrians that look like they are from—"

"From the Edwardian era," Olivia finished his sentence.

"Yes. What I don't understand, Olivia, is your reaction to what you see."

"That's because I'm usually the only one who can see it. I'm trying to figure out how you see it too and, to be honest, I'm scared of what this means."

She walked to one of the sofas and sat down. He sat in a chair next to her.

"Scared of what?" he asked. Chase had seen others express fear when they first realized what was happening, but this seemed different to him.

"Scared that my condition is getting worse. Scared that I'm in some kind of parallel state, outside of reality. I'm not sure if I'm even conscious really. Maybe I've had a stroke. I can't tell if any of this is real."

"What condition, Olivia?"

She looked truly afraid, something Chase had never seen in her face before. He couldn't even imagine her being afraid. She was one of the strongest women he had ever met, but she was clearly shaken when she looked at him and began to fill in the blanks.

"Three years ago I started having headaches and weakness in my right side. I thought it was age at first or my packed schedule, but it wasn't long before other things started happening—things that scared me. One morning I was working in my office at home and I became confused and unsure of what I was doing. I'd been working for a few hours so I decided to take a walk to clear my head and get some fresh air. While I was walking I experienced flashes of places and people who were out of place. Over the next several weeks, this progressed to entire episodes that lasted for hours. During these episodes I would see things like what I've just seen outside the window.

Sometimes it was images of different time periods and other times it was of different places. But it wasn't just hallucinations. I could see these things, but I could also feel, sense, smell and touch them. I could interact like I was really there. Once I spent four hours walking along the Seine in Paris. Another time I spent an hour on a ship in the middle of the ocean."

Chase was listening with rapt attention. He could see that she was troubled by what she was telling him.

"I realized I needed to see a doctor so I made an appointment. Before I could see him I had the first seizure. I ended up in the hospital and went through days of testing. I didn't have any more symptoms while I was there so they sent me home to await the results. During those few days I had more episodes that got longer and more involved. I spent two days in my apartment, but it was my apartment as it appeared fifty years ago. Like today, everything outside the window was of another era and so were my clothes and everything I touched.

My doctor called me to his office and broke the news that there was a tumor growing in my brain. It's not malignant, but it's too intricately placed to be easily removed. Taking it out could cause much greater problems. Since I had an explanation for the symptoms I felt comfortable telling the doctor about the episodes I was having. I was glad to know I wasn't crazy and he didn't think I was either.

It's a little late to make a long story short, Edward, but eventually my doctor and I decided to let things progress and see what happened. I hired my good friend Jane to be my nurse but we don't tell anyone that's her job. I refer to her strictly as a traveling companion and she's the only one besides my medical team who knows the truth. When I have these episodes she helps keep me safe while I wander through an unreal world. She reschedules appointments until I'm feeling better and she makes sure nothing falls through the cracks. She keeps in regular contact with my doctors and I don't know what I would have done without her the last two years."

Chase couldn't believe what he was hearing. He knew Olivia as a take-charge woman who could run an army of people, throw a charity gala, and develop companies from the ground up. He couldn't imagine her being at the mercy of something like this and how she was able to keep it secret. He was also touched that she trusted him enough to tell him about it and she didn't seem to be ready to stop talking yet.

"The truth is, Edward, I came to enjoy these episodes. They seem so real when they're happening that it's a little like traveling through time and space to experience things and people and places I would never get to see. In my life I've seen a lot of the world—more than most. But when this happens it's like going on a magical journey that has endless possibilities. When it happens I'm not scared. But now you tell me you can see the same thing I see outside the window which *does* scare me because it means things are getting worse. Though the tumor is not malignant it is growing and as it does it will take away my mental function as well as physical abilities. You may wonder why I'm not having it removed but I've talked at length with the surgeons about that option and now I've waited so long that the surgery would likely rob me of the essence of who I am. I might live but I probably wouldn't be the "me" that you know. Or that I know. So I opted to let it take its course and to go along for these exciting rides whenever they come. But since you're sitting here telling me that you see it too it's apparent that something more severe is starting. I think perhaps we should get Jane. She can contact my New York doctors and make arrangements to get me home."

Olivia seemed utterly defeated and Chase realized he had a problem on his hands he had never experienced before. He wanted to reassure her that she wasn't having a severe episode, but everything was so complicated now that he hardly knew how to explain the situation to her. The woman was obviously even stronger than he had known. He would start with first things first.

"Olivia, I can't get Jane for you because she's not here."

"But you said she had checked in to the hotel."

"Yes, she checked in but she could not make 'the trip' with you."

"I don't understand, Edward. She should be next door."

Chase realized for the first time how ridiculous his explanations must sound when he has to help travelers understand what's happening.

"Yes, she is next door in 2016. But we're not in 2016 anymore. Today is March 1, 1913."

Olivia stared at him without a response.

"What you're seeing is not a result of a tumor and you aren't experiencing an unreal world, Olivia. Jane isn't here because you and I have gone somewhere she cannot go."

"I don't understand, Edward. It sounds like you're saying we've gone back in time." Olivia was rubbing her temples with her hands and he could see that she was trembling.

"That's exactly what we've done Olivia. And it's all my fault."

CHAPTER 15
CATHERINE PARKER
1865

Catherine opened her eyes and looked around for Laura and Mr. Chase. The cold water and a few minutes rest had perked her up and she was eager to get some answers for the questions swirling around in her head. Nothing made sense, starting with Lawrence Cameron's name on the Italianate house where the shiny glass office building should have been. *My meeting was supposed to be with Lawrence Cameron IV, some sort of descendant maybe?* She shook her head to clear the cobwebs. *Descendant? Am I really thinking that way, like I've somehow traveled back in time? I must still be asleep, but I don't know how to wake up from this dream. I've got to figure a way out of this or I'll sleep through my real meeting. Wake up, Catherine! Nothing.*

She slapped her cheek. "Wake up, Catherine!" she said, this time out loud.

"Are you alright my dear?" It was Laura. She sat down and put her hand to Catherine's forehead, checking for fever.

"Laura, something is happening to me. I think I might be having a dream and I can't wake up."

"Have you been ill?" Laura asked and Catherine's adamant head shaking was her answer.

"I don't mean to be indelicate, dear, but is it possible you have had spirits that might have caused your thoughts to be muddled?" She laughed softly. "It's nothing to be ashamed of if that's the case. I may have done that once or twice myself, by accident of course," Laura said soothingly.

"You think I'm drunk?" Catherine sounded indignant but then realized a hangover sounded more plausible to a stranger than being in a waking dream. "I'm not drunk. I went to my room for a short nap and when I woke up I was here."

"Weren't you here at the hotel when you laid down for your nap?"

Catherine sounded exasperated. "I don't mean *here*, like this place. I mean *HERE*, in this time!" She knew how ridiculous this all sounded and dropped her head into her hands. Just then Mr. Chase returned to her side.

"Ms. Parker, I understand you have had a very trying afternoon. Why don't we let Ms. Keene get back to her business and I will try and help you sort this out. I believe I can explain everything." He turned to Laura. "Ms. Keene, you have a guest waiting in the lobby. Please don't worry about Ms. Parker. I will see to her and find you a bit later to update you on her condition," he said calmly.

Laura hated to leave Catherine when she was so clearly distraught, but she did have an appointment and Mr. Chase seemed to have things in hand. Besides, she wasn't really sure what to say next to calm the young woman.

"Very well, Mr. Chase. I will see to my appointment but when I return I will check in on Ms. Parker. Would that be alright with you, Catherine?" she asked.

Catherine nodded her agreement and Laura went to meet her guest. Chase sat down beside her and poured her another tall glass of water.

"I'm so sorry for your distress, Ms. Parker. I assure you there was no other way to get to this point. And when I have explained everything to you I believe you will understand the importance of having you here at this place at THIS time." He handed her the water glass and she looked at him with eyes that seemed to plead for an explanation, anything to convince her she wasn't going crazy.

Edward Chase took a deep breath and seemed to steady himself for the words he was about to speak.

"Ms. Parker, today is April 12, 1865. In two days the President of the United States, Abraham Lincoln, will go to Ford's Theatre to see your new friend Laura in a play titled *My American Cousin*. While he's there John Wilkes Booth will assassinate him. You are here to make sure that happens."

And with that, Catherine Parker finally fainted.

CHAPTER 16
TOM KELLY
1962

Tom was ushered to a seat on one of the sofas that face each other in front of the fireplace. The president's desk was to his left. Tom remembered photos of little John Kennedy climbing under the desk and through the modesty panel. He also remembered the desk was a gift from Queen Victoria and had something to do with a ship. The *Resolute*, he thought. Jackie had wanted to use it. Jackie! *Is Jackie Kennedy in this house right now?* The thought of it made him smile. He might not have a law degree, but meeting Jackie Kennedy; now *that* would impress his mother.

The room was fairly crowded with men in dark suits huddled in small groups. A man turned to Tom and introduced himself. There really was no need.

"I'm Robert Kennedy, Attorney General," he said as he offered his hand. Same Boston accent. Same distinctive face.

You'll never be president. You're going to be shot dead by a crazy man in a hotel kitchen in a few years. The thoughts were coming fast and furious in Tom's mind. Could he just say it like that? Just blurt it out?

He had a sudden thought. Those bath salts! That must be it. Somebody spiked the salts. Or maybe they were those drug things the kids call bath salts today. Do you put those in bath water or is it just slang for a drug you ingest? It didn't matter. He had to be high. He had never been high, but he had studied the drug culture for a film he worked on in college and he'd interviewed kids who described vivid alternate realities while riding the substance wave.

Leave it to me, Tom thought, *to spend the one drug high of my life on a nerd-dream about politics instead of something like leaping tall buildings or picking Technicolor mushrooms with the rabbit from Alice in Wonderland.*

"Mr. Kelly?"

Tom realized both Kennedys were staring at him and waiting for a response.

"I'm sorry, I was thinking about, um, something I read. What was your question?"

The president responded. "We're just wondering about your initial response to the report. I know you've only had a few minutes to look it over, but your insight is likely to be different from everyone else's in this room and we'd like to hear what you think," he explained.

Tom hadn't read the report but he knew enough about what was happening from history classes that he decided he had no choice but to try and BS his way through until he could figure a way out of this room.

"I think the Russians doubt your resolve, Mr. President," he answered with false confidence.

"Doubt his resolve?" responded the attorney general. "How can they doubt it with all those American ships parked off the coast of their island launch pad?"

Tom was not shaken. He had no idea where the bravado was coming from.

Why yes, White Rabbit, I believe I will have tea at the Mad Hatter's table. Two lumps please.

"They think you'll blink," Tom responded. That's what this was about, right? Brinkmanship? Who blinks first? The world's most dangerous game of chicken, only he already knew the outcome.

Queen? What queen? I like my head right where it is, thank you very much.

The two Kennedys whispered together for a moment and Mrs. Lincoln tapped Tom on the shoulder and handed him a folded sheet of paper. The note read:

Mr. Kelly,

A very urgent matter of a personal nature requires your attention at the Willard at once. Please return at your earliest convenience. (The rabbit says it is not tea time.)

Edward Chase, concierge

Tom stared at the note in his hand in stunned silence. *I am really, really high.*

Just then the Kennedys turned back to Tom. "The problem, Mr. Kelly, is that somebody has to blink first. The question is, how many will die if it's us?"

The room began to spin and Tom heard his own voice.

"Mr. President, I sincerely apologize. Something has come up that I must deal with at once. I beg your pardon but I need one hour for . . .um. . . .further research."

"Of course," said the president. "Take the hour. As you know, Mr. Kelly, we cannot afford to be wrong."

CHAPTER 17
CALVIN WALKER
1963

Calvin was having a terrible time trying to get his head around what Chase was telling him. Chase decided to take him for a walk around the area to help him come to grips with where he was. As they walked up 14th Street, Calvin felt like he was in a dream state. The vehicles, the way people were dressed, the items in the store windows, even the way people spoke to each other. . .it was all different than the day before. He had been to Washington many times and there had always been a cosmopolitan air about the city, but now he noticed there was no mingling of the races and no trace at all of anyone of obviously foreign descent. Most of the well-dressed ladies and gentlemen in this area so near the White House were white. Groups of black men and women moved about, but they kept to themselves and Calvin cringed when he noticed most would put their heads down and step aside for the white citizens to pass on the sidewalk. He couldn't remember enough Jim Crow era history at the moment to know whether or not Washington D.C. establishments were truly segregated in the early 60s, but from his observation it didn't seem to matter what the law said. The races were separating themselves from each other.

Calvin thought about his company, Diagnosis Digital, and the members of his leadership team. He was the founder and CEO, a black man with a good education and no personal frame of reference for discrimination other than some redneck boys in high school. His team was made up of men and women of different races and ethnic backgrounds. Their tech staff was like a melting pot. Every area of the world map was represented plus they had gay and straight staffers, religious and non-religious people, and a couple of leftover counter-culture hippie types from the peace and love generation. His company was well known for recognizing people for their merit and hard work and nothing about where they came from or what they looked like had any bearing on their ability to succeed. Sure, he had grown up in the South, but he was born in 1969 and his upper-middle-class parents plus above average surroundings insulated him from the more gritty aspects of Southern race relations. Everything about what he was hearing from Chase and seeing on the streets of Washington was unsettling him. It was one thing to read about it in a history book, but another thing entirely to see it with your own eyes.

Chase continued talking, but Calvin was becoming lost in his own thoughts. Here he was walking down the street with a hotel concierge explaining to him that he had traveled back in time to 1963, that he had met the real Dr. Martin Luther King outside an elevator this morning, and that the famous March on Washington was in literal danger and he was the only person who could help. It was all so ludicrous and yet Calvin hadn't packed his bags and changed hotels. It had happened the moment he handed that newspaper to the man at the elevator. In spite of the sheer impossibility of the situation, something in Calvin's very being had told him he was talking with the real Dr. King. It might have been the presence the great man exuded or the sound of his voice that Calvin had heard so many times over the years when the famous speeches were played. Those were possibilities, but he felt there was something else and then it came to him. It was color. He almost laughed out loud. The key to him accepting that he was currently in 1963 Washington was all, ironically, about color. Both his meeting at the elevator and the sites he was seeing on the streets were so different than in his mind's eye. Everything was alive, breathing and teeming with unspent action and hope. He realized that everything he had ever known of this time had come from black and white photographs in books. Now he was seeing everything in full color and three dimensions. These people were real and they were walking and talking in a real environment where he could walk and talk with them. He could feel the slight breeze that eased some of the oppressive August heat and he could smell the bacon cooking as they passed a restaurant. He had felt the grip of the handshake Dr. King had offered him and he had seen with his own eyes the way the races interacted with one another here in public. He even believed he'd be able to taste the bacon that was cooking except that, as a black man, he would likely not be welcome in the restaurant. Despite all common sense and the laws of nature, Calvin knew what he was experiencing was real. With that established, he turned his attention back to the conversation.

While they walked, Chase explained to Calvin that there were a lot of different groups within the black community who were against the march because they felt it didn't go far enough for the cause. They thought the policy of peaceful protest was weak and the practice of teaming up with white advocates was selling out to the very people who had kept them in bondage for so many years. These groups took a militant stance and they felt that if the march was successful with its even-handed tactics it would set them back further. They weren't willing to petition for changes. They weren't interested in *asking* the government that had enslaved them to come to their aid now. To them, the time had come for *action,* not words. They wanted to take the rights they were due by force and to make those who would consider them less than equal pay at any cost. Some of the groups were well known and the FBI was monitoring their movements to prevent violence. It was the smaller and lesser-known groups that Chase was concerned about, particularly one that called itself Kifo, which was short for *nyeupe kifo*.

"It means *white death* in Swahili," Chase said.

"Sounds like a fun group," Calvin said sarcastically.

"They're more dangerous than any of the groups you've heard about. They only want one outcome and that's the one their name espouses. They want blood, Mr. Walker. Blood for blood, in their estimation. Anything less, to them, is giving in to the white man."

"So they have plans for this march?" Calvin asked.

"Big plans. They're holed up here in the city with plans to disrupt the proceedings."

"I don't understand the rationale," Calvin said. "How can they go against their own brothers?"

"They believe their 'brothers' have gone soft and are begging at the white man's table for scraps. If the march is successful, as we know it was when it initially happened, it will show that non-violent protest and multi-racial cooperation are viable means to an end. Kifo doesn't want that message to get out. They want a race war and their offensive begins tomorrow."

"What am I supposed to do about it? Look at me, Mr. Chase. I'm the kind of guy they're fighting against. I don't believe in violence and bloodshed. I don't know what you think I can do with people like that," Calvin said.

"Unfortunately, I've told you all I know about the situation. The *how* is for you to figure out. I have two addresses where they might be gathering. Both are in very dangerous parts of the city. I have arranged a change of wardrobe for you so you'll fit in better with where you're going. It won't do for you to come walking in wearing wingtips," Chase told him.

"I don't think it's my shoes that'll make me look like I don't belong."

They arrived back at the Willard and Chase walked Calvin to the elevator.

"The clothes are in your room along with some currency of the proper era and a brief identity I wrote up for you. Basically you keep your own name, but you tell them you come from the streets of Chattanooga, not the suburbs. The fact that you come from a Southern state should help you. Think of all the atrocities you've read about in the history of the civil rights struggle and use those kinds of examples to describe your background. Just don't claim to have been part of any organized group or present at any famous event like the Greensboro sit-ins. They may be able to trip you up and find out you're lying if you go with big name events. Keep it generic, but wear a chip on your shoulder. If you can find out what they're planning, perhaps law enforcement can take it from there. You won't know until you get inside," Chase said.

"I imagine it takes a long time to gain the trust of a group like this. What makes you think they'll warm up to me and share information in a single night?" Calvin asked.

"I think they will because whatever they're planning is imminent. They need as much help as possible to pull it off. If you give them the impression you're ready to do battle they may let their guard down a little. Remember, they'll be on the lookout for informants who may be trying to stop what they're planning."

"What you mean is that I'm walking into a trap," Calvin stated.

"You could be. I don't want you to have any misunderstanding about the stakes here. If they think you're against them they will kill you without a moment's regret."

"Remind me again why I'm doing this, then?"

"Someone has to stop this group. You have a decision to make. You have to decide if the future you know, the freedoms you enjoy and the world your children live in, is more important than your own life. I did some research on you, Mr. Walker, and I know the kind of man you are. I believe you are the perfect person for the job and that's why we're here," Chase answered.

Calvin was silent while he considered what the man had told him.

"There's just one problem with your theory, Chase. If they kill me I won't be able to be that man for my children."

"That's why you can't fail, Mr. Walker."

Chase pushed the button for the elevator and the doors opened. Calvin walked inside and Chase stayed on the lobby side of the doors.

"You have to sell them on the idea that you've come to Washington to kill the people they want dead. In the end, it's the only way to save them."

CHAPTER 18
OLIVIA FORDHAM
1913

Chase had to do something he had never done before. He had to start his explanation at the beginning of everything he knew about traveling through history. A woman with Olivia's intelligence and worldliness who also feared she was losing herself to a brain tumor was not going to be convinced any other way. By the time Chase had told her about his experience in college and all the things he had been party to since coming to the Willard, Olivia had a monster headache. She was teetering between the absurdity of what he was saying *(wouldn't this make him hundreds of years old?)* with the burgeoning hope that maybe there was another explanation for what was happening that didn't mean her lucid time was coming to an end.

Olivia confided that the planned endowment for the Fordham Museum was to be her final act in the public eye. She was planning a graceful retirement once the center's future was secure. She envisioned herself becoming a mysterious hermit who would live out her life in her New York City penthouse enjoying any good days she had left and keeping her declining health from public view. She had it all planned out and now this man was telling her she had another purpose to fulfill before any of that could happen. He kept talking about tears in the fabric of history. Tears she could understand. Hadn't she been having tears in her own mental capacity for three years now? She was willing to grant that it was possible because she was inexplicably excited by the idea. Her life over the past thirty-six months had been in a type of limbo, never knowing when her reality would be upended. She rarely went anywhere without Jane just in case things began to get hazy or she found herself in a full-fledged episode.

The longer Chase talked, the more excited she could feel herself becoming. He explained why she was here and how important it was for her to do what was needed. It appealed to her sense of service and, more importantly, her unquenchable desire for extraordinary experiences.

Her mind couldn't make sense of everything he was telling her. He even admitted such a thing was impossible.

"Olivia, for the people who do these things to do them, they have to suspend part of what they know as reality. Each one has to be willing to go forward with nothing but the unbelievable notion that the impossible is possible."

"It's like faith," Olivia said.

Chase didn't know if she was a woman of faith or not. Her causes had always been secular in nature and he didn't know her personally well enough to determine her private views. But she seemed to grasp that to accept what he was telling her she would have to be willing to accept what cannot be proven.

The worry seemed to disappear from her face and Chase could see that she was relaxing. She couldn't explain what was happening. She didn't know if it was real or her imagination. She didn't know what she was supposed to do or how she could be of use one hundred years in the past. And she didn't care. In the same way she agreed with Robert Fordham that their lives could be best lived together, she decided to lean in to what Chase was telling her. The rest would have to sort itself out.

"What do you need me to do?" she asked.

"In a few days, Woodrow Wilson will be inaugurated as President of the United States. Before that date, thousands of women are planning to come to Washington to demand the right to vote. Two weeks ago, sixteen of them left New York City on horseback and on foot bound for the city. They need your help."

Olivia was silent for a moment. She smiled when she spoke next.

"Well, they're in luck, Edward. They sound like my kind of broads."

CHAPTER 19
CATHERINE PARKER
1865

When Catherine came around, the first thing she noticed was a playbill for *Our American Cousin*. Edward Chase had placed it beside her on the settee in order to wave the smelling salts under her nose. As she pulled herself together he handed her his handkerchief so she could dab at the water she'd spilled on her dress. It was still damp from the soaking she got from the carriage. Chase didn't speak at first and she took her time tending to her dress before she faced him again.

"You were saying something about . . .umm . . .an assassination I believe?" It seemed she could hardly form the words.

Chase searched her eyes but couldn't tell what she was thinking. He'd been in this situation many times and he knew he had to go slowly. Rushing headlong into his explanation would only cause her to shut down or, worse yet, bolt for the door. He knew they didn't have that kind of time. They only had forty-eight hours to go before their date with destiny and there wasn't time to find another person to handle the situation. It had to be Catherine. He gave her a brief explanation of what it meant to have a tear in the fabric of history and how critical it was to make sure everything happened as it had originally. That meant that she had been brought here to see that the president's assassination was not thwarted.

Catherine had been silent, taking in Chase's words all the while trying to wrap her mind around them. *He's saying it again. He's saying I have to make sure the president is assassinated. Perhaps the most beloved president of all time. The man who preserved the union. The one who freed the slaves. The same person who said 'four score and seven years ago' and other stuff like that. The president who was very famously shot and killed already and yet he wants me to make sure it happens again? What the hell kind of dream is this? It has to be a dream. It must be.*

"Mr. Chase, let me see if I understand you. I came here today, and by today I mean in 2016, to attend a job interview. An interview for a job that could change the course of my life, mind you. And now I'm sitting here in a long, dirty dress having just met an actress while I was out dodging horses and buggies on muddy streets and you're telling me I'm about a century and a half in the past and that I'm just going to walk out of here in my buttoned shoes and go make sure somebody kills the president who has been dead for 151 years. Is that about it? Because if it is, I think one of us needs some medical attention."

A hint of a smile crossed Chase's face. "Ah, sarcasm. The twenty-first century practice of stating the absurd. I recognize it."

Catherine didn't smile back. She wasn't giving in so easily to this man who appeared to be deranged. *How does a fancy place like this end up with a nut job for a concierge?*

She sat in silent defiance.

But he didn't make the cars disappear. Or the paved streets. And certainly not the top of the Washington Monument.

She tentatively decided then to give him a chance, not because she was prepared to believe what he was saying, but because she didn't have any other choice.

"All right, I'll play," she said as she picked up the playbill resting between them. She saw the name LAURA KEENE in big, bold letters. The star of the show.

"She was nice to me," Catherine said, almost to herself. "She helped me after a carriage flew out of an alley and splattered me with all this mud." She looked down at her bedraggled attire and thought she must look a mess.

Chase nodded his agreement. "She's a nice lady and a very well-known actress. I suppose you might say she's the Jennifer Aniston of this time. I heard about what happened behind the theatre this afternoon. That's where you were, you know? That's the alley behind Ford's Theatre. Evidently a bit of a kerfuffle erupted between Ms. Keene and Mrs. Aberdeen. It wasn't the first time Mrs. Aberdeen has made a hasty retreat about town with her carriage. I'm sorry you got caught in the flying mud, but it's serendipitous that you met Ms. Keene. You'll have easy access to the theatre through her."

"So she knows about this? She knows I'm. . . .not from here?" Catherine asked.

"No, she has no idea. She was just going through rehearsals this afternoon. She's played this theatre many times, but there are a few areas of the stage that have limited sight lines for some of the seats in the house so they were doing some new blocking. She doesn't know what's going to happen. She doesn't even know the president will be in the theatre in two days. He has not replied and there is even a rumor that he left town to attend the ceremony for the raising of the United States flag over Fort Sumter in Charleston Harbor. Major Anderson hauled it down that awful night four years ago and this will be the first time the union colors have flown over the fort since. No, the president will not make his plans known until the day of the performance when it becomes clear his wife wants to attend with Major Rathbone and Clara Harris."

"Just like that?" Catherine questioned him with a snap of her fingers. "Shouldn't there be Secret Service crawling the place already and getting ready to lock everything down? I know times were different, but I didn't think the president ever went anywhere on the spur of the moment."

"Remember back to your junior high history, Ms. Parker. No president had ever been assassinated before Mr. Lincoln so there is no Secret Service yet. The president comes and goes just as you or I. Even during the war he rode his horse to and from the Soldier's Home outside of the city with just a single sentry most of the time. And now the war is over. Peace is the order of the day for the first time in four contentious years and people are breathing easier. Lincoln is being hailed a hero. He really should be safer than ever."

Catherine jumped in. "Then that's wonderful news! All we have to do is keep him home from the theatre and the Great Emancipator lives to oversee Reconstruction. Simple, right?" Catherine's comment was dripping with sarcasm. "If this is really 1865 and I'm going to be hanging out with the leading lady at Lincoln's last play then why would I do anything OTHER than wave my arms around and tell everyone who'll listen that John Wilkes Booth is up to no good and save the president's life?"

"You're right. You could do that and you'd save a great man's life. But you could also do what the entire Confederacy could not. You might destroy the United States of America."

CHAPTER 20
TOM KELLY
1962

Tom nearly tripped a woman on her way through the revolving doors. As he entered the lobby of the Willard he saw Edward Chase walking toward him.

"What's going on?" The words were out of Tom's mouth before the two met halfway across the lobby.

"Mr. Kelly, please lower your voice. I assure you I can explain everything."

"There was something wrong with those bath salts in my room. I think they had some kind of drug in them. I'm walking around in a dream state and I have a very important meeting in a few hours that I can't afford to mess up. You need to get somebody in here, a doctor or somebody, to help me," Tom was nearly pleading as he ran his hand back and forth through his hair.

"This way, Mr. Kelly." Chase led him through a doorway off the lobby into the Round Robin Bar. "Please have a seat," he said as he poured him a glass of water from a carafe behind the bar.

"I could sue this hotel, you know! How many people take a bath in this place and end up passing out? I could have drowned!" The more he talked the more upset he became but Chase remained calm.

"You are not high, Mr. Kelly. You are in perfect health. The bath salts were a mixture of the finest lavender, heather, and moss from Ireland. There was nothing in them that would cause you any distress," the concierge assured him.

"Then I suppose you have an explanation for whatever the hell is happening to me? Is that right, Chase?"

"It is. But I'm afraid you are going to have to indulge me for a rather lengthy explanation. Please drink some water and try and calm down. The meeting with your investors is not in jeopardy. However, the fate of the world is and you are here to do something about it."

Tom stared at the concierge for a long time, waiting for him to either break up laughing or offer further explanation. He did neither. After a few deep breaths and a full glass of water Tom was no closer to figuring out what was happening.

"All right, I'm listening. Start talking," he said to Mr. Chase.

"Today is October 23, 1962. Last night, President John F. Kennedy went on national television to announce the buildup of offensive missile sites by the Soviet Union on the island of Cuba. He also announced a blockade around the island to stop any Soviet ships attempting to deliver further supplies to Cuba that could make the weapons operational. You know this event as the Cuban Missile Crisis and you know that it ended peacefully with the Russians turning their ships around and the missile sites being dismantled. That's how it happened the first time."

"What do you mean, 'the first time'?" asked Tom.

"Something has happened to the fabric of history, Mr. Kelly, and a significant change has taken place in the run up to the finale of the "game of chicken" as you refer to it. The first time the Soviets blinked. They pulled back and war was averted. This time the course of events has been altered. That's why you're here. You have to find out what has changed and fix it. And before you ask the question let me answer it; if you don't fix it, a first strike order will be issued by one of the nations. Given the circumstances, once it is ordered it cannot be rescinded."

CHAPTER 21
CALVIN WALKER
1963

It was now 9:30 in the morning. For the third time since he woke up, Calvin was walking to the elevator on his floor. He still hadn't had a cup of coffee. The clothes Chase had left with him were fairly nondescript. There was nothing thuggish about them, but they also didn't look like they had come from an expensive store. They were meant to blend in where he was going. To that end, Calvin had taken off his gold wedding band with the row of diamonds across the top. He hated thinking that it might be stolen.

When he got to the lobby Edward Chase was waiting for him. The concierge said he had arranged for a taxi to take Calvin to the general area where the addresses he had given him were located. He warned him that it could be hard to get a taxi on the way back and that he should be careful to get out of the area before it got too late. Calvin didn't understand why getting a taxi in D.C. would be a problem. They were known to be pretty much everywhere looking for fares.

"Mr. Walker, you have to remember this is 1963. Just the color of your skin will be enough for most taxis to pass you by in the better neighborhoods and where you're going they are scarce indeed because the area has a reputation for violence."

Awesome. This is sounding better and better all the time. Calvin got into the cab and headed for the first address on his list in

Washington's Southeast quadrant. The driver dropped him off a few blocks away and said he would go no farther.

Once on the sidewalk, Calvin got his bearings and started walking in the direction of his first stop. On the way there he wondered what kind of heinous activity could be taking place at this time of the morning. In his mind, these things happened in the dark of night, not before lunch on a Tuesday. The neighborhood was a busy one. Mothers were pushing their children in strollers along the sidewalk and stores seemed to be doing good business as he passed by their open doors. Nothing looked particularly dangerous to him. He walked straight for a few blocks and navigated west for a couple more. He'd ventured into the residential areas where he saw people sitting on the steps of walk-ups that had seen better days and in doorways of apartment buildings. Most were men who should have been at work by this time of day, but they seemed to have nowhere to be. There were also quite a few young people in their teens and twenties who eyed Calvin with suspicion as he passed. He was feeling like the farther he walked from where the taxi driver had dropped him off the more sinister the area felt. One other thing he'd noticed in the six blocks he'd walked was that he hadn't seen a single white face. It was the opposite of the nearly all-white environment near the Willard. He couldn't explain why but he felt much more out of place here where the faces looked like his own than he had when he walked up 14th Street with Edward Chase, and he was ashamed of his reaction. Just about the time he had decided to turn back he came to the first address on the note. He wasn't sure what the protocol was for dropping in on a group of radicals so he rang the buzzer until someone released the door and he walked up to the second floor. He did the only thing he knew to do. He knocked. After a few more minutes of knocking and listening for any sound that would betray the inhabitants he decided there was nobody there and he went back to the street. He really wanted to leave the area but the other address was only a block away so he vowed to give it one more try and then hightail it back to the Northwest.

The single block made a world of difference. There were overflowing trash cans on the sidewalk, like the city didn't bother to pick up the trash here. The smell was putrid and some of the lighter waste had blown into the street where it advanced from doorway to doorway with every gust of wind or passing car. The people who were milling about locked onto the newcomer as soon as he rounded the corner and Calvin could feel them watching his every move. *Three times. I'll knock three times and wait thirty seconds and then I'm out of here.*

He came to a walk-up with the address he was looking for above the door. There were three young men sitting on the steps between him and the entrance and they were in no hurry to move to let him pass. He remembered what he'd been told years before that had served him well in business: always walk into a room looking like you belong there and people won't question you. He put on the air of someone who was supposed to be exactly where he was and stepped around the men. Inside the main door there were two doors on the first floor and a staircase leading to two more on the floor above. He was looking for apartment 2A. As he started up the stairs he heard a commotion. When he reached the second floor landing, he saw the door to 2A standing open and several men moving boxes inside that had been sitting outside the door. They all stopped when they saw Calvin. Then they simultaneously pulled handguns from waistbands, coat pockets and other hiding places. Calvin put his hands up as he quickly counted eight barrels aimed at him.

In colorful language they asked him what he was doing standing there. *Act like you belong and nobody will question you.* Calvin barely recognized his own strong and non-wavering voice as he said, "Put the guns down. I'm on your side. I'm here to help you."

CHAPTER 22
OLIVIA FORDHAM
1913

On February 12, sixteen women left New York City bound for Washington, D.C. Many more joined them along the way as they gained publicity for the planned march in the nation's capital the day before the inauguration. They had drawn up a letter for President-Elect Woodrow Wilson informing him that they would be seriously watching his administration to a degree that had never before been seen and they expected him to champion suffrage for women. They requested an audience with him for as soon as possible after he was sworn in.

The women were doing all they could to gain attention for the upcoming march and for their cause at large. One drove a horse-drawn, brightly-colored wagon covered with signs and filled with literature she handed out freely to all who would take it. Some of their participants even recorded a newfangled motion picture promotion that was greeted with boos and hisses when it played in movie houses. Preparation was underway on floats, banners, and all the trappings of a celebratory parade.

Olivia didn't know any of this was happening. As the head of a global business and now a large foundation, she was accustomed to briefings from her trusted staff on any subject she needed to master. She approached the situation she found herself in now with the same attitude. She asked Chase to fill her in on everything.

"I'm happy to share what I know with you, Olivia, but you must understand that my knowledge of the situation is limited."

"How can that be? And what did you mean when you said earlier that my being here is your fault?"

Chase thought carefully about how to explain the next part to her.

"Since I came to the Willard and became the concierge I've been tasked with leading people like you through these points in history. I'm never sure exactly what the problem is or how to solve it. Downstairs, behind the concierge desk, there is a wall of cubbies where messages and mail were collected for guests before the days of voicemail and e-mail. When I first came here I wasn't sure how my job would work. On the first evening I was looking at the cubby wall and something caught my eye. It was a narrow slot that seemed out of place. Upon further examination I found a note that had been left for me. It gave me limited information about the historical tear and a few details and I was instructed to choose a person to travel back in time to try and fix the problem. I wasn't sure what to do at first but I learned over time how to select the right people by examining the hotel's reservation lists. I learned as much as possible about who would be here and whether or not that person would be a good match for the situation. Honestly, Olivia, it's usually just a hunch, although these days with the Internet I can find out quite a bit about a person before they arrive. That leads me to you and to why I said it's my fault you're here."

Olivia sat enthralled by what she was hearing.

"When I found out about this tear I was only told three things. First, that it involved women's suffrage and the 1913 march. Second, that there is a particular woman who is critical to the future of untold numbers of men, women and children in the years to come and that something in this timeline is changed so that she might not fulfill the role she is destined to play. Keep in mind she did fulfill that role initially."

Olivia nodded. "What's the third thing you were told?"

"The last thing I learned from the note is that this lady does not understand her significance in the course of history and that without her involvement the result would be future suffering and untapped potential. When I learned you would be here at the hotel this week the timing seemed providential. I knew you had to be the one to handle this."

"Why do you think it has to be me?"

"You're a strong woman and look at everything you've been able to do with your life. Without women like these pioneers you might not have had those opportunities and I believed, and I still believe, that when you meet them and walk in their shoes you'll be inspired to help overcome any obstacle that's set before them. So, you see, it was my decision to bring you here." Chase was concerned when Olivia didn't respond right away. "I hope you aren't angry with me."

She seemed to be somewhere else entirely but when she spoke Chase realized her analytical mind had been hard at work. "If what you're telling me is true then I'm not having one of my episodes AND you have given me an opportunity to meet and interact with some of the bravest women of the twentieth century. Is that the long and short of it?" she asked with a sly smile.

"Yes, I believe that about covers it," Chase answered. He was pleased to see her looking like her old self.

"Then let's get out of this room and find this mystery woman." She practically sprang to her feet and headed for the bedroom to get changed. From the hallway Chase heard her parting comment.

"I've always wanted to drive a Model T!"

❦

Chase accompanied Olivia to the lobby in her Edwardian finery. They had decided she would visit the headquarters of the National American Woman Suffrage Association (NAWSA) on F Street and introduce herself to Alice Paul who was the driving force behind the march. Olivia didn't see any reason not to start right at the top. Edward walked away momentarily to arrange her transportation and Olivia busied herself watching the exquisitely dressed patrons as they milled about the lobby. She herself was dressed in one of the smart ensembles that had appeared in her closet. She was glad that by this time the use of corsets was optional. She opted to skip that part of the experience. Age did have its advantages.

She was admiring the courtly manners of the gentlemen as they attended the ladies. *It's a pity such niceties were abandoned,* she thought. A young woman entering through the revolving door caught her attention. She was lovely with her dark hair arranged in a complex style and topped with an enormous hat that set off the vibrant blue of her eyes. She appeared to be quite young but it was clear she was comfortable in such opulent surroundings, like she belonged in a place such as this. The sight of her reminded Olivia of the character, Rose, when she steps out of the motorcar in the movie *Titanic.* Olivia watched her as she kindly thanked the bellman who had brought her bags. Her voice was soft and her speech refined.

She has excellent manners. It's apparent she's been raised well, Olivia found herself thinking.

The young woman seemed to be waiting for someone and she made her way to the seating area where Olivia was standing. As she got closer something that felt like a jolt of electricity went straight up Olivia's spine.

"Pardon me, ma'am, would you happen to be Amelia Sutherland?" the young woman asked.

Olivia could not speak. She only managed to stare into the blue eyes before her, but the young woman didn't seem to find her rude.

"Please forgive my manners, ma'am. I didn't introduce myself." She offered her hand. "I'm Victoria Webster."

It cannot be, Olivia thought over and over. As if in slow motion she reached forward and placed her hand into Victoria's. Time seemed to stand still as Olivia Asher Fordham shook hands with her grandmother.

CHAPTER 23
CATHERINE PARKER
1865

"Destroy the United States of America? I'm a Yankee, Mr. Chase, why would I want to do that? And how would saving the life of the man who devoted that life to preserving the union destroy it?" Catherine asked incredulously.

"Do you remember why John Wilkes Booth wanted to kill the president?" Chase let his question hang in the air as he watched Catherine consider her answer.

"He was a Southerner. I remember that," she answered.

"Yes, but not a Southerner whose family farm had been destroyed because there were no men left to work the fields. He didn't have children who were half-starved because their livestock and stored food had been commandeered by the army. He wasn't part of the suffering mass of people whose lives had been given over to fighting for their homes and property because it was the land of their birth. Most were too poor to own slaves and too far removed from the political world to concern themselves with "states rights" and such weighty thoughts. They were farmers and merchants and blacksmiths and riverboat dock stewards. And now they're sick of war. Hundreds of thousands are dead. Families are scattered and the land they fought for is ruined. They didn't want to lose the war, but they've given it all they had and they're tired. They want to go home and start over. But not John Wilkes Booth.

He's an actor from a family of actors. His life is spent on stages and in fine hotels with the public fawning over him. These past four years he's had the luxury of concerning himself with fine clothes, aged whisky, and flaming political rhetoric. He hasn't bled for the cause and he's not prepared to let it die. Originally, he planned a kidnapping but now he believes the South will take up arms again if he *kills* Lincoln. He thinks he'll be heralded as a hero across the Confederacy, and that the fire will be reignited. We know it didn't work out that way. He was called a murderer and he died a coward's death hiding in a barn. The South did not rise up and call him 'son' and the death of Lincoln actually helped heal the nation, not tear it back apart. The Southerner who thought he knew what the people wanted could not have been more wrong."

"I still don't see what any of this has to do with tearing apart the country. You just said yourself that people came together over Lincoln," Catherine countered.

"I said they came together over his *death* because a nation that had seen nothing *but* death for four years recognized the brutality of what he suffered. But what if he had lived? There were others who were attempting to stir factions of the Southern population into new rebellion. Some were saying the Emancipation Proclamation meant nothing to them and abuses of the newly freed slaves were promised. Not every military unit had laid down its arms. Fighting continued for months after the surrender at Appomattox as word of capitulation traveled west. There were still two sides, two ways of life. Each side only saw their own suffering. They needed to come together and heal the wounds, but they didn't have a common experience on which to base those first tentative steps. Lincoln's assassination gave it to them. While he lived he was just a man, but in death he became a martyr. Booth's action achieved the complete opposite of what he intended. For decades, even a hundred years after, Lincoln's words were being used to inspire the hearts of freedom fighters and civil rights leaders. When Lee surrendered to Grant, most in the government wanted the South to pay and pay dearly. Lincoln knew the Southern people had already paid, and that if the union was to truly be reunited mercy and grace would have to rule the day. He put forth lenient terms for those who had worn the gray uniform. They were sent home to begin the process of rebuilding their lives and Lincoln made sure the terms with each state laid out a clear path to reconciliation, not a focus on retribution. He famously said, "Let 'em up easy." He set those things in motion and then just days later he died. In death, he became larger than life and his example of mercy and dedication to the ideals of unity never had to endure testing or scrutiny. His legacy became untouchable and the nation healed."

Catherine looked weary. "Are you saying that if he had lived there might have been more war and that the North and South might not have mended their fences? You really think Lincoln's death and not his life led to reconciliation?"

"I'm saying that Lincoln died and we had reconciliation. We had a hero—a sad-looking man who had persevered during a long, lonely war where he was hated in the South and ridiculed in his own government. He lost a child while in office and seemed to internalize the sacrifice of every mother whose son gave his life on the battlefield on *either* side of the conflict. That much we know. It's what we don't know that could hurt us. What would have happened if he had not been killed? That's the part we don't know and it's much too dangerous to ever find out."

"I'm not saying I'm going along with this and I still hope it's just a bad dream," Catherine's voice trailed off and Chase could tell she was struggling with her thoughts.

She looked him in the eye. "Tell me what you want me to do."

CHAPTER 24
TOM KELLY
1962

The next forty-five minutes went by in a blur as Edward Chase spun an unbelievable tale. He explained to Tom that he was a guest in 1962 Washington and what it meant to have a tear in the fabric of history. It wasn't long before Tom was battling a raging headache for which Chase effortlessly passed him a couple of aspirin without being asked.

This guy knows I have a headache, or should I say he knew I was going to have a headache and he knew I was toying around with Alice in Wonderland imagery and crazy rabbits at tea parties. I'm not sure if he's nuts or if I am, but something is definitely very wrong here.

"So it's 1962 and the Russians want a do-over with the whole Cuban thing. Let's say I buy that theory," Tom said. "That doesn't explain what I'm doing here. I'm pretty low-hanging fruit at my own chosen profession, which happens to have absolutely nothing to do with politics or national defense anyway, so please tell me what a middle-aged man who dabbles with movies can do to help this situation. And don't say anything about "Argo" because I'm pretty sure that ruse only worked once."

Chase was calm, as always. "You are here precisely because of what you do for a living. You may have noticed the White House is full of men in suits and they have every kind of expertise at their fingertips having to do with politics and national defense. They have spies, and people who spy on spies, and there are a lot of things they know. But there's something they don't know that you do," he answered.

"And what's that, Mr. Chase? How much vodka it takes to make you forget you just watched four million dollars of your investor's money go down the drain or how many Russian hookers can fit in a phone booth?"

"You know Nikita Khrushchev and his back channel network," Chase responded.

Tom was slumped in his chair and he let out a chuckle. "And how is it that I came to know this information?"

"You learned about it in your role as a filmmaker." Chase passed a battered script across the table.

Tom looked at the cover. *The "K" Factor.* Under the main title there was a subtitle: *Khrushchev and the KGB.* Tom had never seen the script before, nor heard the title, but his name was on the next line right there on the cover.

"I don't know what this is. I've never seen it before and I certainly didn't write it," he protested. "Let's not forget, I wasn't even born when all this happened."

"None of that really matters now. In this timeline you are still Tom Kelly and you have spent your adult life making films. You're not a big name but some of your work has been noticed by important people. This script is an example. It was never developed into an actual film because there were a lot of people who were pretty nervous about what you had uncovered. The project died before it got off the ground, in large part thanks to some of those dark-suited men down the street who are currently wondering if there's room for them in the nuclear bunker."

Chase continued, "You spent a year on the ground in the Soviet Union developing a network of contacts under the guise of a propaganda film that would be pro-Communist. Nobody there knew you were an American. You worked up a good cover as an eccentric Argentinian with deep pockets and you stayed away from the naturally suspicious types on the Soviet payroll. Instead you courted the fringe. I believe you call them "want-to-bes" who were impressed with your story about glorifying the motherland on the silver screen and they hoped to play a role so to speak. Money talks in a place where the average worker spends more time worrying if he'll be visited in the dark of night by the secret police than whether or not his retirement is looking secure. You passed around the cash and, in return, bought access to the pipeline that rides the fine line between *government-sponsored* and *government-secret*. Some of the information made it into your fictional script, but the powers that be know there is much more that you didn't put on those pages."

Chase passed a file folder across the table. Tom opened it to find pages and pages of notes in his own handwriting. "The rest is in there," Chase pointed to the notes.

Tom was stunned as he flipped through the pages. There were names and dates and aliases. He saw crude drawings of Moscow streets and buildings with lines and arrows pointing to the margins where he had described the things and people to be found in each place. There were letters on official government letterhead that were written in Russian but had the English translation handwritten between the lines, again in his handwriting. And photos. There were photographs of the Soviet premier in public places, but also in private. Some appeared to have been taken in the man's bedroom as he sat in his nightclothes and nursed a tumbler of vodka. There were men in uniforms and other men who had the same G-man look as our American FBI agents, only with a Russian flair. There were women too. Women who were in all forms of dress, both professional and the other kind of professional. There were names written on the backs and descriptions in some kind of shorthand. *Olga, St. Petersburg, 44–61, exit.* Strange though it was, Tom knew what it meant. The woman in the photo was Olga, (an alias), and she could access the back channels via a St. Petersburg contact. Even though the Soviets called the city Leningrad, these loyalist contacts still used the old city name, St. Petersburg. The street address for the drop on her end was 44 and she would drop responses to him two blocks away at number 61. *Exit*, meant that she had gone underground and Tom remembered why. Someone found out about her children who lived with their grandparents in a peasant village hundreds of miles away and sent an unpleasant message regarding what would happen to them if she didn't stop her activities. She disappeared on a Thursday and Tom had hoped it was her own doing and that she hadn't been forcibly silenced. She was one of the nicer ones and could be trusted. He hoped she was somewhere warm and sunny with her children.

He had no idea how he knew these facts, but a cursory glance through the notes and the script seemed to open the floodgates and he suddenly "remembered" everything that was written there.

"There is a lot of communication flowing through unofficial channels between Washington and Moscow," Chase warned. "Think of the game of telephone that you played as a child. How often was the message at the end of the game the same as it was at the beginning? Multiple hands mean multiple opportunities for errors, accidental or otherwise. Somewhere in the communication process there is a problem. I don't know if it's intentional or not and whether or not it has happened yet. What I do know is that getting a message confused when both men have their fingers on the launch buttons can only end in disaster. That's why you're here, to help the White House navigate this communication exchange. You have to find the error and fix it."

Tom could hardly move. "How will I know when I find it? They're not exactly going to hand me a transcript to review."

Chase paused before he answered. "Look carefully, Tom. Because if you don't find it you won't have to worry about disappointing your mother. You'll never be born."

CHAPTER 25
CALVIN WALKER
1963

In rapid succession, four enormous men grabbed Calvin, searched him for weapons, pushed him into a kitchen chair, and re-aimed their weapons at him. During the abrupt welcome someone had finished dragging the boxes inside and closed the door. Calvin was in the belly of the beast now and a single wrong word could mean the end for him. It was no time to show fear. These people thrived on making people fear them.

"I thought I told you to put those down. I'm not armed, as you are well aware."

The quiet one leaning against the stove finally spoke. "As we are well aware. . .fancy, fancy. That's fancy talk you're making there. I don't know if we understand fancy talk like that here in the hood, do we boys?"

The others snickered, but kept their guns pointed at Calvin.

The same one continued to talk, but he had left his perch and was beginning to slowly circle Calvin. "Are you some kind of college boy? Cause we love the college boys down in here." The others laughed, but it was menacing. "Yes, sir, the college boys all want to come in here and help us. But you too old to be a college boy. Maybe you a *pro-fess-a*" the thug said as he strutted around. His underlings kept laughing. They were his audience. "Is that it? You a *pro-fess-a* come down here to teach us how to talk to the white folks? Them college boys and *pro-fess-as*, they wanna talk about stuff and pass out flyers and make speeches. You a speech-maker, boy?" he asked as he kicked the leg of Calvin's chair. "Did you come here to *talk?* Cause you in the wrong damn place for talkin', *Pro-fess-a.*" Suddenly he spun around and came within an inch of Calvin's face. He put his gun under Calvin's chin as the others began to get more excited. "You got one minute to tell me how you found us and why I shouldn't waste you like one of them pigs that's black but thinks they's lily white."

Calvin's head was spinning. He could imagine what the scene looked like and for a split second wondered how any of this was remotely possible. But he had more urgent matters to attend to, including the gun presently pressed into his lower jaw. His instinct for self-preservation took over and he said the only thing that came to his mind.

"It doesn't matter how I found you. The important thing is I can get you Martin Luther King. Tonight."

A look went around the table and the guns went down. As he rubbed his chin where the muzzle had been pressed he wondered what he had just done.

CHAPTER 26
OLIVIA FORDHAM
1913

Olivia regained her composure and introduced herself to Victoria. She had a fleeting thought about the absurdity of her grandmother being a teenager while she herself was a mature woman of seventy. It was topsy-turvy like everything else had been since she had awoken from her nap.

"I'm not acquainted with Ms. Sutherland but, Mr. Chase, the concierge, may be of assistance. He's busy at the desk right now, but he'll be along in a moment and we can ask him," Olivia said.

"That would be wonderful. Thank you."

"Would you like to sit down?"

Victoria smiled. "I would like to sit down very much. The journey from Philadelphia has been a bit hard on my feet I'm afraid." The two women sat down as Olivia thought of her grandmother's house in Philadelphia. It had been in the family for several generations and she loved to visit there when she was a girl. She remembered that her grandmother had lived in the house her entire life. It was strange to think the young girl before her may have just left that same house to come here.

"Did you travel here by yourself?" Olivia asked. She was mentally trying to do the math to figure out how old Victoria was.

"No, a family friend who lives here acted as chaperone, but I'm on my own now. My parents are quite bothered by the idea but I'm seventeen and more than capable of taking care of myself.   And it is 1913 after all, and not 1850," she said defensively. Olivia thought she sounded terribly childlike.

"I meant you no offense, Victoria. What brings you to Washington?"

"I'm sorry if I was defensive. It has taken weeks of arguing with my parents to convince them to let me come. I'm here to take part in the parade for women's suffrage. I think it's time women have an equal voice in their government. Don't you agree?"

My goodness. She certainly has no trouble speaking her mind.

"As a matter of fact, I do agree. Is this Ms. Sutherland part of the group?"

"Yes, and she's an acquaintance of the gentleman who escorted me on the train. He spoke on her behalf and assured my parents she is a quality person. That's what ultimately convinced them to let me come. I've written to her and she is to meet me here at the hotel and instruct me on how I might be of service."

"What do you hope to do with this organization?"

"Well, to tell you the truth, I really don't know. A few months ago I happened upon a rally in Philadelphia where the suffragists were making their pleas to the crowd. Someone handed me a pamphlet and starting talking with me about the issue. I thought it was very important, but Mother was waiting and we had to leave. She told me not to speak to 'such people' as she called them. A day later, one of the members came to our house and asked for me. I suppose someone told them who I was, although I'm not sure why they were interested in talking with me. She left more information and started coming by to see me every couple of days. I attended a few meetings and started to get very interested in what they are doing. Mother says they want to use me because our family name is important in Philadelphia."

"What do you think?"

"I think they need young people like me to help get the word out. The ladies who are in charge are very capable and I think they probably need others like me to help make signs or go door to door and talk with people. I'm happy to do whatever is needed to make a difference."

"Is that your goal? To make a difference?"

Victoria looked confused. "Of course. Doesn't everyone want to make a difference? I just think it's time women had a chance to do more. Mother doesn't think so. She says it's unseemly, what they're doing."

"Your mother sounds like she has a lot of opinions."

"You have no idea."

"I'm sure she's concerned for your safety."

"She's more concerned for my reputation, or rather, our family's reputation. She's afraid I will do something to bring shame on us all."

"You don't strike me as a young woman prone to shameful associations."

Victoria looked pleased by Olivia's compliment. Chase joined them and told Olivia he had arranged for her transportation to the headquarters.

"Edward, I'm pleased to introduce you to Victoria Webster. Victoria, this is Edward Chase, the hotel's concierge." Olivia spoke to Chase. "Ms. Webster is looking for a woman named Amelia Sutherland. Are you familiar with Ms. Sutherland?"

"Yes, in fact. She was here earlier and had to leave for a meeting at the very office you are planning to visit. She asked me to pass along her apologies to Ms. Webster, but I would venture to say that if the two of you would like to ride together you could likely catch Ms. Sutherland at the office."

Victoria looked excited. She turned to Olivia.

"I hope that wouldn't be an imposition, Mrs. Fordham."

"Not at all, dear. It's a splendid idea."

"And one of great economy as well," Victoria added.

What a strange thing to say. This child has likely never had to concern herself with issues of economy. There is indeed more to her than meets the eye.

"It's settled then. We'll be off at once," Olivia said.

"Oh, I almost forgot! My bags are by the door. I have a reservation here for the next several nights," Victoria said to Chase.

"I'll take care of your bags and have your room key for you when you return," Chase said.

Victoria was on her feet, practically bouncing with excitement. "Oh, thank you so much, Mr. Chase. And thank you, Mrs. Fordham. Mother would be so pleased to learn that I've made such providential acquaintances my first hours in town," she gushed.

Providential indeed, Olivia thought.

Together they climbed into the waiting car and headed for F Street.

CHAPTER 27
CATHERINE PARKER
1865

Mr. Chase had a hot bath prepared for Catherine and after a good long soak and a change of clothes she went down to the lobby to meet the carriage that would take her to a late dinner with Laura Keene. They settled into a quiet corner table at a restaurant a few blocks from the Willard. Catherine noticed Laura was still wearing her stage makeup from her dress rehearsal.

"I'm so pleased to see you're feeling better, Ms. Parker," Laura said to the younger woman.

"Please, call me Catherine."

"Of course. And you must call me Laura."

"I'm sorry I didn't recognize you before, Laura. I had a long trip from Ohio and I believe I was just terribly overtired. Of course I know who you are and I'm embarrassed to say I'm a bit star struck to be sitting here with you," Catherine told her. The star struck part was the truth. She'd never met a famous actress before.

"Nonsense. There is no reason to be awed by a woman of the stage, Catherine. After all, we spend our lives pretending to be someone else. I've never understood why that fascinates people so much really," Laura answered.

Catherine had an immediate thought. *Probably because pretending to be someone or something you're not is freaking hard.*

"How do you do it?" Catherine asked. "How do you stand up there and act out scenes when you already know the ending of the play? For example, you are all innocent and tentative about love at the beginning of the play, but you know your paramour is going to die in the final scene. How do you play the happy parts knowing the sad is coming?"

Laura thought about it for a minute. "I guess I've never considered it that way. When I play a character I do my best to really *become* that person in the moment. At the beginning of the play, if my character is falling in love she's at that point and has no idea of the tragedy to come. I don't focus on the tragedy until the character gets to it. That way I can keep my reactions as genuine as possible. I suppose you could say I start the character's journey over every time the curtain goes up."

Catherine was quiet as they ate the tender roast beef and potatoes the waiter had brought. She seemed to be deep in thought, but made all the right responses as Laura kept up the small talk. Laura noticed the silence.

"Are you still tired, my dear? Would you like to go back to the hotel?"

"I'm sorry, Laura. My mind is preoccupied with something I have to do. I didn't mean to be rude. I have a lot on my mind," Catherine apologized.

"It's no problem. I'm ready to head back myself. I have a few costume adjustments to attend to and a short afternoon rehearsal tomorrow. Would you like to meet for dinner again tomorrow evening?"

"Actually, I was wondering if I might stop by and watch your rehearsal. I've never seen anything like that," Catherine wondered if her request was out of line. Big stars are particular about people watching them rehearse. At least that's what she'd heard on TMZ.

"I would love for you to join me. It gets so tedious and I would be happy to give you a tour of the theatre and have you sit in the wings for the rehearsal. And while you're here this week I welcome you to be my guest for Friday's performance. Rehearsals are fine, but you really must see the full show with sets and costumes. This show is quite humorous and the light fare will give you a chance to get your mind off serious things for a few hours," Laura said.

Oh, Laura, you have no idea how serious this is.

"Thank you for the kind invitation. I accept."

I'm in, Catherine thought. *Now what?*

CHAPTER 28
TOM KELLY
1962

Tom cleared security again at the White House gate and found himself waiting outside an unknown meeting room on a lower floor. He had a feeling it was the fabled Situation Room, but nothing about it looked like he expected when he was finally admitted. A quick look around the table confirmed that he was part of something at the highest levels. Seated around the table was the famous "ExComm," the executive committee Kennedy had pulled together to deal with the crisis. Over the next few hours Tom learned firsthand what was happening and some of it differed from the textbook versions he remembered.

About a week before, reconnaissance photos had revealed construction of offensive missile sites on the island nation of Cuba. Information that had come in since then showed the sites had been under construction for several months. While the history books claim the U.S. and the U.S.S.R. were equal in their nuclear capabilities, what that really means is that they had enough between them to blow up the world so there wasn't much point counting beyond that. Where they weren't equal was in delivery methods. The U.S. could fire long-range missiles into the homeland of mother Russia, but the Soviet missiles were only capable of shorter-range deployment, making them a threat to Europe, but not to the continental U.S. The Soviets needed a closer geographic location where their limited flight capability could target American soil and they got that by exploiting the fears of one impressionable Cuban dictator.   Fidel Castro's men had repelled the Bay of Pigs invasion, but he feared a new and more successful invasion by American forces. To add to his own security, he approved the Soviet plan to put missiles in his country and, just like that, the Soviets had their launch pad for North American destruction.

In his address to the nation last night, President Kennedy had announced a naval blockade of Cuba aimed at preventing the Soviets from landing more parts and supplies that could make their sites operational. The scariest thing Tom learned was that Soviet field commanders in Cuba had been given authority to use their battlefield nuclear devices in case of invasion. All it would take was one Rambo-esque commander feeling like he was in the crosshairs of the U.S. military and this tinderbox would be lit. Tom couldn't help thinking about the fog of war and how easily a mistake in judgment could be made. He shivered in his chair, which did not go unnoticed by the military brass in the room. The commanders reported that U2 planes were currently conducting low-level recon flights over the sites every two hours. Analysts were pouring over thousands of frames of film, checking for any change in the readiness of each location. The group in the room with Tom was now on day eight with little sleep and the literal weight of the world on their shoulders. Tensions fluctuated between high and extremely high and tempers were short.   Only the two Kennedys seemed to fly above the fray like kings watching their gladiators fight for supremacy.   They were listening to every point and carefully evaluating the arguments for and against every proposal.   One man in the room would be the ultimate authority and he held tight to his brother's counsel. These two would watch and listen and, when the time came, they would act. Tom was impressed by the questions they asked when they did interject.   The questions were thoughtful and complex. It was clear these two men were imagining changing scenarios and they challenged their team to think beyond step one and step two to steps ten, and eighteen, and twenty-five. What will happen if we do this? What if we do that instead? The elephant in the room, the one who could not be questioned, was the Soviet Union itself and its recalcitrant leader, Nikita Khrushchev.

On the wall, a giant map of the behemoth nation held sway over the room, its sheer size and the unfortunate shade of red that had been used in printing causing it to feel like a sinister monster, the color of blood. All the mystery of the land behind the iron curtain only served to increase the ominous presence felt anytime it was mentioned. Tom knew why they called it cold war now. The very sight of the red map in this environment chilled him to the bone.

One poor general had been tasked with providing potential casualty reports. It was clear right away that his job was a bit like explaining how many grains of sand there are on the earth. It doesn't matter if the estimate is wrong because there's really nobody in the world who can count them anyway.

"For all practical purposes, Mr. President, it will get everyone. Millions in the initial strike, millions more from radiation exposure over time, the rest from sickness, starvation. From suicide." He paused, and then continued. "There might be some left, sir, but the government will be gone as will the food supply and all infrastructure. Those remaining won't be in the Middle Ages. They'll be in the Dark Ages."

Tom sat stunned. *And there will be no one left to count them.*

The marathon session broke for a quick meal. Sandwiches were brought in from the White House mess and the group separated into smaller groups at the president's request. A man with round glasses approached Tom and extended his hand.

"I'm McGeorge Bundy. I'm the one who sent for you. Don't worry about it if you get some flack from McCone. He took over the agency a few months ago and has a different opinion of the Soviet threat than official reports that were issued before he got there. They underestimated the possibility this could happen, but he didn't. He's a sharp guy. I think when he sees what you have to offer he'll be ready to work with you." He motioned for Tom to follow him. "The president would like to see you in the Oval in ten minutes. Walk with me upstairs and I'll park you in a conference room. Someone will come for you when we're ready," he said.

Tom followed the man up the stairs, recognizing that McGeorge Bundy was the president's National Security Adviser. He wasn't positive but he thought "McCone" was John McCone, head of the CIA.

I'll bet he's not happy I'm here. I doubt if the CIA is accustomed to getting advice on covert communications from a Hollywood reject.

Bundy deposited Tom in a room as promised and Tom pulled out a sheet of paper and started making a list of all the people from the meeting.

> *President Kennedy*
> *Bobby Kennedy, Attorney General*
> *McGeorge Bundy, National Security Adviser*
> *John McCone, Director of CIA*
> *Dean Rusk, Secretary of State*
> *C. Douglas Dillon, Secretary of the Treasury*
> *Robert McNamara, Secretary of Defense*
> *General Maxwell D. Taylor, Chairman of the Joint Chiefs of Staff*
> *Assorted deputies and under-secretaries*
> *Vice President Lyndon B. Johnson*

The last one was a surprise, not because he was there but because he was fairly quiet. Everything Tom had ever heard about the bombastic vice president and later president from Texas had prepared him for a loud, bossy, expletive-spewing man, but Johnson had kept his tongue in the meetings. He participated, but he didn't try and take over. Whatever his feelings about the president, he knew better than to overstep in this situation.

Tom was mulling this latest discovery over in his mind when he heard a familiar voice calling to him from the doorway. He turned to find Ethan York standing there.

"Are they ready for me?" he asked the young man.

"Not yet, sir. I asked to be assigned to you for the day so I'll be in charge of getting you from place to place. I thought that way it would be easy if you want to tell me anything," he said with a knowing look.

"Listen, son, I appreciate that you're scared and I'd like to tell you there's nothing to worry about, but you strike me as a smart guy so you've probably figured out there's plenty to worry about. The problem is, if this thing goes down you won't have time to get to South Carolina and it wouldn't matter if you did because it will disappear just like Washington," Tom said matter-of-factly.

Ethan had a look of terror on his face and Tom knew he had gone too far. He tried to do damage control. It wasn't going to do anyone any good to have this kid lose it in the West Wing. Who knew how many others were right on the verge themselves? It could set off a mass panic.

"What I meant to say, Ethan, is that anything that might happen will likely happen fast. On the other hand, as nice as South Carolina is, it's not a strategic location like Washington so it probably wouldn't be a major target. Even so, getting there could take a while and I can't tell you whether or not you should head that way because I'm not sure it would matter where you are. Anyway, this may all blow over instead of blowing up." His attempt at lightheartedness went nowhere.

Ethan sat down in the chair next to Tom, a clear violation of intern protocol, but he wasn't thinking about those things.

"Mr. Kelly, I appreciate what you're telling me and I do understand. We had those nuclear drills when I was in high school and it always seemed stupid to me to get under a desk and expect that to protect me from a hydrogen bomb. I always figured it made the grown-ups feel like they were doing something when there really wasn't anything they could do. I knew that then and I know it now." His thoughts seemed to drift away for a moment.

"I guess I just hate the thought of not being with my family. Dying here or dying there, both options are pretty terrible. I just don't want my mother to worry about me. And I don't want her to be alone."

"How old are you, Ethan?"

"I'm eighteen. I graduated from high school in May. Top of my class at Fort Mill High," he said with pride. "It's just a little place, hardly a dot on the map but it's right beside Charlotte, North Carolina so sometimes I tell people that's where I'm from because they know where that is. But it doesn't feel right to say that because it feels like I'm not proud of where I'm from and I love South Carolina. Especially the beaches. Have you been to the beaches in South Carolina, Mr. Kelly?"

"Ironically, it was a beach in *North* Carolina that brought me here today but I haven't had the pleasure of your South Carolina beaches. I'm sure they're much nicer," he said with a smile.

"I like to think they are, especially down around Charleston. I like to go there with my mom. We both like history and when we go to Charleston she says they're still fighting the war down there," Ethan said.

"You're very close to your mom it seems."

"I am. I'm close to my dad, too. He's a really good guy, but he has more in common with my brother so they do a lot of stuff together. They like to play golf and football and I like to do nerd stuff like read books and talk to grown-ups. I guess I'm a grown-up now too, but I don't feel like one. Anyway, my mom heard me say once that I thought it would be cool to come to Washington and work at the Capitol or the White House. She never forgot it and decided it would help me get into the best college so she's been working for two years to get me this chance. They usually take kids who are already in college, but she wouldn't take no for an answer. She was right, too. Just showing I was going to be an intern here helped me get into the University of Virginia. I kind of wanted to go to Clemson back home but she told me the University of Virginia is the school of Thomas Jefferson and I should aim high. So I'll be going to Charlottesville in January."

"You're a good kid, Ethan. You're doing what your mom wants you to do," Tom said with what he hoped didn't betray a hint of sarcasm as he thought about how disappointed his own mother would be by his life choices.

"No, I'm really doing what I want to do, except maybe the Clemson part. I never thought I could be the best at anything, but she told me I could and she helped me along the way. I'm kind of awkward and shy, not exactly class president, you know? She was always telling me I was as good as everyone else. I didn't believe it, but I decided to work at it and it paid off. It turned out I was a lot smarter than I thought. I owe her a lot. She's really proud that I'm here doing this. I think everyone in Fort Mill is sick of hearing her talk about it. She hasn't stopped since I found out in the summer I had been accepted."

"Why did you wait until October to start?"

"I had to save up the money to live here for a few months. I share a small apartment on the other side of Capitol

Hill with four other interns. I wanted to be able to pay for it myself so I worked at a grocery store back home," he answered. "I won't be here that long but it will be enough to count, Mom says. I just really thought I'd be here longer than a few days." Tom could see the tears forming in the corners of Ethan's eyes.

"When's the last time you spoke to your mom?"

"Ten days ago, when I caught the Greyhound bus in Charlotte. I sent her a letter when I got settled in and I've gotten a couple of letters from her. I can't afford to use the phone for long distance except in an emergency," he said wistfully.

Tom felt a pang of identification with this boy who wanted so much to make his mother proud and was so afraid of failing. He knew the feeling well.

"You said you're assigned to me for the day, right Ethan?"

"That's right, sir," Ethan answered.

"Then I need you to do something for me. It's really important."

Ethan sat up straight in his chair. "What can I do for you, sir?"

Tom held up a brass key. "I need you to go to the Willard Hotel, two blocks east of here. Go to room 1022."

Ethan was all ears, perked up at the thought of doing something important.

Tom continued, "Keep in mind what's happening here is highly classified so you can't give away information or you might scare someone. You have to be upbeat and positive."

"Yes, sir. Of course," Ethan reassured him.

"You can handle this for me? You're sure?"

Ethan nodded his assent.

Tom leaned in closer and pressed the key into Ethan's hand. Ethan leaned in to hear his assignment from this important man who was here to help the world avoid nuclear annihilation.

"Here's what you do when you get to my room: pick up the phone and call your mother."

CHAPTER 29
CALVIN WALKER
1963

The man who had done all the talking was called Fish. Calvin didn't catch any other names, but after they had lowered their weapons a heated discussion had broken out among them and it was clear Fish was their leader. They addressed every question and every objection to him. The last thing he heard was Fish's assurance that if Calvin proved to be full of shit they could draw straws for who would get to off him.

Note to self, avoid the appearance of shit-fullness.

Calvin found himself seated across the table from Fish as the others were relegated to other work around the apartment.

"Start talkin'," Fish said.

"My name is Calvin Williams." The last name was a small lie and he knew the lies were going to get bigger before they were done. He just didn't want them knowing his real name, as though that would somehow protect him from retribution. "I'm from Tennessee and I came here to find a group who would be willing to do something about this march. I'm tired of the bullshit way these guys are sucking up to the police and the government. They're selling us out and we might as well be slaves again if we go around shaking hands and asking them to please give us some rights. Some of these march assholes are acting like we're dogs or something when they go around the white man's table and beg for the scraps." He hoped the brusque language would lend him the necessary street credibility.

Fish wasn't laughing anymore, but he wasn't convinced. He circled the table where Calvin sat, building the tension with his silence. Finally he spoke, "You know what I think you are? I think you a cop. I thought you was a professa but now I think you a cop. You talk all fancy and you walk up in here and won't say how you found us. I suppose you know who we are?"

"I know you're Kifo. But I'm not a cop and I can prove it."

"Well, you better prove it cause there's nothing these boys like better than killin' cops. And the only people, besides us," he said as he used his gun to gesture around the apartment at the rest of the group, "who knows about Kifo is cops."

"I know about it because I'm on the inside with the organizers of the march. That's how I know who you are and that's how I have access to Dr. King. I can tell you exactly where he is and what he's doing. You just tell me what you're planning and I'll figure out a way to get him where you need him to be." Calvin felt sick at his stomach just saying the words. He revered Dr. King and even pretending that he was on the side of these thugs made him sick. He kept reminding himself he just had to find out the plan so the police could take over. He kept talking. "If you want to get attention then you have to make a big splash and you need a big name for that. You want a race war, right?"

"Only way to get what's ours is to fight for it. Talkin' never did no good," Fish said.

Calvin could see he was getting somewhere. "If you take out Dr. King, you'll get the race war you want. He's not the only organizer, but he's the most famous and the most moderate. He's the main voice for peace. If you take out the one calling for peace you'll get war."

Calvin stopped talking because he could see Fish was considering what he had said.

"All right, I won't kill you tonight. But I still don't believe you so you gonna have to prove yourself."

"How?"

"If you so close to King, you be back here at seven o'clock tomorrow morning with proof that you was with him today."

"What kind of proof?" Calvin asked.

"Well, *Pro-fess-a,* you gonna have to figure that out on your own. And you better get it done cause Tiny here is gonna follow you home so we'll know right where to find you if you try to pull anything shady."

Tiny turned out to be anything but. He was a mammoth man with a fierce scowl. Calvin had a feeling Tiny could do unspeakable things to him and not be late for dinner.

After a few more admonishments and reminders of what kinds of horror they would visit on him if he betrayed them, Fish let Calvin leave with Tiny in tow. They started the long walk to the Willard while Calvin tried to figure out a way to explain his new shadow's presence in the grand hotel. He hoped Edward Chase had some tricks up his sleeve.

CHAPTER 30
OLIVIA FORDHAM
1913

From the time Abigail Adams had written to her husband, John, during his attendance at the Continental Congress in Philadelphia in 1776 asking him to "remember the ladies," the role of women in society and in government had been hotly debated. For some it was not a question of if, but when, women would be recognized as fully involved, equal citizens. For others the question was whether or not they were mentally qualified or if the act of political involvement was too rough for their delicate sensibilities. By the time Victoria Webster and Olivia Fordham walked into the NAWSA offices the very idea that women were too delicate to participate fully in society was a notion that was on its way out of popular thinking, although it would take years to completely defeat the idea. Olivia wasn't sure if the notion was ever truly defeated given some of the chauvinists she had known over the course of her career. Still, there was important work being done and Olivia quickly noticed the zeal with which the women went about their duties. It reminded her of the staffs of some of the causes she worked with. They were true believers with no frame of reference for surrender.

Alice Paul was leading the charge for the organization. She was well known in suffrage circles and her methods tended to be more radical than those of other pioneers of the movement. She was officially the chairperson of the Congressional Committee whose members had been known to resort to hunger strikes when picket lines didn't yield the desired results. She was a New Jersey Quaker, twenty-eight years old, and a veteran of the movement in England where she had been imprisoned and later force-fed when she wouldn't end her hunger strike. Paul was a legend in suffrage circles, eclipsing even the work of such earlier luminaries as Lucretia Mott, Elizabeth Cady Stanton, and Susan B. Anthony. Though some states had given women the vote, Paul and her compatriots would not be satisfied until the federal government mandated it from sea to shining sea.

The office was bustling with activity for the march that was just two days away. When Olivia introduced herself to the young girl at the front desk and also gave her Victoria's name, Alice Paul was summoned at once. Olivia found it strange that they would be so quickly and enthusiastically received, but pushed the thought aside as they were led to a rear office. Her uneasiness was soon answered when Amelia Sutherland joined them as well.

"Miss Webster, I'm so pleased to meet you. Please forgive me for not being at the hotel when you arrived. My assistance was needed here and I'm very glad you've made it," Sutherland said as she turned to Paul. "Alice, this is the young lady Sarah was telling us about."

Sarah Lanphear was the woman Victoria had met at the Philadelphia rally and who had visited the Webster home encouraging Victoria to get involved. Alice Paul came forward to shake Victoria's hand. "Yes, of course! Sarah wrote me about you and I'm very happy to meet you. And who is your companion?"

"This is Olivia Fordham, Ms. Paul. I just met her at the hotel and she was planning to come here as well so we rode over together."

Alice and Olivia shook hands and Alice asked Olivia where she was from.

"I'm here from New York and I've heard great things about your organization. I wanted to come by and see for myself."

Alice could see that Olivia was a woman of means. Her appearance and mannerisms were both flawless and she had a New York connection. *Park Avenue,* she thought, *or maybe Fifth. Definitely Upper East Side.* Plus she had Victoria Webster in her office, a coup for the group no doubt. Sarah had told Alice about Victoria's family in Philadelphia. They were an old money, Main Line family with lineage traceable to the early settlers and landed gentry in England before that. A woman of her standing would be an invaluable asset for the movement and Philadelphia was a hard nut to crack. Victoria could be the key. Alice was thrilled to have two well-connected women joining the ranks.

The women talked for a while about plans for the march as well as their intention to meet with President Wilson after the inauguration. Alice told them about efforts in other states and how each could be beneficial in their home cities. Victoria looked uncomfortable and Olivia noticed. When Alice and Amelia stepped out for a moment to tend to business Olivia asked Victoria what was wrong.

"It was just something she said," Victoria said, referring to Alice. "She talked about my family and how important that could be in Philadelphia. But I'm here on my own. My family doesn't support this and I don't think my parents would be happy with their name being used." She looked defeated. "I'm afraid my mother might be right. I'm just a girl. What use could I be to them except for my name?"

"That's nonsense, Victoria. You are your own person and it's your name as well as your family's. I do agree that you have to be careful. A good name is built over a long period of time and torn down in a moment if one is not careful. But you haven't heard yet what they want you to do. You can always say no, but you should determine for yourself if the cause is something you want to lend your name to. It doesn't hurt to hear them out."

"You're right. I am passionate about women having the vote. I've met quite a few young men who, frankly Mrs. Fordham, I don't believe are as intelligent as I am. I know that sounds terribly conceited, but why shouldn't a smart woman have just as much right to a voice as any man has regardless of his education?"

"Victoria, I'm quite certain there are many men and women who are not as learned as you are," Olivia said with a smile. "And I dare say most are not as brave. You seem to have a good head on your shoulders and I believe you can make an informed decision."

Victoria looked much more comfortable when the ladies returned.

"I would be happy to help you this week in any way I can," Victoria said to Ms. Paul. "And when the march is over we can discuss how I might be of service to you in Philadelphia if that is agreeable to us both." Olivia was impressed with the confidence she heard in Victoria's voice.

They left the office with the understanding that both would return to the office the following morning to join the effort.

❧

The afternoon was lovely and they decided to walk back to the hotel. The two women chatted easily and Olivia had to keep reminding herself that this young girl was actually her grandmother. Because of their current ages she found herself mothering the girl while marveling at the courage and fortitude she showed at such a tender age. Seventeen in 1913 was a far cry from seventeen in the twenty-first century. Plus, Victoria had grown up sheltered in a world of class and wealth. She couldn't have seen much of the seedier side of life, but she carried herself with such resolve that it conflicted with her age and circumstances.

After they had walked several blocks and taken in the sights of the city, both women were starting to wish for a taxi to come along. The thought had barely crossed their minds when they came to a street corner and a motorcar came to a screeching halt, sending water from a curbside puddle all over Olivia's dress. Victoria escaped the deluge, but was mortified at the sight before her. The driver of the car leapt out and immediately began apologizing to the women. He was practically stumbling over himself with embarrassment at causing the scene. The car was new to him, he reported, and he was still having difficulty with some of the rigors of driving. He was a terribly kind young man and it was apparent that he felt terrible about the mess.

Victoria was using her white gloves to try and dry some of the fetid water from the shoulders of Olivia's ruined dress. The young man passed his linen handkerchief to Olivia so she could wipe her face. She was struggling with her hat, which was dripping dirty water all over her. She finally got the hat off and wiped her face and when she looked up she had another shock in store. It was a good thing her health problems were limited to her head and not her heart because two shocks in one day would have been more than she could take.

She thanked him for the handkerchief and handed it back, dumbstruck. As she did, she noticed the monogrammed initials, JFA. James Franklin Asher. Her grandfather.

CHAPTER 31
CATHERINE PARKER
1865

Against all odds, Catherine was able to fall asleep without much of a struggle. The situation she found herself in was too big for her mind to comprehend and she just shut down for a few hours. It was the best thing she could have done for herself.

The next morning when she woke up and started to stretch and wipe the sleep from her eyes, she thought for a moment she'd been dreaming until she looked around the room and saw the evidence of a bygone era. A glance out the window confirmed her suspicion. The half-finished monument stared back at her like an omen. She thought about the date. April 13. Not just April 13. . . .April 13, 1865. One day before the Lincoln assassination. She recalled from her school days that Lincoln was shot on Good Friday. That made today Maundy Thursday, the date of remembrance marking the night of the Last Supper. She couldn't get the thought out of her mind.

She took care in her dressing, this time letting the lady's maid Mr. Chase offered help her into the corset. It wasn't quite as painful as she anticipated, but the real shock was how it changed the shape of her body. She admired her hourglass figure in the full-length mirror and pushed the thoughts of women's liberation and so forth to the back of her mind. Even her best push-up bra couldn't do what this had done for her cleavage. After a few more admiring turns before the mirror she got back to business. Chase had spoken of tears in the fabric of history. All through school she'd been an excellent student of history and the law and although she would love to have her laptop and access to Google she knew she would have to reason this out the old-fashioned way. She took out a sheet of heavy paper from the drawer along with the elaborate quill and ink bottle. It looked like a mess waiting to happen. *Oh well, the Lord hates a coward,* she thought. She dipped the nub of the quill into the bottle and after a few blobs and smears, she began to make a list of what she could remember about the assassination and Lincoln's last days. To figure out what she was supposed to do she had to find out where the tear was. What was "off" about the situation? Who wasn't where they were supposed to be? What part of the puzzle was missing? The list began to grow, but she felt like it was done by a seventh grader. These were facts most everyone knew. Was there anything here that would point her in the right direction? She read the list over and over, adding small details as she remembered them.

Lincoln was shot just a few days after Lee surrendered to Grant. John Wilkes Booth was an actor. . .well-known. Ladies' man?

Shot at Ford's Theatre. . .play was "Our American Cousin"
Laura Keene is the star of the play!

The Lincolns attended the play with another couple. . .names?

The assassination was part of a larger plot that included plans to murder the Vice President and other top government officials. Who? Seward? The folly guy?

There was a woman involved. She had a tavern and boarding house. Mary Surratt. What is the address of the boarding house?

Lincoln had a guard with him who left the theatre and went to a tavern, leaving him unguarded.

The opera box Lincoln sat in overlooked the stage. Check out at rehearsal this afternoon.

Booth found out the president was coming when he went to get his mail at the theatre. (He traveled as an actor and had his mail sent there.) Was this the day of?

Even after the official surrender the war still went on in other parts of the country.

Grant went to Washington to sign papers formally ending the business of war. Lots of people wanted to see this hero.

Lincoln was the most hated man in the country.

Vice President Johnson was not popular either because he was a Southerner who sided with the union, but the union didn't trust him because he was from Tennessee.

Booth had a gun that only fired one bullet.

Booth believed he would be hailed a hero for killing the president.

After what felt like the hundredth reading of the list she was no closer to figuring out her next step. She decided the best move would be getting out among the people and trying to observe as much as possible. Maybe something would stand out. She recalled learning that, during this time in history, anyone could just walk into the White House without an appointment. Catherine folded the list and put it in her reticule, added a pair of

delicate lace-trimmed gloves to her ensemble, and headed out the
door for the short walk down Pennsylvania Avenue.

CHAPTER 32
TOM KELLY
1962

Once he had Ethan on his way to the Willard, Tom hung around in the hallway until he was called to the Oval Office. He didn't want anyone yelling at the young man for leaving his post so he made sure to let some higher-ups know he had sent him on a very important errand to retrieve something from his hotel. He hoped the boy was able to get through to his mother and that they could catch up and offer each other some comfort. It would be nice if he could pick up the phone and call his own mother, but at this rate he might be seeing her sooner rather than later. He supposed his apology for skipping out on law school could be delivered once he passed through the pearly gates if it came to that in the next few hours or days.

Mrs. Lincoln ushered him into the Oval where the president, the attorney general, the national security adviser, and the head of the CIA (John McCone, as he had suspected) were waiting to speak with him. The hour was getting late and Tom noticed the long shadows outside the window.

The attorney general spoke first. "Have a seat, Mr. Kelly. Our time is short because the president has to get back to the Sit Room but we'd like to follow up on something you said earlier today."

"Fine," answered Tom.

"You said you think Khrushchev believes the US will blink first. Why do you say that?"

Tom was ready for this question. He had been thinking about it all afternoon. "The Soviet premier believes the U.S. will blink first because of an inherent characteristic in the Russian male nature."

"Go on," the President encouraged.

"Mr. President, you must remember that since the overthrow of the imperial government in 1917 the Soviet state has been challenged with keeping control of its population under a communist system that provides for, ironically, an unequal allocation of resources. The poor are still the poor; the working class is still the working class. Only now, instead of the opulence of a royal family and the trappings of imperialism, the workers labor under the iron fist of a faceless, industrial entity. The proletariat isn't enjoying a better life than they had before, it's just that now they go about their meager existence without a glamorous family to fawn over and with a secret police presence to keep them up worrying at night. This government has little to offer them so they give them heaping doses of something that is *not* in short supply." Tom paused to see if anyone in the room would fill in the blank.

"And what is that, Mr. Kelly?" The question came from the CIA director. "What are they giving them that has anything at all to do with the problem at hand?"

"Propaganda. They're giving them propaganda." Tom could see the director was about to interject with a comment but he kept going. "The Soviet mentality is no accident. For more than forty years, the people have been told by the government that they are superior in every way to the rest of the world's population, especially the Americans."

Now it was the AG who spoke, "How does this factor into Khrushchev's mindset?"

"The Soviet government has kept control in two ways, by force and with public relations. We know about the *force* part. It's the PR that concerns me. They've told the people, 'you're better, stronger, smarter. Your products are superior, your education, your culture, your way of life. . .it's all superior. The Americans are inferior. They are spoon-fed and soft. They lack your inherent intelligence, fortitude, and abilities. As a result, the Soviet Union is better, stronger, and smarter. Our military is unstoppable, our weapons are foolproof. If the Americans want to start a war with us they don't stand a chance. But we're the good guys and the only way we'll use our weapons is to defend ourselves. We will only destroy the world in reaction to an American attack. We are invincible, but the Americans may be too arrogant to realize it so we must remain at the ready to defend our way of life.'"

Director McCone was shaking his head. "This is a wonderful civics lesson, but again I ask what this has to do with Khrushchev?" He turned to the president. "Mr. President, with all due respect, we are wasting our time here. My agency has the best intelligence available and our analysts know everything there is to know about the way the Soviet premier's mind works. What are we gaining by this exercise?"

All eyes turned to Tom. It seemed they might all be wondering the same thing. He knew it was now or never so Tom Kelly stood to his full height and looked the President of the United States in the eye.

"That's what I'm trying to explain, Mr. President. Khrushchev believes you will blink first because that's the message that's been sold to the Soviet people for forty-five years and he inherently believes it himself."

"And what is it that he believes?" the president asked.

"That at the end of the day, you're a coward, sir."

CHAPTER 33
CALVIN WALKER
1963

If Edward Chase was taken aback by the 6'5" scowling man standing in his lobby, his good breeding didn't allow him to show it. Calvin had pulled the concierge aside to explain his predicament while he left Tiny standing near a marble column that somehow didn't seem to dwarf him the way it did most people. However, the looks he was getting from other patrons were enough to make Calvin uncomfortable. He was afraid Tiny might lash out at the well-heeled clientele. They represented everything Kifo was fighting against. Chase quickly made arrangements to give the man a room and was careful to place him far away from Dr. King and his entourage.

Calvin escorted Tiny to his room. The man was clearly impressed by the elegance of the hotel, but he tried not to show it. Calvin thought he could use this to his advantage.

"Ok, Tiny, here's the thing. I can't just walk into the room with Dr. King with you beside me. They know me, but they have no idea who you are and you scare me so I'm sure you'll scare them too. Fish gave me the night to get the proof I need and you know exactly where to find me so I need for you to stay in this room all night and not come out. You can order anything you like to eat from room service. Just pick up the phone. Sign the bill and leave a nice big tip. Everything will be taken care of. At 6 a.m., leave the room and walk outside and across the street. I'll meet you on the corner."

Tiny didn't look too happy about letting Calvin out of his sight for such a long stretch, but the idea of room service, a hot shower, and the very comfortable-looking bed was enough to convince him that it couldn't hurt to give the guy some room to work. After all, he could always find him and hurt him in the morning if he tried a double-cross. He didn't give much thought to the idea that Calvin might sneak out in the night but Kifo didn't keep Tiny around because of his thinking skills. Calvin handed him the room service menu and quietly closed the door behind him. He went back to the lobby to find Edward Chase.

"Is your friend all settled in?" he asked.

"Yes, and I think you're going to be handling some fairly monumental room service charges for the evening." It might be petty but Calvin was pleased to at least stick Chase with the bill for getting him into this mess.

"I need another favor, Chase," Calvin said.

"What can I do for you, Mr. Walker?"

"I need to spend the evening with Dr. King."

Chase was silent for a moment but unruffled as ever. "I have an idea that should work," he noted. "Give me half an hour."

꙳

Thirty minutes later, Calvin had showered and dressed in a suit of the period that Chase had left in his closet. The concierge knocked on his door and Calvin followed him down the hall. They came to a double door marking the entrance to a large suite. Chase knocked and a gentleman answered the door.

"Hello, Mr. Abernathy. This is Calvin Walker, the gentleman I told you about," Chase said by way of introduction.

"Yes, of course.   Please come in," Mr. Abernathy welcomed Calvin into the suite and led him to a sitting room where Dr. King was sitting surrounded by papers. Chase had left when Calvin was invited in. He had done everything he could to help. He just hoped it would be enough and that Calvin could prevent tragedy from marring the monumental occasion.

"Dr. King, this is Calvin Walker, the man Edward Chase sent up."

Dr. King stood to shake Calvin's hand. "We met earlier today at the elevator, I believe."

"Yes, how do you do, Dr. King? I'm honored to meet you. Officially, I mean."

"Mr. Chase tells me you're an educated man of the people and that you are just the person I need to help me," said Dr. King.

"I'm happy to assist you in any way, sir. What can I do for you?"

"I'm working on a little speech for tomorrow's event and I'm concerned about how it will be received by the audience. I'd like for you to read over it and give me any suggestions you might have. I've been rewriting the last couple of paragraphs for a few hours and a fresh set of eyes would be a great help. Would you mind?"

Would I mind? Calvin almost laughed at the absurdity of the situation.

"I would be honored, sir," Calvin managed to say.

Dr. King motioned him to a seat across the table and handed him several handwritten pages. Calvin sat down to read and knew that somewhere in these pages he would eventually come to the words that would define a dream for millions of people just like him – people who would finally believe it was a dream they could achieve.

CHAPTER 34
OLIVIA FORDHAM
1913

James Franklin Asher. Of the Middleburg, Virginia Ashers. Horse breeders and land owners. American landed gentry. Royalty in a land without royals. Olivia had never met him, but she had seen photos of him all over her grandmother's house. One day he would be known as "Senior" when his son and Olivia's father, James Franklin Asher, Jr. was born. He would die in a car accident in 1941 at the age of forty-seven. Her grandmother would mourn his death for the rest of her own life and Olivia's father would swear there had never been a better man. Her family would reap the benefits of his wise counsel for years to come. But today he's only a nineteen-year-old boy with elementary driving skills. This isn't the story Olivia had always heard about the way her grandparents had met but she did recall it had been in Washington, D.C.

In all of the chaos he had offered to drive them back to the Willard. Olivia was so stunned she took him up on his offer and he managed to get them back to the hotel in one piece. Edward Chase met them at the door and escorted Olivia to her suite so she could clean up and get changed. The young man was clearly distraught over the mess he had caused and when Chase heard the boy's name was Asher he knew there was more to the story. Chase was well aware that Olivia Fordham had been an Asher before her marriage. He determined the young man should stay at the hotel until Mrs. Fordham could regain her composure. He settled Victoria and James into a corner booth in the restaurant and told them to please have an early dinner and wait. He sent two maids up to help Olivia and kept an eye on the young people to make sure they stayed put.

It took an hour for Olivia to get cleaned up and changed so that she felt presentable again. The entire time she'd been upstairs she had been thinking about the young people downstairs. Chase told her he was keeping them in the restaurant. She had just witnessed the meeting of her grandparents and she was trying to remember what she had heard before. She recalled a story about how they had met as young people in Washington, D.C., but there had been a carriage accident involved. She supposed that with both horses and the new motorcars on the streets at the same time it could have been a car and not a carriage. Either way, they were downstairs getting to know each other, which was a good sign.

In the restaurant, the two young people found themselves surprisingly shy with one another, as neither was particularly shy normally. They tripped over each other's sentences when the silence between them felt awkward, but eventually they managed to get past the *Who, What, When* and *Where are you from?* parts. James told Victoria he was in the city for a few days with his older brother who was doing some work for their local congressman. James had come along to help with anything his brother might need. The car belonged to the brother and James had been learning to drive before they left Middleburg and thought he was ready for the city traffic, but he told her he was rethinking that now and they both laughed. It seemed to break the tension and conversation flowed more easily after that. Things were going well and Victoria was taken with the handsome gentleman, and he with her. He noticed her stunning eyes and the way her voice seemed to dance across the table toward him. She noticed his strong jaw and elegant hands. *Piano hands,* she thought. He was musical, but it was the trumpet he played, not the piano. Still, she thought he was amazing. She blushed outwardly when she found herself thinking her parents would approve of such a boy. He noticed the blush and asked her about it. She said she was feeling a bit warm and he flagged down the waiter and ordered her a fresh glass of cool water.

What an elegant young lady. Even my mother would approve, he thought and then he reprimanded himself internally for such thoughts about a woman he had only known for an hour.

It wasn't until they got to the *What brings you to Washington?* portion of the conversation that things began to go downhill. In under an hour Victoria had felt she could tell him anything and he would understand and agree, but when she told him she had come for the suffrage march she was surprised at his response.

"Suffrage? Oh my dear, Victoria, please tell me you aren't getting caught up with those busybodies! Those women are not of high repute and they have no business meddling in affairs best handled by men."

Victoria was nearly struck speechless. Nearly, but not quite.

"Busybodies? You believe women who are actively campaigning for rights that they deserve are busybodies?"

"From what I hear they plan to parade themselves down Pennsylvania Avenue and make demands of the new president. I've read that sometimes they carry picket signs or even go to jail. It's not at all ladylike. My mother says these are not women of quality."

"Your *mother* says? And what do you say?"

It was at this moment, when Victoria practically spat the word "mother" at him that Olivia came near the table. The young people didn't seem to notice her, but she clearly saw the anger flashing in Victoria's eyes and the steadfast defiance of James.

"I agree with her! Women of quality, women like her and like you are not the type to parade around making demands when you have everything in life you could possibly need."

He didn't mean to sound smug, but he was infuriating Victoria with every word out of his mouth. She completely changed her opinion of him and thought he belonged back on his horse farm and she told him so.

"Perhaps your horses like to be saddled and directed where to go, but modern women do not require such instruction!"

"My horses are champions and they don't need me to tell them where to go. They know exactly where they are *supposed* to go and where they are *not supposed* to go!"

Victoria was sliding out of the booth and pulling her hat and bag with her as her anger blossomed. Olivia watched in stunned silence.

"Well then, *Mr. Asher,* I'd better go where I'm *supposed* to go which is anywhere you are not! Good day, sir."

And with that Victoria stormed away from the table leaving Olivia and James flabbergasted, and a waiter holding a pitcher of cool water.

"You didn't hear them, Edward. They were going at each other like warring nations."

"I understand, Olivia, but you remember what it's like to be their age. They think they know everything and little disagreements get blown out of proportion. They'll calm down."

"I don't know. Victoria was livid. She went to her room, which is down the hall from my suite. I hope she didn't damage your door because she slammed it quite definitively."

"A lot of doors have been slammed here over the years. You should have been here just before the Civil War when we had to keep Northerners and Southerners on separate floors. You've never heard such door slamming."

Olivia looked at him for a laugh, but he didn't offer one. Then she remembered he was serious. He had been here during the Civil War. She shook her head in disbelief.

"Either way, it seems I have two problems on my hands now. One is whether or not my grandparents will get to be my grandparents and the other is this woman, whoever she is, who has such importance to the movement. The day is almost over. How am I supposed to find her?"

"Olivia, I think you *have* found her."

"What do you mean?"

"Think about it. The woman in question is supposed to be valuable to the movement, but also to the future for women in other ways. Your grandmother is a Philadelphia Webster. She could be invaluable to the movement as she carries with her a cachet because of her name and her background. If she really believes in this cause that can be priceless. On the other hand, she's of tremendous value to women of the future outside of the movement."

"How so?"

"Because of you."

"Me?"

"Yes, you. Think about it. Your work with your husband's company brought millions of dollars to female-led companies all over the world, not to mention helping to break through the glass ceiling for women executives."

"Edward, I didn't have to break the glass ceiling. I married it. I'm no pioneer for women. I just had a wonderful husband who was an excellent businessman and he taught me."

"Maybe he did help you learn, but you've gone far beyond those initial days. He's been gone for years and you've not only grown the company, but also created the institute and given hundreds of millions of dollars to charity."

"Yes, but this movement is about empowering women and I've never thought of myself as an activist. I've just done the best I could with the extraordinary opportunities I've been given."

"I think you're being too modest. In your charitable work alone how many micro-loans have you made possible for women in poor countries to operate a business to put food on the table for their children?"

"That's just a—"

"I'm not finished, Olivia. How many children have been inoculated? How many girls have gone to college? For that matter, how many have gone beyond basic reading and writing training in some countries? And none of this takes into consideration all the women I know you've mentored along the way."

"It's dangerous to believe one's own press, Edward."

"Not when it's all true, Olivia. And all of it is."

"Are you saying you think I was brought here to make sure my own grandmother marches in a parade and also manages to marry my grandfather so I can one day be born? That sounds awfully self-important considering how many groundbreaking women will be part of this event."

"It doesn't matter how it sounds, I believe it is absolutely the reason you're here. When I got this assignment I just knew it had to be you, but I couldn't understand why the feeling was so strong. Now I know. This is more than history. It's personal. And you have to get this done right."

Olivia was quiet for a moment and Chase could see the look of concern on her face.

"That may be easier said than done," she said.

"Why is that?"

"Because I'm pretty sure my grandmother has just decided she hates my grandfather and I have no idea where he went."

"As you know, there is a fine line between love and hate and sometimes the fire of one can ignite the passion of the other. I believe you will find Mr. Asher relaxing in Peacock Alley where he is desperately trying to figure out what just happened to a perfectly lovely conversation."

"I suppose I'll start with him. I never knew him, but I knew my grandmother well and she was not one to back down easily from an argument. Let's hope my grandfather has a bit more of the peacemaker in his nature."

CHAPTER 35
CATHERINE PARKER
1865

"I beg your pardon, ma'am." The apology came from a scruffy man sitting against the wall leading to the staircase. He had his legs out in front of him and Catherine had tripped and nearly fallen. The man pulled his legs under him and allowed Catherine to pass. She could hardly believe her eyes.

In college, Catherine had taken an independent study course that involved a week of seminars in Washington and during that time she had taken the public White House tour. She knew from the tour that she was standing in Cross Hall and that the stairs led to the part of the house known as the residence. Normally, a Marine guard stood sentinel at the foot of the stairs and although it looked like he was the only thing between the hoi polloi and the first family, everyone with a brain knew there was no way to get up those stairs without the Secret Service coming out of the woodwork and suggesting you might be better off turning around. Like now. If you valued your life.

But now there was no guard and the stairs were filled with people coming down and going up and some just lounging and having conversations. She took a tentative step and then another and when no alarm bells went off she picked her way up the stairs, dodging the mass of humanity that seemed to have business with the president. At the top of the stairs she was greeted with another unbelievable scene. There were people everywhere and they were casually seated on the furniture and the floor or wherever there was a place to rest. She found a place against the wall and listened to their conversations.

"Yessir, I came down from Pennsylvania as soon as I heard it. That ole' Lee, man I wish I could have seen his face. He ain't so proud now, is he?" Mr. Pennsylvania grinned a gap-toothed smile and spit—yes spit—into a contraption that seemed to be there for that purpose. "My boy'll be home any day from the fightin' in Kentucky and I aim to get him one of them jobs carryin' the mail."

Another man wearing a suit that was several sizes too large kept combing his oily hair across his forehead and shifting from one foot to the other. He seemed very nervous. Catherine heard him say, "I've slept here the last two nights and I got to see the president today. I got a idea that'll keep these free nigras in line but we got to get it goin' fore any more get to Ohio."

Their conversations were varied, but all had come to get something from the president. Most wanted a job, but some wanted land they believed would be seized from the defeated South. Catherine mingled about the room for a couple of hours, but she never saw the president and the line of people to see him kept growing. She decided this idea was getting her nowhere.

Did I really walk over here expecting to see Abraham Lincoln walk through the door? Or maybe Mary Lincoln walking about and talking to everyone about seeing a play tomorrow night?

The absurdity was almost too much, but as Catherine stepped back outside and smelled the unmistakable stench of nineteenth century urban sanitation and heard the cacophony of horses and wagons beating against the rutted dirt roads she knew she had to keep going. Absurdity be damned.

CHAPTER 36
TOM KELLY
1962

Tom's comment about the president being viewed as a coward had sucked all the air out of the room. President Kennedy broke the tension with his response.

"I think you might be right about the way they view us, Mr. Kelly. Unfortunately, that means we run the risk of this degenerating into a schoolyard pissing contest, which is no way to determine the fate of the modern world."

The others nodded in agreement and the president continued. "How do we overcome the bravado element without weakening our position?" Tom started to respond, but the president cut him off. "Because make no mistake, as horrific as I find this situation, I cannot let their provocation go unanswered. This country will not tolerate a bully in our backyard. He must retreat to his corner."

"Yes, Mr. President, he must. He's made a grand statement by secretly placing these weapons off our coast and in doing so he's shown the Communist world that he's out in front and carrying a big stick. He needs a way to back down without losing face. He can't look weak in front of his countrymen. They would never forgive weakness."

Robert Kennedy spoke up. "Mr. President, we've talked about this possibility since the start of the crisis. Khrushchev thought he could park his nukes in secret, but now that they've

LEANNE BURNETT MORSE

been discovered he's so far out on the limb he's got to show resolve and strength. We need to offer him a way to let the air out of his balloon without sacrificing the dignity of a country whose main currency is national pride."

Bundy was nodding his agreement. "To be victorious we can't appear to be the victors."

"Gentlemen, this is not new thinking. We are already working through our confidential sources and back-channel contacts to communicate with the premier," Director McCone advised.

"Your system is compromised," said Tom.

McCone spun on his heels and leaned toward Tom with his finger just inches from Tom's face. "How in the world could you possibly know if our system is compromised, which it is NOT, I might add!" McCone turned to address the president directly. "Mr. President, with all due respect, we're wasting our time with this nonsense. My men know what they're doing and this is not a movie we're talking about."

Tom knew his credibility was on the line so he laid it all on the table.

"I know your system is compromised because two years ago I breached it myself."

For a moment he wasn't sure who appeared more stunned, the President of the United States or the Director of the Central Intelligence Agency. And things were about to get worse.

CHAPTER 37
CALVIN WALKER
1963

The handwritten speech Dr. King gave Calvin to read talked about how his people had been given a bad check by the American government and about the importance of fighting this battle with dignity and the need for self-discipline.

He touched on what it would take to satisfy an entire race of people that justice belonged to them and likened that experience to the rushing of a mighty stream.

Most symbolically, he spoke of his own children and how he longed for them to be judged by who they were and not by how they looked.

Calvin knew the words by heart. He had studied the famous speech in college and been impressed with the preacher's zeal with which it was both written and delivered. Reading it here in its unfinished form he could already hear the reaction of the crowd, the pauses and the inflection, and the growing tenor of Dr. King's voice as he led up to the iconic peroration that would electrify all who heard it.

There were tears in Calvin's eyes as he finished reading the draft. The line that he loved about the ringing of freedom from his beloved Lookout Mountain in Tennessee wasn't in there yet, but the night was still young and he knew it would find its place. Growing up in Chattanooga, he had visited Lookout Mountain many times and when he was there he always thought of that line and how much the actions of those brave pioneers of the 1960s had changed the life he knew. In his time, freedom did indeed ring from Lookout Mountain. Calvin was nearly overcome with emotion.

Dr. King saw the tears in Calvin's eyes.

"Please, Dr. King. Don't change a word you've written here. When you deliver this speech tomorrow people of all races will hear in it the most compelling argument for freedom ever spoken."

The pastor was touched by Calvin's response. He thanked him and when Calvin reached to hand back the pages Dr. King held up his hand.

"Keep them. Those have already been typed. I hope this speech means as much to those who will hear it tomorrow as it has to you tonight."

You have no idea, Calvin thought.

As he bid King and his entourage goodnight and the door closed behind him he was jolted back to the reality of what he had to do. He held the proof he needed in his hands. Now he just had to convince Kifo that he wanted to kill Dr. King in order to save him and to save the movement.

Calvin had a fleeting thought that if any of this was, in fact, a dream it was quickly turning into a waking nightmare.

CHAPTER 38
OLIVIA FORDHAM
1913

Olivia found James sitting in a chair in Peacock Alley just off the main lobby as Chase had said he would be. He looked despondent. His neckwear had been loosened and he was slouching in the chair rubbing his temples. Olivia could almost hear the wheels turning in his head. When he saw her approaching he stood to his feet and straightened his tie.

"Mrs. Fordham, please allow me to apologize again for causing you such distress. And I insist on taking care of any charges for the cleaning or replacement of your clothing. I'm terribly embarrassed."

She waved her hand as though it was nothing. "Please, Mr. Asher, don't give it another thought. That outfit was not one of my favorites and now I have a perfectly good excuse for a shopping excursion for which I will not allow you to pay. It was simply an accident and I fear I wouldn't have done any better with the motorcar," she said with a smile.

James thought it an odd statement as everyone knew ladies did not drive motorcars, especially ladies of Mrs. Fordham's class who were ferried about by their drivers. He let it go because everyone knew women of a certain age could be eccentric and he imagined she was old enough to be afforded the kind of kid-glove treatment one might offer to a senile aunt. She sat and motioned for him to do the same.

"I hope you don't mind, but I couldn't help overhearing the conversation you were having with Miss Webster."

A black cloud seemed to pass over his face as he answered. "Yes, it was a most unfortunate turn of events. I'm not certain why she got so angry with me."

"Do you think it could have been that you made light of her views on the issue of suffrage for women?"

"Oh, I didn't think she was terribly serious about such a thing. A girl of her standing is unlikely to be so inclined, don't you think?"

"I do not think, as a matter of fact. She seemed perfectly sure of her own mind when she told you about it."

"Well, I just don't know about that, Mrs. Fordham." *Maybe the old woman really is senile. She can't actually be defending such behavior by a proper young lady,* he thought. "My mother says suffragists are malcontents who need to find husbands and be about the business of their homes and children and not out gallivanting around trying to be men."

Olivia bristled at the thought that her own great-grandmother held such antiquated opinions.

"Perhaps it would serve you best, Mr. Asher, if you didn't share your mother's opinions with the young ladies of today. I believe you will find they might disagree more often than not."

James looked momentarily chastised. "I just wish I could talk to Miss Webster again. I think I might make a better impression the second time around. Although I suppose my splashing you with dirty water was really my first impression and the argument the second. I doubt if she'll give me a third try." He stood and collected his hat.

"If you'll excuse me, Mrs. Fordham, I really should be getting back to Capitol Hill to see if my brother needs my assistance. I apologize again for the difficulty this afternoon and I hope that when you see Miss Webster again you will pass along my best wishes and sincerest hope for her happiness."

Olivia thought the young man looked like he was in danger of a decidedly unmanly crying episode, but he straightened himself up and before she could think of anything to say he bid her goodbye and took his leave.

She had struck out with her grandfather. Now she'd have to face her grandmother and, if memory served, attempting to change her mind about anything could be a daunting proposition.

CHAPTER 39
CATHERINE PARKER
1865

Catherine hailed a carriage and asked for the Surratt boarding house. The driver said he knew the way, but wondered if she was sure she wanted to go there.

"It's not in the best neighborhood, ma'am. Are you sure you wouldn't rather wait for your husband?"

She was sick of being asked about a husband or a proper chaperone to accompany her where she needed to go. She wondered what this pimply-faced kid would think if she told him she had flown high up in the sky here to the city on a big metal airplane that brought her all the way from Ohio without a male escort.

"I'm quite certain I want to go there, thank you very much." She sat back on the seat and braced herself for the bumpy ride to 541 H Street.

"Here you are, ma'am. This is the Surratt boarding house," the driver told her.

"Wait for me, no matter how long I'm inside," Catherine told him and walked away before he could argue.

She pushed the door open and heard a bell ring that had been hanging on the knob. A young lady came out and seemed surprised to see Catherine standing there.

"Can I help you?" asked the girl.

"I'm looking for someone who may be staying here," Catherine responded. "He's an actor named John Wilkes Booth." She had no idea what made her ask for him.

The girl seemed surprised. "I know of him but he doesn't stay here ma'am. I believe he lives in a hotel." Catherine searched the girl's face for some sign she was hiding something but couldn't detect a lie.

"Is Mrs. Surratt here?"

"No ma'am. I'm Anna. Mary Surratt is my mother," the girl answered.

For a moment Catherine was stunned. She wasn't sure what she would find when she came here, but for the first time she was face-to-face with someone connected to the conspiracy. Granted, she was the daughter, but her mother was THE Mary Surratt, the only woman hanged for her role in the killing of the president. The woman whose tavern had been used to store the guns for John Wilkes Booth to aid in his escape from the city. *I need to put that on my list,* Catherine remembered.

"She's not here, but she should be back in a few hours. Would you like to wait?" Anna asked.

"No, I was just hoping to locate Mr. Booth. You're sure he isn't staying here?"

"Ma'am, people like Mr. Booth don't stay in places like this." She glanced around and dropped her voice to a whisper. "I have heard that he stays at the National Hotel when he's in town," she blushed.

Of course. She's a fan. He's like Ryan Gosling to this girl.

Catherine could sense the young girl was telling the truth. She didn't know where Booth was and her blush gave away her secret admiration. If Booth was planning something sinister, this girl knew nothing of it.

"I'm sorry to have bothered you. I'll be on my way," Catherine said as she reached for the doorknob.

"Do you have a message for my mother?"

Catherine paused as more of her history lessons came to mind.

Mary Surratt is going to be hanged for her part in the assassination. The young girl standing in front of me will plead for her mother's life. History will never be sure how much involvement Mary had, if she even knew what the men were doing. I can save her. I can tell Anna to get her mother out of town. Whatever she's done so far, nobody has been hurt. It's not too late!

And then she remembered Chase's words of warning. She stood, aching to tell Anna something that could save her mother and save the life the young girl herself knew.

"No. No message," Catherine said. Quickly she walked out the door, hanging her head like the coward she was.

CHAPTER 40
TOM KELLY
1962

The evening of October 23 passed with Tom Kelly sitting on a sofa in the Oval Office explaining to the President of the United States and his brother, the nation's top law enforcer, how he had systematically breached the communication pathway between the world's two superpowers. In spite of much arguing and posturing, Bundy and McCone had been dismissed from the room before the explanation began in earnest, but not before Director McCone assured Tom Kelly he would make sure the full weight of the government was brought to bear against him. Tom had a fleeting thought that for the rest of his life he would probably pay the price for crossing the nation's top spy by being constantly harassed by a CIA grunt whose only job was to make his life miserable.

If I don't go to federal prison or get obliterated by a nuclear bomb first, of course.

"Start at the beginning," said the attorney general. "And forget for the next few hours that you're talking to an officer of the court. I need the full truth."

Oh well, in for a penny, in for a pound.

"Three years ago, I had an idea for a film based on the KGB so I started doing research and found out pretty quickly that there was a more interesting angle to the story. It happened sort of by accident. I was exchanging letters with a professor at Yale who was granted asylum by the U.S. fifteen years before.

He was giving me background information on the growth of the KGB and the changes in the country since the establishment of the Soviet Union. His parents had vivid memories of the overthrow of Nicholas II, and they had shared stories with him of life under the imperial system. They had intimate knowledge of that life because his father was a groundskeeper at Tsarskoe Selo, home of the imperial palaces. When the Romanovs were placed under house arrest, his father continued to work for the family during the time they stayed there. Nicholas sometimes slipped him coded messages to carry to the outside. He was taking them to supporters of the Tsar who responded with messages about what was happening outside the palace gates. These messages warned the Tsar of ominous rumors about the fate of the family. This was during the time the Romanovs sought asylum in England. They were related to the British royal family as descendants of Queen Victoria. King George V was fond of his cousin the Tsar, but the First World War was still raging and the king was leery of revolution in his own country. He believed that while cousin Nikki might lose his crown, he wasn't in danger of losing his life, so he denied the request for sanctuary. Loyalists in St. Petersburg believed the Tsar was in mortal danger and their missives became more and more fevered. Before a viable solution could be reached, the Tsar and his family were moved and eventually ended up at a house in Ekaterinburg in the Ural Mountains. Some of the servants went with them and died alongside them when the entire family was executed in the basement a few months later. The professor's father had begged to be allowed to go with them to continue to serve the Tsar, but it was believed that Nicholas sensed the danger to come and refused to allow him to go along because he had a young son at home. The son was the professor with whom I was now communicating.

   In the years following the assassination of the imperial family, the professor's father had reached out to the loyalists with whom he had exchanged the Tsar's messages. They got together in secret to write a comprehensive history of the last months, believing the monarchy would be restored and the murderers brought to justice. The secret history filled two volumes and his father was given responsibility for hiding them. When his son was ready to defect to the United States he knew the government would be looking at his family carefully and their secret might be discovered. Enough time had passed that he realized the old system was gone for good and he recognized an opportunity to get the books out of the U.S.S.R. so their story could be preserved without threat of discovery. The books went with the professor on his journey to America. Incidentally, his parents were found dead in their home seven months later and the house had been torn apart. The secret hiding place where the books had been kept had been pried open. Thankfully, the books were safe in Brooklyn by that time."

The president had been listening intently and now posed a question to Tom. "I get the feeling there was more to the books than some dusty history. Am I correct, Mr. Kelly?"

"You are, Mr. President. The books were full of names, addresses, dates, and most importantly, code ciphers. The history was extensively documented, but that's not what made the books so dangerous to possess years after the revolution. It was the data on the writers themselves and the organization that had grown from their small beginnings that changed the course of my research and has implications in this room today."

"What was in the books?" asked the attorney general.

"The books were the founding documents of a secret group of loyalist informers, spies, code breakers, and messengers. They styled themselves as the counterpoint to the emerging secret police, the Cheka, which eventually became the KGB. Their goal was to be ready to go fully operational to help rebuild the old Russia when the time came, but it never came." said Tom.

"So, a secret group formed out of the rubble of the last Tsar's government and they existed for several years hoping to see their old way of life returned," Robert Kennedy mulled the idea over.

"Not exactly, sir. The passing of the original group, including the groundskeeper didn't mark the end of the mission," answered Tom.

"What happened to them?" asked the president.

"They regrouped, sir. Over time new contacts were recruited and placed in all the major cities of the Soviet Union as well as in rural villages. They're even active in Siberia. It was through their network that I infiltrated the 'official' clandestine chain of communication between our nations. They call themselves обходной канал информации. It translates in English to *Back Channel*. They've kept up with advances in spycraft and technology and years ago they established a new headquarters."

"Where?" asked the president?

"New Haven, Connecticut, sir."

CHAPTER 41
CALVIN WALKER
1963

At five o'clock in the morning, Calvin finally got out of bed to get ready for his day. He hadn't slept a wink and he couldn't be still any longer. A few minutes before six, he folded Dr. King's handwritten speech draft and put it in his pocket. He hoped it would be enough to get Fish to trust him and give up the information he needed.

By the time he met Tiny across the street from the Willard the scene was pretty spectacular. Buses were backed up on both sides of 14th Street, discharging their passengers for the walk to the Washington Monument where the march was scheduled to begin. Billed as the "March on Washington for Jobs and Freedom," the event had brought people from across the country to the nation's capital. Tens of thousands had already gathered and by the time the speeches were scheduled to be delivered more than 250,000 would line the National Mall. Most of the attendees were black, but there were thousands of white people and some of other races as well. It was their inclusion that rankled the more radical groups including Kifo.

Calvin and Tiny skirted the gathering crowd and walked back to the apartment where the group was huddled together. Fish didn't look surprised to see Calvin. He still feared the man was an undercover police officer or FBI agent, but he was intrigued enough by the possibility of getting close to Dr. King that he let the situation play itself out. He would decide soon whether or not to continue with Calvin or have him dispatched by one of his eager lieutenants.

Calvin approached Fish and held out the sheets of paper.

"What's this?" Fish asked.

"It's the proof you asked for. That is the speech Dr. King will deliver today at the march. I was with him last night when he was working on it."

"And where was this?"

"At the Willard Hotel," Calvin responded.

The answer was apparently humorous to Fish and when he chuckled his acolytes followed suit. "So you and Dr. King were just sittin' around writin' speeches in that fancy place next door to the White House? They must have a colored wing I never heard of."

"It's the truth, Fish," Tiny said. It was only the second time Calvin had heard the man's voice. "I stayed there too and they had the softest bed you ever did lay down on and I ate dinner three times and didn't pay for none of it."

"And what was Williams doing while you were eatin' dinner three times?"

"He had to go to get your proof and he got this speech," Tiny said.

"Did you see him with King?" Fish asked.

"No. He told me to stay in my room and order room service."

Now the others were laughing and Tiny looked like he might take them all out like a giant bowling ball thrown at ten laughing pins.

"So you had yourself a nice evening while Williams wrote himself some notes last night. Is that right?" Fish demanded.

Tiny looked at his shoes and gradually withdrew from the group.

"I didn't write those pages," Calvin said. "Those are the handwritten notes Dr. King made and he will say those words this afternoon in front of the crowd."

"Why should I believe you? How do I know he gonna say this?"

Because everybody in the country knows he said those words, you stupid moron.

But, of course, no one did know. At least not yet. This shifting of time was playing tricks with Calvin's sleep-deprived brain. Fish was right. There was no way to prove who had written the notes. Just then, Calvin had a thought. He went for it.

"Look, I'm pretty sure you know a good bit about Dr. King. As a matter of fact, I'd say you're obsessed with him and with the others. You know what they're preaching from their pulpits. Just take a few minutes and read the speech. You'll recognize the things he's saying."

Fish looked for a moment like he was finished with the conversation and Calvin feared he was about to be turned over to the salivating underlings. But there was something about their leader that gave him a ray of hope that he might survive a few more minutes. Calvin could tell that despite the bad grammar and tough attitude, Fish was not a stupid man. In fact, it almost seemed like he was purposely dumbing himself down to impress the others. He might have been onto something because Fish sat down at the table and began to read. By the end he was angry and he slammed the pages down.

"That's the problem with this whole damn group! All this talk about dreams and dignity. Where is the dignity in bowing down to white men and asking them to please let you walk through the front door of the store? Who gives a damn about dreams for little black boys that grow up in the streets and hope one day to get a job cleaning some white man's office? The time for talkin' and askin' is over. We been free a hundred years and we still got to step aside and put our head down when a white lady cross the street. And they put on bed sheets and burn crosses and say they Christians. No sir, this ain't no time for dreams. Today we gonna bring them something that will haunt their dreams."

Fish had begun pacing the room while he delivered his diatribe. He turned to the group and told them to leave Calvin alone, that he'd be going with them today. The men looked vaguely disappointed, but were quickly fired up by Fish's fervor and they began unpacking the boxes Calvin had seen them carrying in the day before. What Calvin needed to do was nail down Fish's plan for getting Dr. King and get back to the Willard so Chase could get the FBI involved. Even just being around for a couple of days, Calvin recognized the FBI would not take his word, the word of a black man, seriously enough to stop what was going to happen over the next few hours. He needed Chase's help.

He was still thinking about how the FBI would step in to protect Dr. King and the other organizers while they raided this den of would-be assassins. But when he took a closer look at what the men were taking from the boxes his blood ran cold. They didn't have the kind of equipment used to take out a high-value target like rifles and scopes. What they were unpacking was chosen to do damage over a much larger area. They may have hoped to get a Dr. King or a John Lewis in the process, but these men had clearly come prepared to take out as many spectators as possible. Calvin recognized his problem was much bigger than he had thought when he realized he was standing in the center of a room full of bombs.

CHAPTER 42
OLIVIA FORDHAM
1913

Olivia invited Victoria to her suite and when the young woman arrived she could tell the anger that had been stirred up in her was still brewing.

"Please have a seat, Victoria. I understand you had words with the young gentleman."

"I wouldn't call him a gentleman, unless rudeness passes for manners in Virginia," Victoria answered petulantly.

"Well, you only met the man so it's no problem that he turned out to be so wretched. Isn't that right, dear?"

Victoria appeared torn. She was nodding her head like she agreed with that statement but the look on her face betrayed her.

"It's just that he was so smug and so, so. . . . so,"

"So what dear?"

"So old-fashioned!"

"Then it's a good thing you'll never have to see him again. I can see that he upset you, not to mention he's an abominable driver. I suggest we never speak of him again."

"I mean, he was so sure of himself and so interested in what his mother, of all people, thinks. She must be a hundred years old!"

"You're right, darling. He's definitely not worth a moment's worry on your part. Let's talk about something more pleasant."

Olivia could see Victoria considering the idea of never speaking of him again and it wasn't sitting well with her. That was exactly what Olivia was hoping for.

"I don't think he's a bad person, really. He just has old-fashioned ideas."

"All the more reason for a modern young woman like you to stay away from such a cad."

"Oh, he wasn't a cad. He was very kind and solicitous. He was terribly embarrassed by what happened with the car and ever so worried about you."

"As he should be, that irresponsible wretch!"

"No, he's not irresponsible. He's in college and planning to go to law school and his brother is a lawyer who does work with the United States Congress. I think he comes from a very important family in Virginia and they have champion horses. I think they even have a Kentucky Derby winner on their farm."

"My, but you learned a great deal about the young man while I was changing clothes."

"Yes, and he asked all about me and seemed very interested until I told him why I'd come to Washington. But I just told you myself that I wasn't sure why I had come or what I hoped to do here. I just said that to you this very afternoon and then I jumped all over him when he didn't seem to understand why a woman would want to have the vote."

"Do you think it's possible you might have jumped to the wrong conclusion about his attitude?" Olivia asked.

"I suppose so. But he did talk about horses knowing where they were supposed to go and I think he was talking about women knowing their place."

"That's quite an assumption. Did he actually say that?"

Victoria thought about it and her face began to change.

"No, he didn't say that exactly and I was being awfully rude to him."

Olivia decided to move in for the goal.

"Well, it doesn't matter because it's unlikely you'll ever see him again. I'm sure it's just as well."

Victoria looked stricken. "Never?" Her mind was spinning. Olivia offered a solution.

"I suppose it's possible Mr. Chase might know how to reach him. That is, if you fancy him and would like to see him again."

Victoria's face lit up and a blush rose to her cheeks.

"It wouldn't be the most terrible idea to invite him to dinner tonight to thank him for driving us to the hotel and to clear up any misunderstandings, would it?"

Olivia answered. "No, I don't think it would be the most terrible idea."

"I'll call Mr. Chase right away." She ran for the phone and made the arrangements. Chase said he should have no problem getting in touch with Mr. Asher.

On her way out the door to get ready for dinner Victoria made one more statement.

"I'm sure when we talk it over tonight he'll be reasonable and see things my way."

She bounded down the hall and left Olivia holding the door and shaking her head.

❧

James was thrilled to receive word from Edward Chase that Mrs. Fordham and Miss Webster had requested the pleasure of his company for dinner. His brother had work for him to do, but when he saw the hangdog look James was wearing he told him to get out of the office and go see the girl. James took his time dressing and left with extra time in case he had issues with the motorcar. He arrived early at the Willard and was seated in the dining room where he was joined by the ladies.

Olivia had changed into a lovely black dress with an open collar. With her silver hair she was striking, but it was Victoria who turned heads all through the lobby and the dining room. She had put on her best pale blue gown and woven a string of beads through her hair, which was pulled away from her face and left to cascade down her back. James felt his breath catch and he stood there stupidly silent as they approached. He came to himself when he realized he hadn't pulled out a chair for either of the ladies. He seated Olivia first and then gallantly held the chair for Victoria.

Dinner was served and the conversation stayed in the safe realm of *Who's Who* in Middleburg, Philadelphia, and New York. It turned out James and Victoria had many acquaintances in common. The longer they talked, the more enamored each seemed to be of the other. Olivia was feeling good about things and was about to excuse herself from the table when the first hint of trouble started. James had mentioned he'd be on the Hill in the morning working with his brother and Victoria said she was planning to report for duty at the NAWSA office. That sparked another round of criticism on his part and, contrary to Victoria's earlier prediction, he never did see things her way. If the young woman had come to Washington unsure of her place in the movement her stubborn streak had risen up and solidified her resolve after she heard James continue to put down the group.

Olivia tried to intervene to keep the peace, but by that time both young people had decided they weren't giving an inch. The only bright spot was when James had looked at Victoria and said, "A girl like you is too special and too lovely to put herself at risk at such an event."

If that statement was meant to pacify Victoria it had the opposite effect.

"For your information, a *girl like me* is *exactly* the type and you will see me marching down Pennsylvania Avenue two days from now with other girls like me!"

They were both standing now and their voices were raised enough to draw the attention of the other diners.

"I won't see any such thing because I have better things to do than watch a bunch of busybodies parading themselves about."

"That's just as well.   I'm sure your *mother* wouldn't approve!"

"No, she would not!"

"Good evening, Mr. Asher."

"Good evening, Miss Webster."

Once they had stormed out Chase brought Olivia a glass of red wine and she drank the whole thing and asked him to send the rest of the bottle to her suite.

CHAPTER 43
CATHERINE PARKER
1865

Edward Chase saw Catherine walk through the revolving door and start across the lobby. She seemed to be carrying the weight of the world on her shoulders as she sat down in a chair under an elaborate chandelier.

In fact, Catherine was feeling numb from her encounter with Anna Surratt. All the way back she had wanted to tell the driver to turn around, to go back. But she knew she couldn't go back, and she felt like she had condemned a woman to her death. She sank into the chair in the lobby and soon sensed the presence of Chase beside her.

"A difficult morning, Ms. Parker?"

"I don't think I can do this," she answered without looking up at him. The lobby was very crowded but she didn't even look around to see if anyone might overhear her next comment. "If there is a chance to save the president how can I not take it?"

Suddenly she was angry and she looked right into Chase's eyes as he sat down in the chair next to her. She laid into him in a fervent whisper. "I'm a good person. I have spent my life preparing to do something good for other people, or taking care of people, or thinking about ways to help people!" She knew she was starting to ramble. "What I mean is, I'm the kind of person who does the right thing, Mr. Chase, even when I really, *really* don't want to."

Chase nodded, but he didn't interrupt her. She was on a roll.

"My father never spent one moment wondering how to help me get through school and my mother didn't let it trouble her that one day their problems would fall on me. My brother is spineless and his wife is evil and it did fall on me. All of it! I didn't want to go back to Dayton but I went! I didn't want to give up my own dreams to spend my life picking up the pieces of someone else's, but I did that too! And now I have this one amazing chance to help people and, yes, to better my own life in the process, and here you come all *one thousand years old* and tell me I have to hang around in this stinking nineteenth century mud hole and, oh yeah, make sure the most beloved president of all time gets shot in the head. That there is even a chance of that NOT happening is beyond the scope of rational thought and, yet, you want me to do what is absolutely foreign to me and that's to see to it that someone who doesn't deserve to die does, in fact, die at the hands of a narcissistic madman! Well, I can't do it, Mr. Chase! And I *won't* do it, so figure some way out of this and let me get back to my life!" Catherine was spent from the effort but she felt a sudden lightness. It was that simple, she just wasn't going to do it.

She looked defiantly to Chase for a reaction, but before he could say a word they were both distracted by a commotion at the door. A crowd of people was circling a couple who had just entered. Voices were raised and a few cheers went up. Chase stood and told Catherine to please stay put and he would be right back with her as soon as possible. As he walked toward the guests causing the clamor the crowd parted to make way for the concierge. Catherine's earlier diatribe was temporarily forgotten as she found herself watching the pleasant looking woman and the man Catherine assumed was her husband. He looked familiar. Of course he did. But it couldn't be. Could it?

Just then she heard Edward Chase welcome the man. "General Grant, it is my pleasure to welcome you and Mrs. Grant to the Willard."

CHAPTER 44
TOM KELLY
1962

The note was on Willard Hotel stationary and proved the boy had been raised with good Southern manners. Ethan York had taken the time to leave an effusive "thank you" for letting him use the phone to call his mother. They had talked and she had assured him he was doing the right thing by staying at his post and she had reiterated how proud she was of him. She had also asked him to pass along her thanks to the nice man who had offered the use of the phone and shared her opinion that this whole crazy missile thing was going to be worked out just fine because, after all, we *are* a civilized people, you know.

Tom had read the note when he returned to the hotel in the wee hours of the morning. After tossing and turning for hours he finally dropped off to sleep around dawn, only to be plagued by nightmares involving sleazy back rooms with smoking Russians and mushroom clouds in the distance. He gave up hope of any rest around nine o'clock and rang for a late breakfast from room service. He didn't say so, but he had every intention of making sure Edward Chase comp'd it on his bill.

Over exquisite eggs and less impressive bacon he read through his notes. Today was going to be a touchy day. Once the president and attorney general had gotten over the shock of learning a secret Russian spy ring (Russian, yes, but anti-Soviet, he reminded them) was operating out of Connecticut, a game plan was put into place.

Tom's job today would be to make contact with the organization and find out what communication was going back and forth. There was no doubt in his mind they would have their fingers all over it and he hoped to use the access to find the message that could be historically wrong. To do that he needed to know what had actually been sent back and forth eight years before he was born. In 2016, that would have been an easy Google search because a great number of those messages had been declassified. But sitting in 1962 as things were still unfolding, the lack of Internet access was just one of his problems. Thankfully he had a plan to overcome the information vacuum.

After the meeting in the Oval Office, Tom had seen John McCone furiously pacing the West Wing halls. The hours he'd been locked out of the meeting had only served to torque him up and he made a beeline for the president as soon as he realized the meeting had broken up. Tom didn't know what the two Kennedys were planning to tell him to get him to back off, but they had made it clear they wanted the Director's operation to continue as planned and that Tom was to access his alternative organization to see if there was anything to be gained there. As far as they were concerned it was a system of checks and balances and all options were on the table. He couldn't blame McCone for being furious, but he couldn't worry about it either. The CIA man was their problem. Tom had his own problems to deal with.

He made the first phone call using a series of rings and hang-ups before it was finally answered after the fourth ring combination. The connection was made but there was no greeting from the other end, only silence. Tom said "Victoria" then paused and said "Alexandra." It was the code he had been given to use when contacting Professor Volkov. Victoria was chosen because Queen Victoria was grandmother to Tsar

Nicholas' wife, who was named Alexandra. The code was instantly recognized and a raspy voice came over the line.

"Hello, Thomas, my friend. I had a feeling I might be hearing from you."

"Anatoly, how are you, sir?" Tom asked of the man with a million secrets.

"I'm old, Thomas—and getting older by the minute. Our two homelands seem determined to find a way to kill each other once and for all. But that's why you're calling on my secure line I presume."

"It is, Anatoly. But it's not just for research purposes. Are you certain this line is secure?"

"As certain as one can be in this life, Thomas. The KGB hasn't come for me in the middle of the night yet so I assume they don't know where I am. What's on your mind?"

"As crazy as this sounds, I'm calling on behalf of President Kennedy. I'm in Washington and my old script led some people to my door for insight on the current conflict," Tom said tentatively.

"Well, my friend, since they are unlikely to call you to talk about movies over a bucket of popcorn it seems your real purpose must have been discovered," said the professor.

"Yes," said Thomas. "But not all because of the script. They thought I might have some anecdotal advice to share, but they know about Back Channel because I filled them in. I'm afraid I got a little overwhelmed by the circumstances and offered more information than I probably should have, but they don't know who you really are, of course." He was quiet for a couple of seconds. "Now I realize why you insisted on the contact protocol. I can't tell them who you are if I don't know myself."

The man who Tom knew as Professor Anatoly Volkov sighed before he spoke. "I knew it bothered you that I wouldn't reveal certain things, but we've been doing this a long time and the reason Back Channel has survived is that we learned the hard way early on that secrecy and compartmentalization is a must. It's for our safety and yours, but mostly it's to protect the mission. The mission must outlive us all," he said.

Everything Tom had told the two Kennedys was the truth as he knew it. However, he knew that this "truth" was peppered with falsehoods and cover stories to protect the identities of the members of Back Channel. Anatoly Volkov was not his real name. His father was not the groundskeeper at Tsarskoe Selo, although he did work for the imperial family in some capacity and he *was* the messenger between the Tsar and the world outside captivity. He did request to stay with the Tsar when they were taken away, but Nicholas sent him home to take care of his family and also to safeguard the beginnings of the secret organization. The professor's parents were mysteriously murdered in their home and the place was ripped apart, but the volumes had disappeared with him when he defected. The defection was arranged and funded by Back Channel. They knew there had been a leak about their existence and that they were all likely to be killed. Safeguarding the mission was entrusted to the young man who would rebuild from a foreign land, the United States. Tom had no idea whether or not the man was actually a professor. Volkov had a series of secure phone lines that appeared to ring in and out of New Haven, Connecticut near the campus of Yale, but he could just as easily be in a mountain retreat in Colorado or overlooking the beach in Miami. Most importantly, the members of Back Channel didn't know themselves who the other members were. They had aliases and covert means of communication and their individual roles were only pieces of the puzzle. The only person who knew all their actual names was Volkov. The man had lost his parents, his home, and his adulthood to this mission. He would protect it with his life and to that end he carried an ampule of cyanide under his shirt on a thin chain. If caught, he would bite down on the glass and take his secrets to the grave. A special protocol set in motion in case of his failure to check in would elevate a new leader into position. The mission would continue. Until the land of their fathers was restored, the mission would always continue.

"What do you need from me?" asked Volkov.

"Is the channel actively working on the crisis?"

"What do you think, Thomas?"

"I think you've had more mail going around the world than the post office for the last few days," Thomas answered.

"There are a lot of deliveries, yes. From what we can gather the president and the premier are playing a coy game of patriotic pronouncements right now while being careful not to wave either flag too forcefully," Volkov responded.

"Anatoly, I can't explain everything right now, but I have reason to believe there is something in that line of communication that has been sent or will be sent soon that stands the chance of turning the tide in the wrong direction. I need to get into the chain and monitor the messages."

"You don't ask for much, do you, Thomas? You know this isn't Hollywood where you snap your fingers and a beautiful woman brings you a drink on a silver platter," the old man said with a chuckle.

"I know I'm asking for a lot but the stakes don't get any higher," Tom said.

"Can you tell me what you're looking for?"

"I wish I knew. I can only tell you I think I'll know it when I see it. Can you get me in?"

"This isn't a fishing expedition for the sake of finding out if it can be done as it was two years ago. Everything is more dangerous now. Besides the obvious, there is also more risk of our operatives being exposed because all eyes are on this communication. They won't be happy about letting an outsider in under these circumstances. Let me see what I can do. It would go a long way if I had something of good faith to offer them. Just give me something to prove you are as connected as you say you are, something they can verify."

"Give me a couple of hours and I'll see what I can come up with," said Tom.

☙

After an impromptu trip to the White House, Tom returned to the Willard and dialed the special phone the attorney general had arranged to have installed in his room. He gave the code. "Victoria." Pause. "Alexandra."

"You have something for me?" Volkov asked.

"The president has moved back the line of quarantine to five hundred miles," said Tom.

"Yes, we are aware of that. I'm afraid that's not information that will make your case. It's common knowledge now," said Volkov.

"Yes, but are your sources aware that the president has also called for a 'fast pace?'" asked Tom.

"Let me check." Tom heard paper rustling and a minute later the professor came back on the line. "Yes. There is mention of executing at a fast pace."

"It's code, Anatoly."

"Code for what?"

"The highest state of military readiness this country has outside of nuclear war."

There was silence on the other end of the phone.

"Talk to your people, Anatoly. The president has just moved us to DEFCON 2."

CHAPTER 45
CALVIN WALKER
1963

Things began to move quickly once all the boxed were unpacked. This group that had seemed like they were just a bunch of outcasts sitting around complaining about the status quo suddenly morphed into an organized machine. Everyone knew where to go and they began to divvy up their supplies. Orders were given and groups of two and three men began leaving the apartment. Calvin could see the dangerous weapons beginning to disperse and he felt the panic rise within him as he realized he couldn't contain it all to one place for the authorities to handle. He knew he had to move quickly.

"What's the plan, Fish? I need to know what's going down," he said.

"You're with me, Williams. Grab that duffel bag and put everything that came out of this box in it," Fish indicated.

"Where are we going? What's the plan?" Calvin's voice betrayed his rising fear.

Fish turned on him. "You do what you're told! Maybe you did come here to help us and maybe you didn't. Just because you showed up with some scribbles on a page don't mean I'm convinced you're clean. You do what I tell you and I'll decide when you get in on the action. Understand?" Fish was inches from Calvin's face and his demeanor left no room for argument, but there was too much on the line to back down.

Calvin matched Fish's attitude. "Look here! I came to *you* and proved I can get access that you won't have without me. You can't expect me to be able to get your guys close to the organizers without letting me in on the plan. I've got to get back to the hotel so I can blend in with the entourage as they head over to the event. I have to do this my way or you won't get anywhere near them!"

Fish dropped what he was holding and grabbed Calvin by the throat. He pushed him up against the wall. "You don't understand me do you, Professa? You ain't leavin' this room 'cept with me. You think I'll just tell you what we doin' and let you run out of here and tell it? You gonna be right by my side this whole day. I know just how I wanna use you. And if you try to rat us out, you be the first one down." He let go and backed away just far enough that Calvin could barely pass through. He gestured toward a duffel bag on the floor. "Now you pack that bag and be careful. We don't want nothin' goin' off before it s'posed to," he said, with the most sinister look on his face Calvin had ever seen.

Calvin did as he was told and carefully placed the homemade device inside the bag. He put the strap over his shoulder and sat down while the others finished loading up.

CHAPTER 46
OLIVIA FORDHAM
1913

March 2 dawned cold and clear. Olivia hadn't slept well, but over the years she had found she needed less and less sleep. One of the benefits of age she supposed. A quick peek out the window showed the preparations for the inauguration that was to be held March 4. With modern inaugurations falling on January 20, this was a reminder that it hadn't always been that way.

All the preparations she saw weren't for the inauguration though. The suffrage parade would happen before the inaugural events, and it had been scheduled for maximum exposure. In a city that saw no shortage of marches and events, the organizers had made sure theirs wouldn't be short of an audience.

Olivia dressed and met up with Victoria for the ride to NAWSA headquarters. Once there, they were given a comprehensive lesson on the history of women's suffrage initiatives over the past decades. They learned about Sarah Grimke who had begun speaking out against slavery and later included women's rights in her messages. They heard about the establishment of female colleges and the arrest of Susan B. Anthony in 1872 for attempting to vote in the presidential election. It was all very enlightening for Victoria and the more she heard the more she was sure this was something she had to do. Olivia feared for her as she watched the rhetoric building its fire behind her young eyes. In other parts of the city final touches were being put on floats and banners. Participants were arriving and gatherings were popping up all over the city. In many a parlor, ladies were talking about the march. Some were dismissive and others secretly wanted to join in.

On Capitol Hill, James was serving as courier for his brother and the congressman, carrying documents from building to building as they wrapped up their business in preparation for the arrival of the new president. As he walked, he thought only of Victoria. Of the way she looked in that blue dress. Of how her eyes sparkled when she laughed and flashed when she was angry. And boy, could she get angry. He was frustrated with her because he couldn't understand what she could possibly stand to gain by aligning herself with radicals. She had been taken care of her entire life and she would continue to be. She would become a good man's wife and raise a family and preside over an important home. Maybe *his* wife. He was a good man. Why did she need to concern herself with speeches and marches? He could take care of her and those things would never matter.

Twenty-four hours had not passed since he had met her and he was thinking about marriage and what was good for her. He couldn't understand what was happening to him. He had plenty of nice, quality girls back home who were interested in landing him as a husband and would never dream of getting involved in something like suffrage. Their husbands would vote for whatever was best for them. But none of those girls had captured his attention like Victoria. Not even close.

All day he had heard negative remarks about the suffragists and threats of violence and mayhem. The more he walked and the more packages he delivered the more certain he became. If the stubborn girl was determined to take part in this ridiculous parade tomorrow, then he would be there to make sure nothing happened to her. She would probably hate the idea, thinking it terribly old-fashioned, but that was too bad. He had decided.

CHAPTER 47
CATHERINE PARKER
1865

As it turned out, General Ulysses S. Grant and his wife Julia had come to Washington in route to their home in New Jersey after the surrender at Appomattox Court House. They didn't have a reservation, but the Willard wasn't about to turn away the man who had finally done what more respected generals before him could not. This was the man who had stopped General Lee and his Army of Northern Virginia and ended the war. Though the hotel was booked to capacity, Chase had worked his magic and cleared an appropriate suite for the Grants. They were upstairs presently getting freshened up for a meeting with the president. This afternoon Grant would sign the official documents ending the draft and recruiting efforts for the army and sending war-hardened veterans back to their homes and lives.

Catherine had also learned while waiting for Chase to secure accommodations for the Grants that the city itself was preparing for a spectacular celebration this very night. They were calling it the Grand Illumination and every building, from the windows of private homes to the enormous banner declaring UNION being affixed to the Willard roof at this very moment, was to be lit tonight to celebrate the hard-won victory. Even the Capitol dome, which had been kept dark during the war so as not to make it a tempting target since its completion, would be ablaze in glorious light. Thousands of people had descended on the city to cheer and dance and drink and all around party.

Tonight would be the biggest party of them all and the only man the public wanted to see as much as the president was his top general. The man who was thought unfit to lead the nation's army because he enjoyed hard liquor would be toasted tonight as its greatest hero.

When Chase returned to speak with Catherine he found she had disappeared. She wanted to walk and to think. Things were happening so fast and it was time for the rehearsal at Ford's. She walked the entire way, turning her ankles from time to time on the rutted streets.

When she arrived at the theatre she found that Laura had given her name to the man at the box office window and she was allowed entry. She crossed the small red-carpeted lobby and entered the back of the auditorium itself. She had never been to Ford's before. It seemed much smaller than she imagined with its wooden chairs in a semi-circle facing the stage. She looked up and to the right and saw the opera box where the Lincolns would be seated and noticed there was no bunting across the front. In all the photos she'd ever seen of Ford's, the flag bunting and the portrait of George Washington were always there. It dawned on her then that those items were there in her day because they were commemorating what happened here when Lincoln was shot. She guessed, correctly, that before the assassination the opera box was only the state box when the president was in it, sort of like Air Force One. Tomorrow, when they learned he was coming they would be draping it for his use.

They'll never take it down again. That was the thought burning in her mind.

The rehearsal was in full swing. Laura saw Catherine standing in back and motioned her to come on stage. Catherine held up a finger to indicate she'd be back in a minute. She went back into the lobby and climbed the stairs leading to the second level. This level was called the dress circle and once Catherine stepped into the area she could see the easy pathway around to the small door that led to the state box. She walked around and opened the door. No one paid her any attention. She stepped inside the door and found a second door. Opening that one she found the large box that the president and his party would occupy. She stepped forward and looked down at the stage. It seemed to be about ten or twelve feet below her and, if memory served, this is where John Wilkes Booth would leap to the stage as part of his dramatic exit. He would break his leg in the process.

Break a leg, huh, Booth? How many times did someone tell you to do that before you went on stage?

Once again, Laura spotted Catherine and this time she spoke to her from the stage.

"I see you've found the best seat in the house. I've heard Mr. Ford has been hoping the president might turn up tomorrow night. I know he's looking to fill seats. Attendance has been dismal here lately. Come on down and see the view from the stage," she said.

Catherine slowly backed out of the box and closed both doors behind her. She felt a chill and wanted to get away quickly. Even now it seemed like a creepy place.

Laura invited Catherine up some temporary stairs on the front of the stage. From there she turned her around and let her look out over the orchestra level with the footlights in her eyes. Even without an audience it was a surreal experience. The gaslights made a hissing sound and their blue flames danced across the bottom edge of the stage like a borderline to the abyss.

"Those aren't usually turned on for rehearsals, but I thought you might like to see what it's like," Laura said. She motioned offstage to a stagehand and the lights dimmed and went out. The hissing stopped, but the smell of gas lingered in the air mixed with the fragrance of greasepaint and freshly cut lumber that had been used to build scenery. She pointed to an area in the audience section on the stage right side a few rows back.

"I've arranged for you to have a seat there. It's a wonderful view of the stage and you might also be able to catch a glimpse of the president if he does come," Laura told her proudly.

"That's very kind of you. Do I understand correctly that it's a special night, your 1000th performance in this role?" Catherine asked.

"Yes. I know this character as well as I know myself. I believe it will be a night we can tell our grandchildren about," Laura remarked.

"Yes," Catherine answered. "I think you might be right."

Chapter 48
TOM KELLY
1962

DEFCON 2. It was the highest state of military readiness the United States had seen since the system was implemented. Only DEFCON 1 was higher, and it meant imminent nuclear war. After Tom had given Volkov the classified information the president had given him to pass along, several hours passed while Volkov had his network run the information through and verify that Tom did indeed have extraordinary access. Back Channel was sitting on the information when they saw it come through the governmental clandestine network. This proved Tom was telling the truth and they gave Volkov the green light to work with him. Over the next twenty-four hours, messages went through the clandestine network and Back Channel reviewed them and double-checked them with Tom. So far, it seemed the accuracy of the information was holding. There was nothing Tom could identify that might be the catalyst for a change in history.

On October 26th a letter came through from the Soviet premier that indicated he would remove the missiles and personnel from Cuba in exchange for a United States guarantee not to invade the island nation. It looked like de-escalation was to be the word of the day and everyone settled in for a night's sleep in the wee hours of Saturday morning with high hopes, but they would be dashed the following day.

The new day dawned clear and hopeful. Tom slept in and left his room at the Willard just after 9 o'clock. He ran into Edward Chase in the lobby.

"Mr. Kelly, how are things progressing?" asked the concierge.

"Things are going well, Mr. Chase. I think it will all be over today. Communication has been smooth and I think the crisis has been averted yet again."

The concierge didn't look convinced. "Do you know the date, Mr. Kelly?"

Tom paused to think about the question. "The days have all run together but I think it's Saturday. That would make it October 27th, I think," Tom said.

"That's right, today is October 27. It's been twelve days since the first photos of the missile sites came to light. Twelve days, Mr. Kelly."

Tom could see that Chase was hinting at something but he was too tired to pick up on it.

"What are you getting at, Chase? You think we're not out of the woods yet?"

"Mr. Kelly, did you happen to see the movie with Kevin Costner that was made about the crisis? I believe it was around the year 2000 and I know you are very familiar with movies."

"Yes, I saw it," answered Tom. "It was called *Thirteen Days*. If today is day number twelve it stands to reason that we're close to the end." Tom didn't see the problem.

Chase continued, "Perhaps you should think back to the movie you saw. Day twelve wasn't the wrap-up, Mr. Kelly. It was, in fact, the most dangerous day of the crisis. I believe you should get over to the White House right away. I have a feeling you will be quite busy today. I will continue to make sure no hotel staff enters your room and your secure communication equipment is not disturbed. I'm here if you need me."

Tom couldn't remember anything about day twelve, but just the thought of it made him feel sick. He said goodbye to Chase and headed for the revolving door of the hotel. He passed a well-dressed gentleman reading the morning paper. Nothing about the front page looked exceptionally worse than it had over the past few days. The masthead listed the date as October 27, 1962. After today it would be referred to as "Black Saturday," but Tom didn't know that.

He stepped outside and turned right for the short walk to the White House.

CHAPTER 49
CALVIN WALKER
1963

At the Washington Monument the crowd that had been gathering got tired of waiting for directions and began the march to the Lincoln Memorial without the organizers of the event. As they walked along they sang songs and waved signs. The closer they got to the Lincoln Memorial the more electric the atmosphere became. It was clear to all present that something extraordinary was happening. They had marched, sat at lunch counters, quietly protested at courthouses, and petitioned school boards, but nothing had felt like what they were doing today. Buses continued to arrive and the crowds grew as they began to assemble around the reflecting pool and up on the steps of the monument. They were standing shoulder to shoulder, pressing together to get as close as possible to the platform. To those looking back on the crowd from the stage area it looked like a sea of people with no end. And somewhere in that crowd there were members of a radical organization whose name literally meant *white death*. But they were surrounded predominately by black people, the same brothers and sisters they claimed they supported. What good could come of killing these innocents? The answer was simple and Calvin had figured it out on the walk here with a bomb slung over his shoulder in a duffle bag. Kifo thought of these people as lemmings. To them, the marchers were not the thinkers and the doers that they themselves were. The marchers were blindly following charismatic leaders who stood to enrich themselves and gain nothing for their people. The marchers were collateral damage in a war. Collateral damage was expected in war. It was accepted. It was even factored into battle plans. Today these lemmings would die in order to inflame the black population to take up arms with Kifo. The world would see that non-violence was nothing but a waste of time. The marchers even looked like they were out for a Sunday afternoon social. No, they couldn't be taken seriously. But Kifo would be. After today they would not be overlooked. The Black Panthers might have Malcolm X, but Kifo would forever have the aftermath of the march. They planned to lead the way in reforming public life for the black race.

Calvin had no idea where the others had been stationed, but he and Fish pushed their way to within a few yards of the stage. Something about Fish's countenance caused people to make way for him. A few even gave up their prime viewing spots and left the immediate area, sensing he might be a danger.

Calvin placed the bag by his feet. A few yards away he saw a couple of police officers. He quickly came up with a plan.

"I'm going over to those cops to tell them the organizer's motorcade needs assistance at the corner of Constitution and 17th. I'll tell them I'm Dr. King's assistant and that the police chief doesn't want to radio for them because he's afraid word will get out that he doesn't have control of the crowd. I can get them out of the area," Calvin said.

Fish looked unconvinced, but he had noticed the wide berth some had given him. He hadn't gone to any trouble to try and blend in and his black leather attire and menacing scowl had frightened some. He thought Calvin's professorial look might help him convince them to move, which was a good thing because they might finger Fish for a troublemaker if they noticed him there. Reluctantly he let Calvin go, but told him he was watching him for any sign he was up to something dirty.

Calvin navigated the crowd and approached the officers.

"Excuse me, officers, I need your help."

The two white officers looked at Calvin dismissively.

"What do you want?" one of them asked.

"There are men in this crowd with bombs in duffel bags. One of them is ten yards behind me right now and there are at least seven other groups spread out in the area," Calvin said as calmly as possible. He even managed to gesture in the direction of Constitution Avenue and 17th Street while he talked because he knew Fish was watching.

The men seemed unimpressed. "Bombs, eh? Twenty minutes ago it was rifles on top of the monument and this morning it was gonna to be tear gas," one officer said.

The other officer joined in. "Don't forget the kidnappers."

"Right. I forgot about the kidnappers. We've been warned all about the schemes you malcontents aim to use to get us to wade into that crowd and make it look like the big, bad, white police are trying to keep you from making your little speeches. Go back to your place, boy," the bigger officer said. It must have been funny to the other cop because they got a good laugh from it.

Calvin could feel Fish's hard stare boring into the back of his skull. These knuckleheads needed to listen and it was clear they had no intention of taking him seriously.

"I'm not kidding, fellas. If you don't listen to me you're going to have dozens of dead spectators on your hands in about an hour. Not to mention they might just get one of the organizers. Do you want that to happen on your watch?"

"I told you to get back to your place, boy!" the officer made a move toward Calvin with his hand on his nightstick. This was going nowhere fast. Calvin knew he had to talk to someone higher up. At that moment he heard the opening bars of the national anthem. The program was starting. It was now or never.

Fish was watching from his position near the stage. He had a bad feeling that Williams, as he knew him, was ratting them out to the cops. But it was too late now. The anthem was starting and his boys were in place. They wouldn't be deterred. Even if the cops grabbed him right now it wouldn't matter. The duffel bag he had with him was just a ruse, like all the others. None of them had working bombs. The real action had been placed the day before when the stage was being built. He had arranged to have some of his boys from out of state on the set-up crew. He knew nobody would recognize them. They had planted the explosives directly on the support structure of the stage and the surrounding steel, and a trusted member of Fish's group was standing by to detonate them on his signal. The duffel bags were decoys to bring the cops, nearly all white, into the crowd to see what was up. The Kifo boys had planned to fan out in the crowd and open the bags to reveal the "bombs" during the song by Mahalia Jackson. It was scheduled late in the program and all the principals would be on stage. The pandemonium would send the marchers running out and the cops running in. Before anyone could fully react, the stage charge would be fired. That way they could take out everyone on stage, plenty of spectators, and most importantly, the cops who would rush in to protect the organizers. Fish was the only one close enough to be in danger from the blast and he was just about to start making his way out of the area.

For a second he thought it was a shame that Williams might turn out to be a rat. Fish thought he could be a useful resource in a later operation if he was a true believer in their cause. So what he saw next shocked him and seemed to prove Calvin was no snitch. Just as Fish had started to push his way through the crowd to get to a safe spot he saw Calvin, the suspected rat, pull back a fist and punch the strutting officer in the jaw. They had him on the ground with a knee at his throat in record time. The police had just made their first arrest of the

day. And they had cuffed the only man who could have helped
them.

CHAPTER 50
OLIVIA FORDHAM
1913

The telegram had been delivered to Victoria when she stopped at the hotel for lunch and a brief rest midday. She'd been having a wonderful morning with the other ladies preparing for the march, the only dark spot being the memory of her argument with James the night before. She didn't know why she cared so much what a virtual stranger thought about her, but she couldn't shake the disappointment that she was unlikely to see him again. All in all, the morning had been energizing and inspiring, but the message she read sent her spirits plummeting.

Victoria
Deeply concerned by the news from Washington stop insist you return home at once stop ticket on five oclock train arranged Union Station stop obedience expected stop
Father

Victoria felt deflated by the message. All the excitement of the morning was wiped away. It was one thing to come to the city with her parents' grudging, tentative permission, but another matter entirely to defy a direct order to return home. She had never defied her parents' wishes and knew that doing so now would have serious consequences. Sadly she began packing her things and left them with the bellman before returning to F Street to say goodbye to her new friends and explain why she couldn't help them after all.

Olivia had stayed at headquarters while Victoria was at the hotel and she had no knowledge of the letter. She noticed the change in Victoria's demeanor the moment she walked through the doors of the bustling office.

"What's wrong, dear?"

"My father sent a telegram ordering me home on the five o'clock train. He's heard some kind of news about the event and he refuses to allow me to be part of it. My things are packed and I've come to say goodbye."

Olivia felt her heart sink. If Victoria left she would fail the task Edward had given her, not to mention change the course of her own life. But it was more than that. Though she had never had children, this strange situation had her feeling like a mother to Victoria and she could feel the deep disappointment the girl was carrying.

"Do you want to go home, Victoria?"

"Of course not! I want to be here and be part of the march! I've seen so much these last two days. How can I go home and immerse myself in debutante balls and the social register when I know what I know now? I can't turn my back on this work." She paused. "And I don't know why I care because he's an insufferable fool, but I wouldn't mind seeing James again."

There it was. Proof that Victoria herself had strong feelings about both her political advocacy and the young man with the old-fashioned opinions. Olivia felt she would be doing the right thing for all the right reasons if she encouraged her to defy her parents and stay. But it was much harder than she thought. She had no experience with the life of an early twentieth century upper-class girl whose parents held total sway over her choices. The more she encouraged Victoria, the deeper the girl dug in her heels saying there was no way she could defy their direct order to return. It simply wasn't done. Olivia had to remind herself that times were different and she was beginning to lose hope as she watched Victoria make the rounds to say her goodbyes and offer apologies that she couldn't stay. Alice Paul had been terribly disappointed and Amelia had tried everything she could to change the girl's mind. Nothing was working and Victoria was making her way to Olivia to say a final goodbye and thank her for her kindness when the door opened and a woman neither had met walked through.

She looked to be in her early thirties with a vibrant smile and when she came into the room a crowd of women gathered around to welcome her. There was something familiar in her appearance and Olivia felt she should recognize the woman. All activity in the office stopped as she was greeted with a great deal of enthusiasm. Olivia and Victoria watched the scene unfold and finally Olivia noticed something slightly amiss about the interaction between the woman and those around her. It was so slight it could be attributed to the chaotic scene, but it jogged Olivia's memory and she realized at once who the woman was. As if she'd been summoned for this very purpose, the woman made her way from the crowd toward Olivia and Victoria. An aide walked with her and Alice Paul stepped up beside her to make the introductions.

"This is Olivia Fordham of New York and this is the young lady I was telling you about from Philadelphia. This is Victoria Webster." She paused and turned toward Olivia to continue the introductions but the woman took over.

She extended her hand toward Victoria. "It is my pleasure to meet you. I'm Helen Keller."

Victoria and Helen spent the better part of an hour together. Olivia wanted to be a fly on the wall and hear their conversation, but she gave them privacy with the hope that this great woman could be the catalyst to help Victoria make the right choice. As she watched the interaction from across the room she saw Victoria wipe tears from her eyes, at times looking distressed as she told her story, and other times laughing and nodding her head in agreement. Even with the aide translating through sign language it seemed like there was no barrier in their communication. They looked like old friends catching up and when the conversation ended Victoria excused herself to freshen up. Olivia took the opportunity to speak with Helen through her aide. Though Helen struggled with speech, Olivia was impressed with her diligent efforts as the heroic woman shared her thoughts about Victoria.

"She's an extraordinary young woman."

"Yes, she is. And so are you, Miss Keller. It's my honor to meet you."

"The honor is mine. I understand you are from New York."

"Yes, I'm visiting this week and I actually didn't know about the march, I'm embarrassed to say."

"But you've gotten involved now and you've been a great influence on young Miss Webster. I dare say she would have already fled home without you here."

Olivia didn't have a ready answer.

"I understand the young lady's concerns, but there is something in her, some kind of fire, that mustn't be snuffed out. I know all the nonsense about her family name and connections, but even without that there is something about her that makes me think she has an important voice that needs to be heard."

"Do you think she'll stay?" Olivia asked.

"I hope so. Mrs. Fordham, I cannot see and I cannot hear in the way you do, but there are things that I know just the same as if I could see them with my own eyes. Miss Webster has a destiny to fulfill. I hope you will be her champion and help her fulfill it."

"I will certainly try, Miss Keller. And your words mean more than you may ever know."

Helen had been taken to a back office to meet privately with committee members by the time Victoria returned. The look of resolve was back in her eyes.

"Mrs. Fordham, would you mind to accompany me to the telegraph office?"

"Of course. May I ask why?"

"I must let my father know I will not be on the five o'clock train."

CHAPTER 51
CATHERINE PARKER
1865

Laura and Catherine arrived back at the Willard after rehearsal. The city was so crowded with people coming to the Grand Illumination that the ladies decided to have dinner in the hotel dining room rather than braving the crowds at restaurants. They had a nice dinner and Laura retired early to get her rest for the coming day.

Catherine was restless. The crowds were out in force and the city was lit up beautifully. Candles and gas lamps flickered and the public displays were unlike anything that had ever been seen. She walked down the street to the White House and back and still she had no idea what she was supposed to do.

All this celebration, what will it become tomorrow night? Will there be panic? Will there be riots? No, she remembered, there had been no riots. *But people will greet the news with shock and all the red, white, and blue bunting that adorns the buildings will be replaced with black crepe. This celebrating city will be thrust into mourning in little more than twenty-four hours.*

She could still stop it. Or she could do her part to make sure it happened as it did. She still didn't know how to do either one. And she didn't know if she had the courage to do either. She kept walking. Amidst the celebration, the gaiety, and the fireworks she was a lone figure, walking the night away.

CHAPTER 52
TOM KELLY
1962

South Carolina kept factoring into Tom's life all week. Ethan York had told him of his desire to attend Clemson University and it was a Clemson alumnus who grabbed headlines on this twelfth day of the crisis. Early in the morning, a textile management major from the class of 1948 climbed into the cockpit of his U2 plane and set off on a reconnaissance mission like many that had been flown in recent days. But his mission didn't end with rolls of film being developed for analysis. Major Rudy Anderson, now of the United States Air Force, was shot down by a surface-to-air missile over Banes, Cuba. The theoretical had just become the reality.

The mood at the White House was so tense Tom felt that a loud noise might send them all ducking for cover. As if the shooting down of an American warplane wasn't enough, Defense Secretary Robert McNamara had the unenviable task of reporting to President Kennedy that a completely unrelated problem had crept up over Alaska as a second U2 had gone missing and possibly strayed into Soviet airspace.

When Tom had left the White House the night before, he thought they were on good footing with Khrushchev offering to pull out the missiles and personnel in exchange for an American promise not to invade Cuba. All that had changed when a second letter came through clandestine channels that now required the U.S. to remove their missiles from Turkey. The game had changed and the Soviet premier was coming out charging. Now with a downed plane on Cuban soil and one missing off the Alaskan coast, the fuse was closer than ever to being lit. Tom gathered all the intelligence he could and hurried back to the Willard to communicate with Volkov and his network.

After establishing their bona fides as they did with each new transmission, Tom sent a series of coded lines that made up an incomplete message. It was enough for Back Channel to use to compare against chatter they were monitoring from the "official" clandestine pipeline. Everything was checking out at first. Khrushchev wanted the missiles out of Turkey and he would leave Cuba in return. But the messages began to show some deviation and after a few hours of back and forth between the White House and the Willard, Tom could see that something was off in the way the messages were being interpreted. He couldn't be sure if it was a language issue or something more serious.

"Thomas, my boy. Do you think us incapable of translating Russian to English?" Volkov asked.

"Of course not, Anatoly. But there could be a cipher problem," Tom answered.

"There is no problem with the code translation, Thomas. Your messages are tracking perfectly except for this single line. You have someone working an angle that is different from the official party line."

"Can you trace it? Do any of your people know where it's coming from?" Tom asked.

"It appears just like the other transmissions as far as we can tell. There is no difference in the way it is encoded or the origination," Volkov answered.

"I don't understand. Why would they be proposing two different options?"

"I don't think *they* are, Thomas. I don't think your organization is as cohesive as you thought. It might be a group or just one person working alone, but there are definitely two plans here and they could have very different outcomes," Volkov said.

"Have your people been able to finish the translation?" asked Tom.

"It's just coming in now." Volkov paused to read the teletype he received. "The first one is as we thought. You take the missiles out of Turkey and they take the missiles out of Cuba."

"And the second one?"

"It doesn't make sense," Volkov said.

"What does it say?" asked Tom.

"It says that to make the missiles in Turkey part of the withdrawal package the Soviet Union must remove more than just their existing missiles and personnel from Cuba."

"What else do they want?" Tom asked.

"The message says there is no deal unless the Soviets take out Fidel Castro."

CHAPTER 53
CALVIN WALKER
1963

From the window of the police wagon where he was being held, Calvin could hear the "Tribute to Negro Women" portion of the program. He remembered from his study of the event in college that Myrlie Evers, the widow of Medgar Evers, was supposed to lead this part, but she was unable to attend. Calvin found himself glad that she wouldn't be here to see more brutal violence. He expected to hear explosions any second and the longer the program went without incident the more tense he became. He knew Kifo had to be waiting for something specific, some trigger designed to inflict maximum damage.

When he was carted away by the officer with the bruised and bloody mouth, he kept spouting off as loud as he could that he was a member of Dr. King's entourage and demanding to see the chief of police. He didn't figure it would get the chief there, but he hoped it would be enough to get someone with authority to come and talk to him, if for no other reason than to cover their own asses in case he was telling the truth.

Finally, he was rewarded for his patience when a police captain named Perry introduced himself and asked Calvin his name. The program was moving on. John Lewis had taken the podium and was delivering his remarks. Time was running out.

"My name is Calvin Walker. I know this sounds like a hoax and I'm very sorry I punched your officer. I needed to get to someone in authority and it seemed like the only way."

Captain Perry didn't look like he believed Calvin's story either. Calvin could see he was losing him.

"Last night, I was with Dr. King when he was working on his speech at the Willard Hotel. You can call the concierge, Edward Chase, to verify my story." Calvin said.

The captain no longer looked disinterested. He knew Dr. King was a guest at the Willard, however it wasn't common knowledge. If this guy knew where he was staying and was willing to offer a witness he might be telling the truth.

"What did you say your name was?" Perry asked.

"Calvin Walker."

Captain Perry stepped aside and made a quick call on his radio.

"What's this about bombs, Mr. Walker? How would you know about that from working on a speech?"

"I don't have time to explain everything, Captain, but please believe me when I tell you there is a group of radicals here at the march and they are armed with bombs. I came into the information and I was following up on it this morning."

"Why didn't you alert the police?" asked Captain Perry.

"I planned to, but the leader of the group, a guy they call Fish, was suspicious of me and wouldn't let me out of his sight. I convinced him I was going to get your officers to leave the area where he was setting up and then I went directly to them to explain what was going on. They didn't believe me." He shot a sideways glance at the officer who was rubbing his sore jaw.

"So you punched an officer and claimed to be part of Dr. King's entourage so I would come and talk to you. Is that about right?"

"Yes. I know it sounds ridiculous. Please call the Willard and ask for Mr. Chase. He'll vouch for me. But do it quickly because I don't know when those bombs are going to be detonated but it can't be long now."

"Mr. Chase called headquarters this morning with a story about this but he didn't have enough information to go on. He did give us your name, though, and given the stature of the Willard we gave it more credence than we might otherwise have." He turned to the officers who had taken Calvin into custody. "Take the cuffs off him."

The one with the injured jaw looked ready to protest, but Perry stopped him. "Do it!" He gathered a group of officers around and starting issuing orders. He told them about the bombs and assigned them to various areas to start searching. He motioned for Calvin and the two officers who had detained him to follow.

"All right, Mr. Walker. Show me the man you call Fish."

CHAPTER 54
OLIVIA FORDHAM
1913

James had made the mistake of telling his brother and the others at the upscale gathering about Victoria and her involvement with the march. He had been so excited about seeing her again and his decision to look after her well-being and now he was being taken to task for it. The men at the club were having a heyday with him as they swirled their expensive brandy.

"Watch out, son, she'll make a woman of you yet!"

"We know who'll wear the pants in your house!"

His brother joined in on the action. "Can't wait for Mother to hear about this one. Promise me, brother, that you won't tell her until I can be there to see her face!"

Some of the comments weren't meant as light-hearted jokes.

"Those women need to remember their place. I wouldn't be surprised if something happened tomorrow to remind them they belong at home."

"I'd never let my wife or daughter anywhere near those harlots. I hear they like each other, if you know what I mean. Can't get a man, I guess."

"Who would want any of them anyway? A bunch of harpies! Mr. Asher, I hope you like asking a woman for permission to put on your pants!"

"Maybe she won't let him wear pants. She'll wear them instead!"

They were having a grand time at his expense. There was much laughter, but also an undercurrent of something ugly. James didn't know what he'd been thinking. They were right. No man in his right mind would get mixed up with this group, especially not when he had his pick of lovely young things back at home who had no interest in such matters. He doubted if he would ever be able to hold his head up high again if he brought home such a woman.

Someone passed him a brandy and then another. After the fourth one James was pretty sure he wouldn't be anywhere near the parade route tomorrow. No matter how lovely she was or how much he secretly enjoyed her fiery convictions, he *was* a man after all and it wouldn't do for a girl of his to be known as a harpy.

He ordered another brandy.

CHAPTER 55
CATHERINE PARKER
1865

Good Friday. The sun was up but Catherine had not closed her eyes all night. She had walked all the way to the Capitol and along the streets lined with extravagant displays of lights and when she was too tired to take another step she collapsed on her bed and sobbed until dawn. Eventually the stress of what she had to do overcame her and she began vomiting. Exhausted and spent, she took a hot bath and washed her hair. Then she sat by the open window and let the cool breeze soothe her, but her nerves remained frayed. Finally, when she couldn't put off the day any longer she dressed in a simple gown and went down to the restaurant for some dry toast and tea to try and settle her stomach. She was seated there picking tiny pieces of bread off her plate when she overheard the conversation at the next table and noticed she was seated next to Julia Grant and another lady.

"I thought he would be back by now. I am determined to be on that train, but I fear my husband may give in to the president's invitation to the theatre tonight. I simply cannot bear to spend an evening with that insufferable Mary Lincoln. She's a terrible gossip and I do not wish to spend another moment away from my children, especially in the company of so distasteful a companion," Mrs. Grant explained.

"Do you dare send such a note to your husband while he has an audience with the president?" asked her companion.

"I have found that a man may lead other men in battle with great decisiveness, but when it comes to navigating his home life he can use a bit of prompting. I hate to interrupt his meeting, but he's been there for hours," she responded. "I suppose it might be the height of bad manners to send a note. But if I don't do it I just know I'm going to end up watching a play tonight instead of traveling home," she responded.

At that moment Mrs. Grant's companion excused herself to join her husband and Mrs. Grant was left alone at her table. She was holding a note but seemed unsure of what to do with it. The bile in Catherine's stomach began to roll again. This was her moment. She could see the tear as clear as day. If Julia Grant sent that note, her husband would likely join her on the evening train and be on his way home. But if she didn't, he might capitulate and accept the invitation to see the play. Catherine knew the Grants had not attended the theatre with the Lincolns on the night the president was shot. But here was Julia Grant saying she thought her husband was going to agree to go. Ulysses S. Grant was a warrior who had spent four long years on high alert in the theatre of war. His instincts were good and his reflexes were sharpened on the battlefield. If he accompanied Lincoln to the theatre he would be more likely to detect the intruder in the box and to be quick in his response to disarm him. The scene played itself out in Catherine's mind.

If General Grant is Lincoln's guest he may be able to stop the assassin.

Catherine knew her moment had come. She looked around for Edward Chase. He always seemed to be near and yet he was nowhere to be found now. She sent a waiter to the lobby to find him and he returned a moment later reporting Mr. Chase was not at his post. She closed her eyes and did something she hadn't done since before her father had died. She prayed. For guidance. For deliverance. For anything that would take this decision out of her hands. She tore at the gloves in her lap and finally she turned to Mrs. Grant.

"I beg your pardon, Mrs. Grant, I couldn't help but overhear your dilemma," she said softly.

"Yes, I'm not usually so wishy-washy, but I know the general is needed at the White House now. I just really don't want to miss that train. I'm sorry you overheard the unkind things I said about Mrs. Lincoln. I know it's not very ladylike," she sighed and looked down at the note.

"It's been a long war, Mrs. Grant. I don't think the president would begrudge you wanting to get home to your family," Catherine consoled her.

"I believe you're right Miss. . ."

"Parker. My name is Catherine Parker."

"Miss Parker. Thank you very much for speaking to me. I was about to change my mind about sending the note, but you have bolstered my resolve," said Mrs. Grant.

She summoned the waiter and asked him to take the note to a messenger and have it delivered to the White House right away. Catherine watched as Mrs. Grant carefully placed the note in the waiter's hand. The missive was small, barely four inches square, and it was addressed in a fine hand. The waiter placed it on a silver tray and left the dining room in search of the messenger.

"I'm so pleased to have made your acquaintance, Miss Parker. I'm going to go and finish my packing. I have high hopes the general and I will be on the six o'clock train, thanks to you." Julia Grant smiled and started to walk away, but turned back to say one more thing to Catherine. "Thank you again, my dear. I believe you have saved me from a most disagreeable evening."

Her thanks felt like a dagger to Catherine's heart. Mrs. Grant left the dining room and just beyond her Catherine saw the messenger leave the lobby with her note in hand. She watched him turn right and start toward the White House and kept watching until he was lost in the crowd on the street. She kept watching because she couldn't stand, couldn't walk. She could only stare; stare and tremble with the knowledge she had surely signed the death warrant of the President of the United States.

CHAPTER 56
TOM KELLY
1962

There it was. Tom now knew the message that threatened to plunge the world into nuclear holocaust. Somewhere inside his own government someone, or some group, was looking to take advantage of an already dangerous situation to take out an old enemy. The fate of the world had come down to one man. Missiles were in place, the country was at DEFCON 2, recon planes were being shot down, and now someone was interjecting a poison pill into the negotiations.

There was no way Khrushchev could agree to take out Castro. He would look like a puppet of the West, and he would hand his biggest foe a victory they had been unable to achieve on their own with Operation Mongoose. It was the potential for a second attempt on his life that had persuaded Castro to go along with Khrushchev's plan to put missiles in his country in the first place. Castro had the worldwide distinction of being the little dictator who had repelled the big, bad, American wolf. How would it look now for the head of the Communist world to appear to bow before the Americans and remove from their hemisphere the thorn in their side? It was a proposition that was sure to stall peaceful negotiations, or worse, escalate the conflict beyond repair.

Tom had to find out where this was coming from and how to stop it. He went to the White House and told an assistant it was urgent that he see the president. He waited in the outer office for two hours until the president returned from the Situation Room. The attorney general was with him, as usual. Tom addressed both Kennedys.

"Someone in your administration is proffering a second option," Tom said without preamble.

The attorney general spoke first. "Tom, I spoke with the Soviet ambassador an hour ago. He doesn't know about Khrushchev's second letter addressing the missiles in Turkey. We offered to accept the premier's conditions in the first letter, which proposed removal of his missiles and personnel in exchange for our pledge not to invade Cuba. The hope is that he will agree and not press the second letter."

"I'm not talking about the Jupiter missiles, sir."

"How did you know there are Jupiter missiles in Turkey?" the president asked.

Tom realized he knew the type of missiles from studying the crisis in school. The name had just popped into his head, but he couldn't say that to the two Kennedys. "It must have been in one of the Back Channel messages, sir."

Both Kennedys seemed satisfied with his answer. They weren't sure how deep this Back Channel went and they knew if they survived the current crisis they would have to find out, but for now all of Tom's information had been solid and this wasn't the time to question it.

"What second option are you referring to if it's not the second letter?" asked Robert Kennedy.

"Someone is proposing that to reach an agreement the Soviets must also remove Fidel Castro from power. Specifically, sirs, they want him killed."

There was silence in the room. There was nothing in the world that John Kennedy wanted more than the removal of Fidel Castro from Cuba. The problem was, he hadn't asked for it as part of the negotiations. Who was doing this?

Tom explained all that he knew and showed them a copy of the teletype he had obtained from Volkov. The president picked up the phone on his desk and within two minutes the men of the ExComm were seated around the room. Tom stood off to one side as the president stood to address them.

"Gentlemen, we have a new problem. I don't know if it started with one of you or not, but nobody is leaving this office until we find the hole and plug it."

CHAPTER 57
CALVIN WALKER
1963

Calvin, Captain Perry, and the two officers walked through the crowd during the remarks of the next two speakers and a song by a gospel choir. So far they had seen nothing, no duffel bags and no Fish. Perry had Calvin and his group concentrating near the stage since Fish had been seen there last. A rabbi took the stage to offer a prayer and the men continued searching.

In the meantime, the men with the duffel bags had entrenched themselves in strategic spots. There were six around the reflecting pool, one at each corner and one on each side in the middle. One was in the area closer to Constitution Avenue where the police would come running through when the chaos began. The final bag was still with Fish. He had it slung over his shoulder and was watching from his perch in the tree line near the area that would one day become the Vietnam Veterans Memorial. He had actually climbed up into the lower branches, but he didn't look out of place because many others had done the same. In fact, he had a Kifo brother there all morning holding the spot until he could get there. He wasn't about to miss the show and this would give him a bird's eye view.

While he waited in his elevated position he took in the sea of people who were looking with such rapture at the stage. Most couldn't even see the participants from where they stood, but they were nonetheless enthralled with what they were hearing. Fish thought they looked pathetic, like peasants who would dance for the king to make him laugh just to get the crumbs from his table. He thought about how they would panic and trample each other in their attempt to get away from the fake bombs. He planned it that way so they would literally crush the life out of any who were too slow to get out of the way. He wouldn't need the slow ones for the movement he planned to start from the ashes of this one.

The disdain he felt as he watched them was palpable. They weren't his people. They had ceased being his people when he had gotten radicalized years before. That Fish came to be at this place with murderous intent was a tragic twist of fate. He wasn't a son of the South with firsthand experience of the atrocities of prejudice. Fish, born Henry Dockins, had been raised in arguably the most diverse city in America. He was the son of educated, upper-middle-class parents in Brooklyn, who gave him every advantage. They stressed education and raised him to believe that even though their struggle was hard, nothing was truly out of reach. He had an outgoing personality with plenty of friends and plenty of girlfriends. Nothing about him suggested he wouldn't follow along in the footsteps of his proud parents and achieve all that he could imagine.

The break with the life he had known came five years ago. At the tender age of seventeen he had watched as his father became increasingly involved in the quiet, non-violent actions of the early civil rights advocates. It was nothing major, no speeches or long bus rides to the Deep South to sign up voters. He went to a few meetings and offered his reasoned thinking to their collective development. For two years, everything had moved along quietly until a business rival learned of his involvement. Although it wasn't something he wore on his sleeve, his activism wasn't secret either. But his rival saw it as a chance to paint the man as a subversive troublemaker bent on forced equality. The myth that racism was just a Southern problem could be easily debunked in 1950s New York. It was in this environment that a group of "colleagues" of this rival showed up at the Dockins apartment. They said they had come to talk to Mr. Dockins, but they brought baseball bats with them. Fish's father and younger sister weren't home when his mother answered the knock at the door. He heard the men demand to see his father and his mother's insistence that he wasn't home. They didn't believe her and forced their way inside. Fish came out of his room and saw the terror-stricken look on his mother's face. That was the last thing he remembered until he woke up in the hospital. One of the men had bashed him over the head with a bat and while he lay unconscious on the floor his mother was repeatedly raped and then beaten to death. His father and sister had arrived home to find the carnage and believed both to be dead. The fact that his son had survived only strengthened Mr. Dockins' devotion to non-violent protest, but it had been the breaking point for young Henry.

After his recovery, his father moved the family to a new home several blocks away, but Fish was repeatedly drawn back to the scene of the crime. He walked the streets for hours on end, stoking his rage with every step. He drifted away from his father who could see the hate taking over his beloved son's life. It wasn't long before he was venturing beyond the confines of his privileged neighborhood to the darker and seedier parts of the city. It was on one of these long walks that he met up with a group of like-minded men. They believed answering violence with violence was the only path to equality. In truth, they were more interested in exacting revenge than in equal rights and none had more cause to want a bloody battle than the young man whose last memory of his mother was the look of terror on her face.

His mother had given him the nickname, Fish, when he was a child because he loved the water and was an excellent swimmer. It had always been a sweet name, one that conjured up thoughts of a happy childhood and loving family. Now it would become a sinister moniker for a man filled with hate—one who vowed to avenge the mother who had given him the name, and avenge her in blood.

Five white men had spilled the blood of his innocent mother. Today he would spill the blood of innocents in pursuit of a larger goal—full-scale race war. He knew his mother would not be proud, but he had enough pride for all of them.

CHAPTER 58
OLIVIA FORDHAM
1913

Olivia left Victoria at the office working diligently alongside the other women. She returned to the Willard with plans to speak with Chase about the morning's events. On the sidewalk in front of the hotel she noticed a disheveled James leaning against an iron rail. As she got closer she smelled alcohol and noticed he was weaving slightly.

"Mr. Asher, I see you've been imbibing rather early today." She wondered briefly if there was a legal drinking age in 1913. He looked embarrassed to see her.

"I have, Mrs. Fordham. I do beg your pardon."

"Why are you here? You're not a guest at the Willard as I understand it."

"I was hoping to run into Victoria."

"In your condition? I don't think she would be impressed with you under the circumstances."

James blushed. "No, I don't suppose she would. I guess I wasn't thinking straight."

"Would you like to come into the lobby for a cup of coffee?"

"No, thank you, ma'am. I have to be going. I just wanted to see her one more time."

"You're leaving town?"

"Yes, ma'am. I'm going back to Middleburg tomorrow afternoon and I don't plan to be at the parade."

"I believe you were clear in your feelings about the parade. I don't think Victoria is expecting to see you there."

"But that's just it, Mrs. Fordham. I had decided to go and to make sure she stayed safe and to see her again and maybe talk to her even though the things she says make me furious." He was rambling.

"If you decided to go to the parade why have you changed your mind?"

"You wouldn't believe the beating I took this afternoon from my brother and his friends. They were teasing me about liking a girl like that who would want to wear the pants and not let me wear pants and harpies and harlots." He wasn't making sense.

"I beg your pardon? I understand you are impaired at this moment, but I hope you do not expect me to stand here and allow you to speak of Miss Webster as a harlot."

"Oh, no, ma'am, I didn't mean Miss Webster. No, ma'am, she's a lady for sure. Why, you can just see that she's a fine lady from a good family. But they were calling the suffragists those names and saying they like each other in the boy-girl way."

"And you let them say those things about a respectable lady like Miss Webster?"

"I couldn't say anything! Maybe they're right. I couldn't take a girl like that home to meet my mother. And the other girls in Middleburg would think I'd gone crazy when they're so docile and 'yes, James' and 'of course, James' and all that."

Olivia was livid and forgot about this being her grandfather and any implications it might have for her personally.

"If that's the way you feel, Mr. Asher, then I suggest you catch the next train home to your mother and your docile imbeciles and leave a strong and vibrant young woman like Miss Webster alone. She is clearly out of your league. And do sober up.   It's terribly unbecoming for such an *upstanding* Southern gentleman. Good day, sir!"

Olivia left James standing there with his mouth gaping as she stormed into the Willard. She hadn't noticed Edward Chase on the sidewalk, but he had heard every word. He caught up with her as she was angrily crossing the lobby and he grabbed her by the elbow.

"Olivia! What have you just done?"

CHAPTER 59
CATHERINE PARKER
1865

Before Catherine had even come down for toast and tea that afternoon, President Lincoln had sent a messenger to Ford's Theatre requesting the state box for the evening's performance of *Our American Cousin*. Mr. Ford was thrilled to oblige. Ticket sales at his theatre had been dismal of late and having the president in the audience was sure to fill the seats. He wasted no time in having a new playbill printed touting the president's attendance and sending the story to the newspapers. The afternoon papers all reported that the Lincolns and the Grants would be in attendance at Ford's that very evening. When General Grant received his wife's note urging him not to be late for the evening train he knew he could not impose on her any longer. They had been apart from each other and from their beloved children for too long. She wanted to go home and home she would go. He offered his apologies. The Grants would be on the evening train to New Jersey and unable to accept the president's kind invitation.

After his meetings President Lincoln took his wife on a promised carriage ride around the city. Onlookers remarked how they heard the First Lady laughing as she rode alongside her husband. When they got back to the White House the exertions seemed to have taken a toll on the fragile woman. She reported that she had a headache and would like to cancel their theatre plans. While Lincoln would loved to have skipped it as well, he knew the word had been spread and that people were expecting him to be there and he didn't want to let them down. He told Mary they must attend and she found alternate guests to accompany them. Prior to this night, Abraham Lincoln had never met Major Henry Rathbone or his fiancée, Clara Harris, but their names would be forever linked with his because they accepted the late invitation from Mary Lincoln. The show would go on with the Lincolns in attendance.

∽

Catherine had finally found the strength to leave the table some time after Mrs. Grant's departure. She had looked in vain for Edward Chase and had no idea where he could have gone. What a terrible time to disappear! Eventually she went back to her room and reclined on her bed as day faded into evening. The lady's maid came again to help her dress for the theatre. Catherine was like a rag doll, moving as the maid told her to and letting her push and pull and lace and button her until she was properly outfitted in a beautiful deep blue velvet gown that had been hanging in her closet. The maid had been prattling on non-stop about all kinds of goings-on, including the earlier departure of General Grant and his wife. Laura Keene had been receiving lovely bouquets all afternoon and she sent a few over to Catherine's room for her to enjoy. Catherine didn't notice the heady fragrance as the maid wove some of the smaller ones into an elaborate braided bun.

"Miss, would you like to wear this?" the maid asked.

Catherine snapped out of her daze and noticed the maid was holding her grandmother's diamond brooch. It was the one Catherine herself had pinned on her navy suit just before she had taken a nap that first day here.

"Where did you get this?" she asked the maid.

"It was here," the maid indicated a rosewood box on the dresser Catherine had not noticed before. The brooch was the only thing in the box. "It's so beautiful."

Catherine looked at her grandmother's pin and felt tears come to her eyes.

"Yes. I would like to wear it," she said.

The maid pinned the delicate brooch on the neckline of her mantua where it sparkled in the lamplight.

What have I done, Gramma?

Whatever she must face this night she would face with her grandmother's strength. She took her wrap and went to meet the carriage that would take her to Ford's.

CHAPTER 60
TOM KELLY
1962

The Soviets were furious. The messages coming back and forth were getting more heated and trigger fingers were getting itchy. The official clandestine pipeline was bogged down with Khrushchev insisting the Turkish missiles were non-negotiable. But that was only one channel and nobody on either side seemed sure which one was truly "official." Back Channel was pulling missives off the line showing the contentious exchange over the suggestion that Khrushchev take out Castro. The first responses simply ignored that part of the message, but someone on the American end kept putting it back on the table. Finally, the Soviets addressed it and said there would be no deal. The American side reported the president was considering bringing the blockade ships closer to Cuba to aid in a possible invasion and that American submarines were being redeployed to join in the effort. None of this was true, which made it all the more frightening because every man on the ExComm swore on his sainted mother's grave that he knew nothing of these messages. It quickly became clear that someone had gone rogue and was threatening the safety of the world.

Officials began trying to mitigate the damage by adding assurances to the official clandestine messages that the negotiations were still on track, but they couldn't outright say there was someone outside their control sending the messages. There was simply no way to know who it was or what the final agenda might be. Every hour the clock ticked closer toward Armageddon.

Tom was moving back and forth between the Willard and the White House, but he needed help. He had asked to have Ethan be a runner for him. At first the officials balked at sending Top Secret information out with an intern, but Tom argued that Ethan would have no idea what he was carrying or what any message he might send meant. In the end, they didn't have anyone of the right clearance who could be spared so the young man from Fort Mill became Tom's courier.

CHAPTER 61
CALVIN WALKER
1963

It was like they had disappeared; they had simply vanished into the crowd. Or more likely they just blended into the sea of people, just as they had planned to do. Calvin couldn't find any of the men he had seen at the apartment. The police were executing a grid search as effectively as they could, given the enormous crowd. Once or twice they thought they had found something, but came up empty. The program had moved on and Roy Wilkins of the NAACP was addressing the crowd.

Calvin and Captain Perry had covered the area where Fish was last seen. Their actions didn't go unnoticed. From his perch in the tree, Fish could see them. He wasn't surprised Calvin had turned, but he was angry at himself for not completely trusting his gut with regard to the man who had shown up at the eleventh hour claiming he could get to Dr. King. Fish knew it was his own ego that had caused him to let down his guard. He had briefly entertained the idea of a one-on-one confrontation with the movement's most heralded leader. During the night that Calvin had gone to get his proof, Fish had chastised himself for such hubris and vowed that if Calvin returned he wouldn't be swayed by his claims of insider status. He'd keep the man close in case he turned out to be a traitor, which he had. By that time, Fish knew his plans had already been successfully put in place so he wasn't concerned about any damage Calvin might be able to do. On the contrary, the stupid man was right in the blast zone and had brought three cops with him. Yes, everything was working out exactly as Fish had planned, even with the diversion of Calvin.

Roy Wilkins concluded his speech and the crowd was getting restless. Four speakers had taken the podium since a choir had performed and it was time for more music to stir the souls of the crowd. The great Mahalia Jackson took the stage and Calvin heard the opening bars of her song.

He was briefly distracted by the music and stopped to see who was about to perform. From his vantage point something caught his eye as he turned to look at the stage. A man off to the side of the crowd, a good distance from the stage but not too far to be out of Calvin's line of sight, was unwrapping something. It looked to be a small box with wire around it. He seemed nervous, fidgety almost. But when he finished unwrapping the wire he looked back at the stage and that's when Calvin got a look at his face. He had seen it in the apartment that morning and now it bore the same look of hatred and resolve that the other Kifo members wore. In a split second Calvin realized the wire he had unwrapped was part of a long run that headed off in the direction of the stage. With all the people around and the technical equipment nobody had noticed a thin wire that had been carefully placed to protect it from being pulled loose. Calvin's eyes moved in the direction of where the man was intently staring. He looked all the way to the stage and that's when he saw it. Just below the podium, on the structure under the stage, was a black box. It blended in with the rest of the apparatus but Calvin instinctively knew what it was.

Mahalia Jackson started to sing "How I Got Over." Calvin knew the bombs were about to explode, including this new one he had just discovered. He still believed the duffel bags were real bombs. Even though they weren't, they still had a role to play and the men who carried them began placing them on the ground at their feet and preparing to open them at the first chorus of the song. This would start the panic and once it began the man with the detonator would slowly count down from fifteen and fire the switch.

Calvin had no idea where the other "bombs" were but he knew he had to stop the man with the detonator. It was the only thing he could do. There was no time to explain to the Captain as Calvin pushed his way to the edge of the crowd and sprinted for the man with the tiny box in his hand.

Mahalia Jackson approached the chorus of the song with gusto and the men with duffel bags bent and prepared to open them. Calvin lunged for the det man and, in what seemed like slow motion, he felt his feet leave the ground.

CHAPTER 62
OLIVIA FORDHAM
1913

All afternoon Olivia had paced and worried about the scene outside. Things could not be more messed up. The situation felt a bit like trying to nail Jell-O to a tree; you can't do it because pieces of it keep falling off. Victoria was leaving and now she's staying. James was gone, then back, then drunk and confused, and now Olivia had more or less told him to take a hike. And Edward had been uncharacteristically stern with her about keeping her focus on the big picture. Yes, it was important for Victoria to be part of the movement, but it was equally important for her grandparents to get together. That part was bothering Olivia because she remembered specifically hearing that her grandparents had met in Washington as the result of a carriage accident, not a motorcar spewing dirty water and not because of some political event. None of it made sense and Olivia was out of ideas for how to fix it. Her grandparents were turning out to be very stubborn young people.

There was a knock at the suite door and Olivia found Victoria standing there looking tired, but happy. She'd been working all day at the office and looked like she was ready to drop.

"I ran into Mr. Chase downstairs and he told me you wanted to speak with me."

"Yes, please come in. Would you like something to eat? I had a few things sent up."

"Now that you mention it I didn't actually eat lunch today. Once that telegram occupied my mind I forgot all about it." They each filled a plate and sat at the dining room table.

Olivia saw no way around what she had to do. "I saw James this afternoon. He was looking for you outside the hotel." Victoria's eyes lit up. "But before you get excited you should know I told him to go home to Middleburg and leave you alone."

"Why? Why would you do something like that?"

"Because he was talking nonsense about what other men would think of him if he took up with a woman who would devote herself to causes like this one."

Victoria visibly deflated. "Oh. I see."

"No, you don't see, Victoria, and neither did I. He came here, quite a bit past tipsy I might add, because it bothered him that he was concerned with such things."

"I don't understand."

"He was disappointed in himself that it mattered what they thought and I didn't see that he needed to be encouraged and not scolded for how he was feeling. He likes you, Victoria. In fact, I think he likes you so much he's looking for a reason to tell everyone else to go fly a kite. But I jumped to the conclusion that he was somehow judging you unfairly and I'm afraid I was unkind to him."

Tears were welling up in Victoria's eyes. She looked for all the world like a child, and Olivia had to remind herself she wasn't. She was a young woman who knew her own mind enough to defy her parents to be here and she was capable of deciding for herself whether or not James Asher was worth her time.

"He's like every other well-bred young man in this day and age. He's been raised to see things only one way, just as you have. But now you've been exposed to other ideas and started to see the value in them while this is all new to him. He only knows the opinions he's been taught to have. I believe that, given time, he will come to see things as you do and be a support for you, and you for him, as time goes on. I urge you to give him another chance."

"But you said he's gone home."

"No, he hasn't left yet to the best of my knowledge. He's planning to leave tomorrow afternoon, but that gives you enough time to get a message to him if you want to. Mr. Chase will arrange to have it delivered."

Victoria looked torn. Her head and heart were fighting for dominance. She felt she barely knew her own mind and recognized there was so much more for her to learn and to see and do. She was already fighting her parents for the right to do it. Did she really want to take up a fight with a man she barely knew? What right did he have to a say in her life?

On the other hand, she couldn't shake the feeling that she had met the man she would one day marry when he screeched to a halt at the corner. He had come to the hotel with no idea what to say to her but at least he had made the effort. Wasn't it up to her now to make an effort of her own or let him leave and accept that she would likely never see him again?

"I don't know what to do, Olivia. And I have a terrible headache. I think I'll go to my room and lie down if you don't mind."

Olivia walked her to the door and gave her a warm hug. "I'll support whatever you decide. Just don't wait too long. You know they say lightning never strikes the same place twice."

Victoria thanked her and left. On the way to her room she thought how appropriate Olivia's words had been.

I feel like I'm in the midst of a storm and calamity is on the horizon.

CHAPTER 63
CATHERINE PARKER
1865

Catherine arrived at Ford's before the official opening of the doors for the audience. As Laura's guest she was allowed entry and shown to the star's dressing room where she found her new friend in costume and makeup and astonishingly nervous in spite of her familiarity with the role.

Laura wasn't just the star of the show. She had bought the rights to the play a few years before and she was also a theatre owner herself so she took a great deal of responsibility on her shoulders knowing the combination of this being the 1000th performance and having the president in the audience would bring added attention to the stage tonight. Catherine wished her well and left the dressing room to find her seat.

When an usher showed her to the house she was virtually alone in the great space, as the audience had still not been allowed inside. There were a few ushers milling about and some last-minute work going on onstage, but Catherine's attention was captured by the now decorated state box. She had been seen in the company of Ms. Keene over the past couple of days so no one stopped her as she made her way to the private box. Once again she entered through the unlocked doors and found herself standing where the president would stand to acknowledge the crowd in just a short while. She ran her hand along the deep red upholstery of the chair where he would take his ease for the final time and she looked around the box contemplating the horror that was to take place there. Absentmindedly she reached forward and touched the flag that was gathered into bunting on the front of the box. She ran her hand along it, feeling the folds and noticing the texture under her fingers. Without thinking, she straightened the framed portrait of George Washington and continued to smooth and straighten the fabric of the draped and upright flags. She wanted to them to be perfect and found herself lost in the act like a mother fussing over a daughter's wedding dress and veil. It kept her busy for a moment and gave her a purpose—something good that she could do in a situation so terrible.

Finally, she knew she had to leave the box and she did, closing each door carefully behind her. The house doors were now open and the audience was filing in to find their seats. She returned to orchestra level and made her way to the left of the house where Laura had reserved a place for her. Soon the theatre was filled, announcements were made and the entertainment began. Catherine found she couldn't focus on what was happening onstage. She kept looking up to the state box, but she wasn't the only one. Everyone kept monitoring the area as though the president might sneak in there unnoticed. A few patrons were getting visibly antsy that the president had not arrived as the play progressed until suddenly Laura Keene noticed action in the balcony and improvised a line to draw the audience's attention to the entrance of the president. The orchestra struck up "Hail to the Chief" as the group made their way into the state box and suddenly there he was. Though she had accepted this moment would come, Catherine was unprepared for her reaction to seeing it with her own eyes. There, standing at the edge of the box where she had smoothed the flag not an hour before, was Abraham Lincoln. He held his signature stovepipe hat in his hand as he acknowledged the crowd with a smile, something not seen in photographs of the great man. Catherine could see his wife, Mary, beside him and two other people taking their seats in the box. Major Rathbone and Clara Harris took their places on the settee as the president continued to thrill the crowd with his acknowledgment before taking his own seat so the performance could resume. Catherine was amazed. She felt like she had been on a merry-go-round that was spinning too fast. The man revered for preserving the union and freeing the slaves, the one in the giant sculpture at the Lincoln Memorial, was sitting less than the length of a football field from her. He was there in the flesh, alive and well.

Alive. Catherine's earlier nausea returned and she fidgeted in her seat.

The audience was once again attentive to the action onstage though there were many stolen glances at the state box. Everything was normal for a little while. Intermission came and went and with it went the only security guard Lincoln had between him and an assassin. The derelict guard abandoned his post and went drinking at the tavern next door.

As the play continued its second act Catherine kept stealing glances at the box and the area leading to it. When her nerves were almost beyond frayed she saw him, a figure in black approaching an usher and handing him a card. The usher allowed him to pass and John Wilkes Booth reached for the handle of the outer door to the state box. Before he entered, he looked around to see if anyone was watching and as he glanced back his eyes swept the orchestra level. He did a double take and locked eyes with the lovely young woman in the deep blue dress sitting house left a few rows from the stage. Catherine felt her breath catch in her throat. His eyes were black and soulless. They reflected the gaslights like onyx and she felt he could see through her, that he knew that she knew. She sat paralyzed like a statue as he turned the knob and passed through the outer door.

A fan. The women always find me, even in the dark. Especially in the dark, Booth almost chuckled to himself. He knew his fame was about to grow exponentially.

As Booth was carefully opening the inner door and slipping silently into the back of the box Catherine was coming apart in her seat downstairs. The man to her right noticed her distress.

"Are you quite all right, Miss?" he inquired.

"I'm not feeling well." She stood abruptly and everyone in her row adjusted to allow her to pass to the aisle. It was apparent she needed to get out of the room. She walked quickly up the aisle and into the lobby. Laura did not see her retreat. The actor on stage was gearing up for a well-known line using some of the play's folksy language. Catherine ignored the ushers who inquired about her condition and flew up the stairs to the dress circle. She topped the stairs and started around the outer wall toward the box, determined now to stop the would-be assassin.

"Don't know the manners of good society, eh? Well, I guess I know enough to turn you inside out, old gal—you sockdologizing old man-trap," came the line from the stage, followed by an eruption of laughter from the audience and a sound that didn't fit the scene. It was a gunshot. Catherine stopped in her tracks and sank down against the wall, just steps away from the door to the state box.

CHAPTER 64
TOM KELLY
1962

What I would give for Google and e-mail right now, Tom thought as he slogged his way through messages from both the "official" clandestine pipeline and from Back Channel. He had to find out who was sending these rogue demands. Each member of the ExComm had issued a lockdown on his own staff and the number of people who were involved in the negotiations was cut to bare bones. Virtually no one outside of the president's trusted circle was in the know now, but the messages continued. *Kill Castro. Take him out or the president will move the ships in closer to Cuba and prepare for a ground invasion.* None of it made sense. If this person had a death wish it looked like he might just get his way.

Volkov kept sending translated cables and Tom began to compare the time stamps against the messages the United States government was getting from their own contacts. Something about the timing of the messages bothered Tom. Rather than waiting for a response from the Soviets as one would expect when a demand is made, reiterations of the demand were coming fast and furiously. This wasn't the work of a seasoned diplomat. Tom wasn't one either, but he could tell from the timing of the government messages that they were very careful to allow enough time for consideration and response. Nobody wanted to increase the pressure that could result in a tragic outcome. But these rogue messages were relentless in their aggressiveness.

Whoever was sending these seemed to know he wouldn't stay hidden for long and he was pushing hard to get the Soviet premier to buckle under his frequent demands.

For all the initial mistrust between Director McCone and himself, Tom had recognized quickly that the CIA leader was a thoughtful and reasonable man with a strong grasp on the Soviet mindset. Anyone working in lockstep with him would not be pursuing an agenda in this way. Tom mentally crossed the CIA off the list of possible leaks and moved on to the National Security Director's staff. No matter how much he dug or how cynically he viewed high-level government agencies, he just couldn't pin the action to a probable group.

There had to be a third party involved, someone outside the president's sphere of influence. But how did someone get in at this level? The thought struck him as ironic as he had been the outsider who infiltrated Back Channel. That had to be it. There was a government outsider injecting himself into these proceedings with the potential for dangerous consequences. Who was he and would there be time to find him before the damage was done?

Tom whipped open his hotel room door and summoned Ethan York from the hallway. He wrote a quick note to Robert Kennedy with his latest hypothesis and suggested they were looking for someone on the fringe of the agencies of the ExComm. It had to be someone with either past access or enough insider knowledge to know how to get into the pipeline. When he was finished he sealed the note inside an envelope and wrote the word "confidential" across the seam of the seal.

"Take this directly to the attorney general," he told the young intern. "Don't give it to anyone else under any circumstances."

Ethan was nodding his head eagerly, but Tom wasn't finished admonishing him.

"I'm serious, Ethan.   If the Secretary of Defense, National Security Advisor, president's secretary, *and* the Secret Service tell you to hand this over you smile politely and refuse to hand it to anyone but Robert Kennedy himself. You put this into his hands. Do you understand?"

"I understand, Mr. Kelly. I will give this envelope to no one except AG Kennedy, even if I have to eat it to protect it. I won't let you down," Ethan answered.

Before Tom had left the White House for the Willard, the two Kennedys had determined that Tom would send messages hand-delivered by Ethan York and that only Robert Kennedy would be allowed to receive them. The president indicated he would not ask for the messages so there would be no conflict as to chain of command. This would allow for a direct line between Tom and Robert Kennedy and nobody could try to pull rank by saying "the president said to give it to me." Both Kennedys were prepared to back the intern if it turned into a showdown between him and half the cabinet. There could be no more leaks.

Ethan put the envelope in his coat pocket and walked quickly to the White House. His pass allowed him to come and go quickly from the West Wing and within moments he was standing by, waiting for Robert Kennedy to pen his response to Tom, which would be sealed in the same manner. Once he had it, he returned to the Willard and put the return envelope into Tom's hands. He had been gone for less than thirty minutes total. Tom sent Ethan back into the hallway and read the message.

Understood. Will have personnel records for the past five years examined for possibilities. We can't discount the possibility this could be a Soviet spy trying to create the illusion that we have a rogue agent. Official messages will continue to reassure Khrushchev that the Castro demand is not coming from us. Report back ASAP.

Tom thought about the possibility of a Soviet spy trying to make it look like the United States was demanding action on Castro. He just couldn't figure out what the end game would be for that kind of demand from their standpoint. He knew he was in way over his head. The only thing he knew to do was to put on his writer's hat and try and imagine what scenarios might exist. If he was going to write the story, who would this character be and what did he stand to gain? It was a long shot with no viable possibility of success, but it was all he had. He kept digging and over the next few hours sent Ethan back and forth to the White House several times. Against all protocol he eventually invited the young man into his suite and started to bounce theories off him. Pretty soon Tom realized that being top of his class at Fort Mill High School was a bigger deal than he had thought. Ethan was smart and highly versed in history and government. He was also very deliberate in his thought process and some of the questions he asked sent Tom down a different path than he had considered before. It was a path he desperately wanted to avoid because if this line of thinking was correct then everything they were doing could be playing right into the hands of a madman.

CHAPTER 65
CALVIN WALKER
1963

As he lunged at the man with the detonator, Calvin's life seemed to morph into slow motion. He felt his feet leave the ground and saw the man turn to him with a look of panic on his face. He held the box in his left hand and as Calvin soared through the air at him he brought his right hand up and put his finger over the button.

At that moment, Calvin felt something hot hit him in the abdomen. It ripped and tore through him, blazing a path through his flesh. At the same time he felt the skin on his legs heating up and being torn from the bone. The wind was knocked out of him and he saw blood spraying everywhere. He didn't feel anything else, nor did he comprehend the blood that now seemed to be all around him was actually pouring from multiple wounds to his own body. He had been too late, and as he lay dying the last thought that went through his mind was of his family all together the last time they visited Lookout Mountain.

CHAPTER 66
OLIVIA FORDHAM
1913

Edward Chase arrived at the Jefferson Suite with a bottle of wine and two exquisite glasses.

"It's not ladylike in 1913 to get drunk," Olivia said dryly.

"Is that a concern for you?"

"Hell, no. I just wanted you to know I recognize that. Come in, Edward."

They sat in the first parlor and toasted the end of the long day.

"I don't suppose Victoria sent a message for you to deliver?" Olivia asked.

"No. She hasn't come downstairs since she got in."

"If she hasn't done it by now she probably won't. I guess that means I've failed at least part of the task."

"I'm never told for sure what the task is, Olivia. Perhaps it was only to get her to stay and be part of the march. Maybe that's all you had to do and I believe you've done that."

"But you know that's not all."

"I know."

"Have you ever had anyone fail what they've been sent back to do?"

Chase looked away. He *had* experienced a failure. Many years had passed since it had happened, but the consequences were catastrophic and he couldn't tell her that. He didn't have to. She could almost read his mind.

"Have you ever had someone negate their own existence?"

He kept sitting there staring into his glass. "No. I've never seen this happen before."

"And you don't know what will happen to me."

"I don't."

"What usually happens when this is over?"

"Typically, you would fall asleep again and wake up back where you were when this all started. You would lose no time and go about the business you came for. Some people don't even realize they've been anywhere. Most just think they've had a vivid dream, but others assume they had too much wine with dinner or some bad fish," he said in a halfhearted attempt to lighten the mood.

"What about the others? There have to be some who question the experience."

"Yes, there are some. Occasionally they seek me out to see if I give anything away and other times they go back to the scene of the experience to see if they can make sense of it."

"Have any gone to the lengths you went to in order to understand it? To maybe become like you?"

"None that I know of. And I hope that never happens. I'm not sure if this is a life I would wish on another person."

They were silent for a few moments, each lost in private thought. Olivia spoke first.

"So maybe I just won't wake up. Just cease to exist." She paused. "Will there be any sign I was ever here in the hotel? What happens to my things?"

More silence.

"There won't be any sign of me anywhere, will there? No life lived in New York. No business, no institute. I guess with my health condition I eventually wouldn't remember those things anyway. I guess I always thought someone would."

"I can't say for sure, Olivia, but I have to believe that there's still a chance we're missing something."

"It's been bothering me that the story I always heard about my grandparents meeting involved a carriage accident. I remembered it because I thought it was special that they lived in a time people still traveled around in carriages. It didn't happen that way yesterday so maybe this whole thing was already decided."

"I'm so sorry, Olivia. It's my fault that you're here and if I could change this please know I would do it in a second."

The man looked distraught and Olivia felt for him. Strangely, she felt peaceful about her own situation.

"I don't think I would change it Edward. I never knew my grandfather and I could never have imagined my grandmother as a young, impressionable girl full of fire and zeal. I don't know how much more of life as I've known it I really had left anyway so this has been a gift in a way." She reached out and touched his hand. "You cannot blame yourself, my dear friend. Tomorrow I will spend another day with my grandmother and I'll watch her becoming the woman she grew to be."

"This is not over, Olivia. I will spend every moment tomorrow looking for that missing element."

"Please do. And if you don't find it we must both accept it and move on."

He stood to leave and asked if there was anything else she needed for the evening.

"I'm fine, but I would appreciate if you could send up the maids to help me dress in the morning. There is a splendidly fashionable concoction in the closet and I can't think of a better day to wear it."

"Consider it done. Goodnight, Olivia."

"Goodnight, Edward."

CHAPTER 67
CATHERINE PARKER
1865

The shouting. The screaming. "Sic semper tyrannis!"
Thus always to tyrants. Catherine had seen Booth's awkward
landing on the stage and heard him shout his battle cry. She
heard the agonized screams of Mary Lincoln and the shouts of
Major Rathbone. The outer door to the state box had been
barred from the inside and Rathbone swung it open, screaming
for help and bleeding. Confusion reigned as the audience tried
to figure out what had happened. Was this part of the play?
Soon enough it was obvious it wasn't and panic set in. Catherine
saw Laura Keene run to center stage and plead with the audience
to remain calm. Booth had disappeared backstage and the
realization was becoming clear that the president had been
attacked. The call for a doctor rang out and a man ran into the
box.

Without thinking, Catherine got to her feet and started
walking as though she was being drawn to the scene of the
crime. She entered the box and pressed herself against the back
wall watching the surreal images play out before her. Major
Rathbone was standing against the front rail of the box wrapping
his bleeding arm. Mary Lincoln had been moved from her
husband's side when the doctor got there. She was seated on the
settee alternating between moments of shock and others of
agonizing keening. Clara Harris was by her side doing all she
could to comfort the traumatized woman. And there, on the

floor at her feet, was the president. He was so tall he seemed to take up most of the floor space. Blood seeped into the red carpet as the doctor probed his body looking for the wound. He soon found it, a single hole in the president's skull. Dr. Leale removed the clot that had formed and the blood flowed more quickly. The face Catherine knew so well from photos was drawn and pale. She could see the life draining from him. The doctor spoke, but to Catherine's ears it sounded like he was underwater.

"His wound is mortal. It is impossible for him to recover," he said simply.

Just then Laura appeared in the doorway. In a strange turn of events she moved to the president's side. The doctor backed away and Laura Keene, the most famous actress in the world, cradled the president's bleeding head in her lap while his wife sobbed at the news he had been fatally injured.

The roaring in Catherine's ears got louder and louder until all she could hear was the sound of her own heart beating. *Do they know this is my fault? That I could have stopped it? That I'm the reason this man's blood is spilling onto the floor and this woman who has suffered the loss of two children is now facing the tragedy that will finally send her over the edge? They don't even know my name, but this is my doing.* She wanted to faint, maybe even to die. Anything to stop the rising sense of shame and remorse she felt. The cries of Mary Lincoln condemned her by their very rawness.

Some men arrived to carry the president from the box to a place where he could be more comfortable. A place to die away from the scene of violence. Catherine felt herself moving toward Laura. As she laid the president's head down on the floor and backed away Catherine was there to help her to her feet. Laura looked at her with unseeing eyes and the two women embraced. Catherine felt Laura's knees buckle and as she started to fall Catherine caught her and lent her support as she walked her out of the state box to a seat in the dress circle.

The president was carried down the stairs and across the street to a boarding house. Catherine knew from the history books that he would languish all night and die early the next morning. There was nothing she could do now. Her deed was done and the blood could never be washed from her hands.

As the crowd left the theatre to stand in the street outside the boarding house, the cast of the play and the theatre staff became concerned about repercussions. They hustled the rest of the patrons outside and locked the doors. Laura had been in shock and was led away by one of her dressers. Catherine watched her walk away and then left with the other patrons. Laura had not looked back. Though she could not have known, Catherine felt her only friend knew she was to blame. Out on the street now herself she couldn't bear to stand with the crowd. As she made her way from the vicinity of the theatre she waded through a mass of people just arriving as the news spread. Word was getting around about Secretary of State William Seward being attacked at his home. Rumors were rampant, some true and others clearly embellished. But nothing could be worse than the truth. She was bumped and jostled for several blocks until she broke free and for the second night in a row she walked the streets of the nation's capital alone.

CHAPTER 68
TOM KELLY
1962

"Run it again, Ethan. Tell me why you think it could be him," Tom said as he paced from one side of the room to the other.

"It's the pacing. The messages only take into account one line of communication when clearly there are two going on simultaneously. Everything in 'channel one' checks out with 'channel two' but everything in 'channel two' doesn't check out with 'channel one.'" He picked up a stack of messages and laid them out two at a time, side by side until he had two columns of seven messages each.

"Here, look at the way these line up. The time stamps are within a couple of minutes of each other and they relate to one another, see?" Ethan asked.

"Right," Tom answered.

"But these four," Ethan pulled four slips of paper from the columns and put them in a grouping of their own. "These don't relate at all to the others. There's a check and balance going on everywhere else, but not with these. And it's not just what they say, it's how and when they say it."

Tom leaned over the four messages and instantly he saw what Ethan was talking about. The thought crossed his mind that he was taking advice from a teenager using highly classified documents, but he figured it wasn't the strangest thing that had happened to him all week to be sure. And he couldn't argue with what he was seeing. Maybe he'd just been too tired to see it before. Or, more likely, he didn't want to see it.

"I'm not sure there's another explanation, Mr. Kelly. Maybe if you let me take this to the guys at the White House they can make sense of it," Ethan offered.

Tom didn't say it out loud, but suddenly it all made perfect sense to him. And the last thing he wanted was for the men at the White House to know until he could be absolutely sure. Even then, he had no idea what would happen when he told them.

"Ethan, I'm starving. Could you go down to the lobby and ask the concierge, Mr. Chase, to send up a meal for the two of us? I need a few minutes to gather my thoughts and I'll prepare something for you to take to the White House."

Ethan went downstairs to find Chase. Tom sat on the edge of the bed trying to gather his thoughts as he had said he would do, but his mind could only conjure up one word over and over. Treason.

CHAPTER 69
CALVIN WALKER
1963

Something had gone terribly wrong at the Lincoln Memorial. As the police secured the area, Fish climbed down from his perch in the tree. He had to get away before he was rounded up, but his retreat couldn't go as planned because of Calvin's interference.

As he had watched from the tree Fish had seen Calvin trailed by a police captain and a couple of beat cops. They appeared to be searching for him, scouring the area where he had been standing when Calvin threw his punch. They were also paying close attention to the ground, obviously looking for the duffel bags. Fish had been content to let them look all they wanted. The closer they got to the stage the better he liked it because they were putting themselves right where the blast zone was going to be.

Everything was going according to plan and when Mahalia Jackson's song had started Fish could hardly contain his excitement. He glanced at the areas where he knew his boys would be with their duffels and, although he couldn't pick them out in the crowd he knew without a doubt they would be ready when the time came. They were just like him, completely devoted to the cause. Actually, they were even better because they were willing to give their lives for it. Fish wasn't ready to take things that far. He didn't have a death wish. What good was changing things in society if he wouldn't be around to enjoy the fruits of his labor? No, Fish was content to let his foot soldiers bleed if necessary. Of course, he fed them fiery rhetoric about how they would all, himself included, be lauded as heroes for the cause if they were to die in pursuit of their goals. They were simpletons, he thought. He was the leader, the one with the ability to lead the troops through battle after battle until they won the war. He was too valuable to give himself up so easily. He could always find more foot soldiers. He was the general.

Still, he liked the boys who were willing to take up arms with him and he hoped they would all come out of today's event alive and well. There would be much celebration for their success. That was another promise he had made them.

Mahalia had been singing and it was clear the crowd was with her for every note. Fish had looked down to see the man who would trigger the explosion. He had chosen the spot in the tree because he could see the stage, but also because he'd be able to see the detonation with his own eyes. He was more than just the general; he was the conductor. The panic started by the fake bombs would be the signal that would start the countdown to detonation, but the man with the button knew Fish was in the tree behind him and that he was to look in that direction when he got to the count of twelve just to make sure there was no change in plans. If Fish wasn't giving him a pre-arranged signal he was to continue the count from fifteen and blow the charge. Before that they were not to look at each other at all.

Mahalia had approached the chorus of the song. Fish, the conductor, glanced once more at the reflecting pool where the panic was about to start, and then looked back to check on Calvin's position. That's when everything went wrong. He saw that Calvin was standing still and facing *away* from the stage. He was staring at something and when Fish looked in the direction he was facing he saw the det man unrolling his cord. In just a matter of seconds, Fish looked from Calvin back to the det man and like watching a movie he saw Calvin take it all in: the man with the little box, the cord, the stage, the package under the stage, the black box. He put it all together quickly and Fish saw him push his way free of the crowd and sprint for the man with the detonator.

The only actual bomb had been discovered and the panic hadn't started yet. It was too soon to blow the charge. It was all a well-written symphony with different parts and they had to happen in order for maximum carnage. As he saw Calvin sprinting he knew he had only seconds to stop him. He saw his det man register Calvin's intent and raise his other hand to push the button. At the same time the man turned to look at Fish for any sign of what he should do in this unexpected circumstance. Seeing nothing, he turned his head back to the stage and brought his finger down to the button. As he did he felt like a warrior of olden days. This was his moment of destiny. Like Sparta. Like the Romans.

In the tree, Fish had pulled the gun from his waistband and quickly fired three shots just as Calvin leapt into the air at the det man. The shots hit their targets and Fish saw blood explode from Calvin's wounds as he fell to the ground on top of the man. Fish had taken him down, but there was no explosion on stage. Calvin's desperate leap had hit its mark in time, and the sound of gunfire had alerted the men with the duffels that there was a problem. They had looked toward Fish's tree and seen fire shoot from the barrel of his gun. Most of the crowd hadn't noticed a thing. Only those in the immediate area had seen the crazed man run and jump on another man and assumed the police had shot him. The scene was quickly forgotten by all but the police as Mahalia Jackson's song came to a rousing end and the sea of people sang and raised their hands and waved their signs. The commotion was just one isolated incident among a few isolated incidents taking place around the event perimeter that day. Fish didn't have the element of mass chaos to cover his exit, but he managed to escape by doing what Calvin had done at his apartment the day before. He walked like he belonged and nobody questioned him.

At the site of the shooting, Captain Perry took the det man into custody and someone covered Calvin's face with a jacket.

The gunning down of Calvin Walker wouldn't even make the news because the most anticipated speaker of the day had taken the podium. Martin Luther King, Jr. had no idea the man who had been so moved by his speech the night before had been murdered within sight of where he now stood. The microphone carried the sound of his voice across the vast crowd, through the trees where people anxious to be part of the day had climbed to watch, echoing against the white marble of the memorial to the man who had freed his people a century before. He spoke of justice and equality and dreams.

As Calvin's blood stained the ground, Dr. King's words delivered with passion from the steps of the memorial sprang forth to be carried in the heart of activists for generations. Despite their best attempts, Kifo had been unable to keep the most iconic entreaty ever spoken about freedom from ringing across the national mall and into the very fabric of American culture.

CHAPTER 70
OLIVIA FORDHAM
1913

Olivia woke early on the morning of March 3. She had slept better than she thought she would, probably a result of the red wine. The maids assisted her in donning a beautiful dress and matching coat of yellow silk. The coordinating hat was nothing short of a spectacular confection and she paired it with simple white gloves, a long and a short strand of pearls, and low-heeled slippers. She knew they would hurt her feet with all the walking she would have to do, but she couldn't pass up the opportunity to wear them.

Edward Chase met her in the lobby. "Victoria left early this morning before I arrived."

"She's eager to get to work I suppose. I'm sure I'll see her at the headquarters."

Chase assured Olivia he was going to keep working on any angle that might help her situation and then he put her in a car for the trip to the office. When she arrived the scene was utter pandemonium. After making several inquiries she could find no one who had seen Victoria that morning.

"She might be at the starting point for the parade. Several of the ladies who came early were sent over," one staffer reported.

Olivia made her way to the meeting point for the parade participants. She saw more people than she anticipated along with a couple dozen floats and several marching bands. There were women in the clothing of their occupations like nurses and others in commencement gowns signifying higher education. She was also surprised to see so many women of foreign descent. Her main concern was the growing crowd on the sidewalks. A great number of them didn't look friendly to the cause and she worried there could be trouble.

The parade was scheduled to end its run at the Treasury Building, which was right between the Willard and the White House. Organizers were staging a pageant with women in costume representing Columbia, Charity, Liberty, Justice, Peace, and Hope. It was to be a stunning finish to the event, but Olivia wondered if the growing crowd would interfere with those plans.

She looked everywhere for Victoria with no luck. After an hour of searching, the parade was about to begin and Olivia wondered if the poor girl had given up and gone home after all. Just then, a woman wearing a white cape and riding a white horse came to the front of the parade line and began the procession. Five thousand marchers were now on the move toward the Treasury and Victoria was nowhere to be found.

Olivia cut across a few side streets to make her way back to the Willard ahead of the march. Her last hope was that Edward had information that could help. When she emerged on 14th street she was two blocks north of the hotel. As she started walking she could hear the jeers from the crowd. They were yelling at the approaching marchers, calling out terrible names and pushing and shoving. When she got close enough to see Pennsylvania Avenue she could see the spectators had crowded into the street and there was barely enough room for the procession to pass through. The lady on the horse came through just as Olivia made it to the corner. She hurried into the hotel but couldn't locate Edward. She waited for him for about ten minutes and then went back outside to watch the parade. The bands passed by along with the floats, and Olivia heard someone calling her name. She looked around as the person continued to call out to her and eventually followed the voice to the oncoming float. High atop the signage and banners she saw Victoria riding joyfully and waving. Olivia was very relieved to see her and she waved back eagerly. She could see that Victoria was trying to tell her something but she couldn't hear her over the noise of the bands and the crowd. Olivia walked along beside the float as it approached 15th street. She was motioning with her hands that she would follow her to the ending spot so they could talk.

Victoria nodded her understanding and then started waving at the crowds around her again. Suddenly she had a look of terror on her face. Olivia looked in the direction Victoria was looking to see what had scared her so, and that's when she saw it. The float had just entered the intersection of Pennsylvania Avenue and 15th street and there was a carriage barreling down 15th with no sign of stopping. The driver pulled at the reins but was unable to avoid a collision. Olivia watched in horror as the carriage and the float collided and Victoria disappeared from view.

CHAPTER 71
CATHERINE PARKER
1865

At five o'clock in the morning Catherine finally walked through the doors of the Willard. Ignoring the grieving guests milling about the lobby, she climbed the stairs and locked herself in her room. She didn't want to see anyone. For three hours she paced, wept, and retched. In alternating waves of rage and desperation she beat her fists against the bed, against the wall, and across the dresser. She couldn't even summon the strength to change her dress, which was now dotted with the president's blood transferred from Laura Keene's gown when she had kept her from collapsing. As far as she was concerned it was her just punishment—actual blood staining her instead of just metaphorical blood. Her own scarlet letter.

At eight o'clock there was a knock at her door.

"You." Catherine stood in the open doorway face to face with Edward Chase. There was an accusation in her tone. "Have you come to see the grisly proof of my complicity?" She was almost shouting as she gestured at her stained dress.

"Ms. Parker, I know you are understandably upset. I've brought you some tea. May I come in?"

"Of course. Because all I need is some tea and everything will be A-OK," she said sarcastically with a grand sweep of her arm indicating he could enter.

"I waited for you outside the theatre, but I couldn't find you in the crowd. Nor could I find you anywhere else I looked.

My assistant said you returned a few hours ago. I thought you would benefit from some time alone, but I see you've used the time to convict yourself," he told her with a frown.

"You thought I'd be celebrating? Or sleeping? The president is DYING, Mr. Chase and he wouldn't be if I had not listened to you!"

Chase took Catherine by the hand and led her to the chair by the window. When she was seated he spoke again.

"Ms. Parker, the president died less than an hour ago." He let the news sink in as Catherine dropped her head into her hands. "But you are not to blame."

She looked up. "I told Julia Grant to send the note. If she hadn't, General Grant would have been with the president and he could have protected him. I didn't pull the trigger, but I'm responsible. The tear you talk about could have saved him, but I got involved and now he's dead! And I don't care what you say about the consequences of changing history. He wanted to reunify the country. How can you say his death helped to do that rather than hurt it? Maybe if he had lived he would have had a better plan for helping newly freed slaves integrate into society and it wouldn't have taken a hundred years for them to be able to use the same restrooms we use! He could have used his influence to prevent some of the abuses of reconstruction! And maybe his wife wouldn't have gone bonkers and landed in an asylum! I can't believe I went along with this." She was pacing now and worked up into a terrible fit. "Yes, history would have been different, but maybe it would have been better, did you ever think of that? It wasn't my place to interfere. It wasn't my place. . ." The tears were rolling down her face and she sat dejectedly on the edge of the bed.

Chase could see she had finally spent her rage. It was important that she do that so she could hear what he had to tell her.

"Catherine," he had never called her that. "Black integration was a tough pill to swallow for most people at that time, both North and South. It wasn't going to happen overnight and Reconstruction would have been much worse if Lincoln and Grant had not already set the tone. As for Mrs. Lincoln, she was already suffering from instability. I'm sure the loss of her husband made it worse, but she was already traveling that road. And I have it on pretty good authority that General Grant was already well aware his wife did not want to delay their trip and was going to decline the invitation. Even so, none of that should matter to you," he said.

"Not matter to me? How can you say that? I'm —"

Chase cut her off before she could continue. "Hear me out, Catherine. I'm saying it shouldn't matter to you because it wasn't your fault. And it wasn't your fault because the note Mrs. Grant sent wasn't the tear."

Catherine looked at him with wide eyes.

"What do you mean, that wasn't the tear? I heard her debating whether or not to send the note," Catherine responded.

"Yes, but you never heard her say she had decided against it, did you?"

Catherine thought about it and shook her head no. She hadn't heard that.

Chase continued, "You were looking so intently for what you were supposed to do that you assumed that was it, but it wasn't. Mrs. Grant was always going to send that note. She wanted to go home to see her children and she was adamant about not spending the evening with Mary Lincoln. She couldn't stand the woman. You probably helped ease her mind about interrupting the meeting between the president and the general, but you didn't cause her to send the note. With or without your intervention, the Grants were not going to be in that theatre."

Catherine's mind was reeling and she was pacing again. What did this mean? *But the president is still dead so what did I do that caused it to happen that way?* She was searching her memory for every step she had taken over the past two days.

"Catherine, when these events happen I only know there is a tear in the fabric of history. I don't know what the tear is and I'm looking for it just as you are. That's why you didn't see me yesterday. I had a hunch it might have something to do with the carriage ride and I had gone in search of clues. We kept missing each other all day. But when the tear has been "repaired" I get another message letting me know what it was and how it was fixed. That's what I've come to tell you. Please, Catherine, come and sit down," he requested.

She sat on the bed beside him again and waited for him to speak.

"Your task here was to make sure the Lincoln assassination happened exactly as it truly did in 1865 and you have done that. You assumed, and I confess I did as well, that meant you were to make sure events lined up to assure the president was shot. Ironically, that part of the event was still intact. But you did repair the tear in the fabric in the theatre tonight. In fact, you did so by so tenderly caring for the fabric," he said.

She looked at him, confusion apparent on her face. "I don't understand," she said.

He continued speaking in a soothing and comforting voice.

"Before the performance you went to the state box and while you were there you carefully smoothed the fabric of the flag that had been fashioned into a swag across the front. You also straightened the portrait of George Washington and tended the folds in the flag. When you were doing this you inadvertently pulled some extra fabric behind the portrait. It wasn't much and wasn't noticeable to anyone looking at the flag, but it was enough to cause Booth's boot to get tangled and turn his theatrical leap to the stage into a leg-breaking fall."

She was still staring at him without comprehension.

"Don't you see Catherine? That was the tear. Without your interference, the flag bunting would have been smooth and Booth would have achieved his daring leap unscathed. It was his boot that ultimately gave him away. Think back to your history. Because of the broken leg, Booth sought care from Dr. Samuel Mudd during his escape. Eventually the boot, with his name inside for all to see, was discovered by authorities and led them to Booth and helped unravel the conspiracy. If he had not snagged his foot on the fabric and broken the leg he might have gotten away with murder and possibly built support for his goal of restarting the war. Your actions made sure he wasn't able to make a clean break of it, so to speak."

Catherine was in disbelief and started firing off questions in what seemed to be an attempt to continue to pin the blame on her own actions. At every turn, Chase was able to reassure her that her role had been much different than she thought. She was beginning to cry again, but this time the tears were of a different type. "Are you saying you're absolutely sure I'm not responsible for the president's death?" she asked hopefully.

"No, my dear. You most certainly are not. You are, however, responsible for the broken leg that led to the discovery of the assassin."

Catherine was finally crying with full force, but the relief in her eyes was palpable. She and Chase talked for another hour going over all the facts he knew about the situation. They stopped briefly while he had the lady's maid come and help her get cleaned up and into a comfortable lounging dress and robe. He returned a few minutes later with a tray of food and more tea. She was in much higher spirits.

"Mr. Chase, I'm sorry I took my anger out on you. I was so torn about what I thought I had caused. I'm still not sure how I feel about my decision to try and influence Mrs. Grant, but I'm so relieved to know that wasn't the deciding factor," she told him.

"Ms. Parker, (they were back to formalities again it seemed), these things are never easy. And you cannot blame yourself for doing what you thought you had to do in an impossible situation. We are only human after all," he reassured her.

"Are you, Mr. Chase? Are you only human?"

"Indeed, Ms. Parker. I won't trouble you with the specifics of my strange existence, but I assure you, I am only human. Now, you must be famished and I've brought you some of the chef's most delightful creations. Do sit and have something to eat," he urged.

"Thank you for bringing this. It looks delicious, but what I need more than anything right now is some rest. I think I'll relax for a little while and then I'll find you and you can tell me what happens next. I don't think I've ever been this tired. I'm utterly exhausted," she responded.

"Of course, Ms. Parker." Chase reached for the door, but turned to face Catherine once more. "It has been a pleasure getting to know you. You are an extraordinary woman with a bright future ahead of you," he said with genuine emotion.

"Thank you, Mr. Chase. I do, of course, hope that future involves motor vehicles and the Internet. I'll see you in a couple of hours and you can tell me where I might find 2016."

"Sleep well, Ms. Parker." He closed the door.

Catherine put the chain on the door and laid her robe across the chair. She crawled between the cotton sheets and snuggled her weary head into the feather pillow. Two nights without sleep and the spectacular events she had experienced had drained all her energy. Her last thought before falling asleep was of Laura Keene.

I hope you're okay. I'll find you tomorrow and make sure.

And with her friend's wellbeing considered, Catherine fell into a deep, dreamless sleep.

CHAPTER 72
TOM KELLY
1962

When Ethan returned from delivering the latest message to the White House, Tom was nowhere to be found. It was almost dinner time and the sun was hanging low in the sky. Ethan waited outside the door of Tom's suite for a few minutes and then went to find Edward Chase. The concierge knew where Tom was, but didn't think he should share the information with Ethan in case the boy felt obligated to tell others.

At that same time, Tom was getting out of a taxi at National Airport. Chase had arranged a flight for him and he had just minutes to make it before the plane left the gate. An hour later, he felt the wheels touch down and he sprinted down the jetway as soon as the plane door was opened. After another cab ride he stood on the sidewalk and pushed a button to gain entrance to an apartment building two blocks from the vaunted university. He pushed the buttons for residents on the third floor and below so he wouldn't alert those on the upper floors. Someone buzzed him inside and he took the elevator to the fifth floor. When he arrived at apartment 512, he gave three short knocks, paused, and gave four more short knocks in a distinctive pattern. There was no answer. He made a second attempt and when he still got no answer he put his shoulder into the door with all the force he had in him until it broke open.

The professor's apartment was just as he had imagined it would be. There were books everywhere. They were on shelves and tables and in stacks on the floor. A lingering smell of pipe smoke hung in the air along with the musty smell of the books. Everything was neat and orderly except for a hastily arranged pile of discarded papers on a table by the radiator. To anyone else the letters and numbers on them could have been anything or nothing at all. To Tom they were proof that he was in the right place. He was standing in the private home of Professor Anatoly Volkov. Only he wasn't in New Haven, Connecticut. He was on 115th street in New York City, just blocks from Columbia University. A trash can on the floor held remnants of burned papers and Tom was sure Volkov would have burned the rest if he hadn't left in a hurry. Where was the professor? Better yet, *who* was the professor? To Tom he had been friend, but now he feared that all along he had actually been foe.

Tom had stood in this room before, two years ago. At the time he was meeting with an informant who was passing along information Tom would need while traveling in the Soviet Union posing as an Argentinian citizen. The man he had met was definitely not the same person he'd been speaking with on the telephone, not the man who called himself Volkov. His contact had told him this was his sister's apartment that he used when he needed to have in-person meetings in the city. He said her husband was an administrator at Columbia and that she taught literature in a public high school. Now that Tom thought back on it he realized it should have seemed strange that a person in a covert organization would offer so much tangential information about his own family. At the time it didn't strike him strangely because Tom was just a writer looking for a story he could make a movie about. He thought they were being honest with him—that they understood he was one of the good guys.

How incredibly stupid I was. I thought this nice Russian spy was making small talk with me when he was really hiding his trail. And I bought every word.

Everything had clicked when Ethan pulled the four messages from the table and put them aside in a group. Tom noticed something about the typeface of those four. There was something wrong with the letter "H." Part of the upper left of the letter was missing and it looked sort of like a straight-backed chair against a right-hand wall. When he met with his contact, who had called himself Minsky, the written information he had been given had this identical problem with the letter. It had bugged Tom when he came across it on page after page so he had started drawing in the missing section whenever he saw one. In all the correspondence he had ever seen from Back Channel the deformed "H" had never reappeared, until today.

Tom searched through closets until he found a loose board in the floor of the one in the hallway. He opened it and found two teletype machines. One was clearly newer and in better condition than the other. However, he realized quickly that particular machine had a space bar problem; it was jammed and couldn't be used. That must have been the primary machine. The older machine had not been maintained well and he wasn't sure it would even work. Tom stuck the corner of a sheet of paper into the machine and typed an "H." It was missing the upper left section just like he thought it would.

Whoever was sending those messages was doing it with this machine, from this apartment. The knot that had been growing in his stomach since Ethan pulled the four messages was getting bigger and bigger. In his gut he knew who the sender was. But how did he know Tom was on to him and where had he gone?

Tom heard footsteps in the hallway and knew the neighbors would have called the police by now having heard him break down the door. He slipped out the kitchen window and went down the fire escape. Before he left, he took the only possible clue he could find anywhere. It was a university identification card for Dr. Hamish McAdams, Department Chairman, Literature and Letters.

When he hit the street he ducked through the rear alley and headed for the building that housed the English department. He hoped Dr. McAdams was working late because he was the only link Tom had to the elusive Anatoly Volkov.

CHAPTER 73
CALVIN WALKER
1963

Southeast Washington D.C.—the evening of the March on Washington, from the police blotter:

Henry Dockins, aka Fish, was found dead of multiple gunshot wounds in an apartment believed to be the headquarters of a radical group known as Nyeupe Kifo (*white death* in Swahili) that planned to disrupt the events of the day at the Lincoln Memorial. The attempt was thwarted by police.

When Fish left them at the event to save his own skin he signed his death warrant. They were brothers-in-arms. Foot soldiers for a cause. Warriors for freedom. They were willing to die for the cause. Their leader may not have been willing but, in the end, he died for it anyway.

CHAPTER 74
OLIVIA FORDHAM
1913

Olivia pushed and shoved her way through the crowd to the scene of the accident. When she got there she was pleased to see it was not nearly as bad as she'd feared. In fact, the float was still limping along to its place in front of the Treasury Building and the carriage driver had managed to back the horses out of the way. There was no sign of Victoria on top of the float and Olivia looked around frantically for her.

They didn't see her, but she saw them. Victoria was standing on the sidewalk supported by James. She was brushing off her dress, but seemed to be none the worse for wear. He was beside himself asking over and over if she was alright.

Olivia reached them just as she heard Victoria answer his question.

"Yes, James. I'm okay! Despite the fact that you have nearly run me over twice now!" The two young people laughed as their terrified granddaughter looked on.

CHAPTER 75
CATHERINE PARKER
2016

Catherine woke slowly, her sleep resisting the pull toward consciousness. She stretched and rubbed her eyes before sitting up in bed. She looked across the room and saw her blue interview suit hanging where she had placed it before her nap the day she arrived. She saw the flat-screen TV and the modern phone by the bed. A glance out the window showed her the Washington Monument was at its full height and surrounded by American flags, not grazing cows.

It was a dream. The whole thing was just a dream.

She sat there leaning against the headboard contemplating how it could have been a dream when it was so real. Just then the phone next to the bed rang. She picked it up.

"Ms. Parker, this is your wake-up call. Your car will be ready to take you to your appointment at two o'clock as promised. Is there anything else I can do for you?" asked the efficient voice.

"Yes, could you have Mr. Chase come up to my room please?"

"I'm sorry, ma'am, whom did you wish to see?"

"The concierge, Edward Chase," she answered.

"I'm sorry, Ms. Parker. He's helping a guest with an urgent matter down near the Treasury Building. Is there anything I can do for you?"

"No, thank you. I'll be down to meet the car at two." She put the phone back in the cradle and grabbed a bottle of water from the nightstand. She still had an uneasy feeling, but tried to shake it off as she dressed in her suit and heels and arranged her hair in a professional and flattering knot at the base of her neck. She grabbed her bag and went downstairs to the waiting Town Car.

"Good afternoon, Ms. Parker," said the driver. "I have the address of your appointment. Traffic is a bit heavy this afternoon, but we'll be there in plenty of time."

She thanked him and settled into the leather seat. A few minutes later they arrived in front of the glass and steel building with the beautiful view of the Capitol. *Cameron, Hanson and Smith* read the elegant and understated sign above the massive doors.

Cameron, Hanson and Smith. Lawrence Cameron. She sat there lost in thought while the driver held her door open. She took out her phone and pressed the contact number for their receptionist.

"I need to reschedule," she told the driver as she waited for the call to be answered. "Please take me to Ford's Theatre."

CHAPTER 76
TOM KELLY
1962

Tom asked some students where he could find the English department and from there he found a faculty directory that led him to the office of Dr. Hamish McAdams. Walking down the hall he could see the door was ajar and a light was on. From inside the office he heard the sounds of someone hastily moving things about and talking on the phone. Tom peeked through the crack in the doorway and saw a man packing an old valise with the handset of his office phone tucked under his chin as he spoke rapidly. The words were foreign to Tom, but the voice was not. He waited until the man hung up the phone before he pushed the door open and stood face to face with the man as he fastened the buckles on the bag. The man must have heard the creak of the door because he turned around and saw Tom standing there.

"You don't look like a Scotsman to me, Anatoly," Tom calmly said.

If Volkov was surprised to see Tom standing there he didn't show it.

"I'm anyone I need to be, Thomas. I always have been," the old man said.

He wasn't what Tom had expected. Volkov, aka McAdams was short, not more than 5'4", and he couldn't have weighed more than a hundred pounds. He was stooped over with age and his hands shook slightly as they hung by his side. He looked to be decades older than he should have been, given the timeline of his defection to America. But it was his eyes that fascinated Tom. They were bright green and they nearly danced with life. It was easy to see there was much going on behind those eyes. Whatever his body was lacking he more than made up for with a sharp mind. That part Tom knew well.

"I don't know where you think you could run that would be safe, Anatoly. Or Hamish. Or whatever your name is. What you've set in motion will ensure that you can't run far enough, fast enough to save yourself," Tom said.

"I'm not trying to save myself, Thomas. I'm too old to run and if you think that's what this is you aren't as bright as I thought you were. I've been here for forty-two years. I don't see any reason to leave now."

Tom's head was spinning with mathematical calculations. Something didn't add up. The professor said he had come to America only fifteen years before, when he was old enough to take on the mantle of protecting the secret organization. The young son of Nicholas' messenger couldn't be a man of more than about fifty years of age, but the man before him was clearly much older. And he just said he had been here forty-two years? That means he would have to have come to the United States in 1920, just two years after the assassination of the Tsar.

Volkov could see that Tom was struggling to make sense of things. Suddenly things began to fall into place. Tom raised his head to look the old man in the eye.

"It was you. It was you all along," he said incredulously.

"Sit, Thomas. I'll tell you everything. We have nothing to hide anymore and time is short."

CHAPTER 77
CALVIN WALKER
2016

When he opened his eyes he was afraid to move. He wasn't sure if he was dead or alive, in this world or the next. As his surroundings came into focus he pushed himself upright and felt something fall from his chest. He picked up the papers that had fallen and looked at them. Columns and columns of data. Specs for the new software that Diagnosis Digital was having patent problems with.

Calvin rubbed his eyes and stood up from the chair where he had fallen asleep while reviewing the data. He was standing in his room at the Willard, but he couldn't understand how that was possible. Only moments earlier he had felt the life drain from his body as he lay on the ground at the Lincoln Memorial. He remembered the searing pain and the hands of strangers as they worked to assess his wounds. He remembered the sound of Dr. King's voice as he began his iconic speech. Had it all been a dream?

His cell phone rang from the nightstand where he had put it to charge the night before. He spoke briefly with an assistant back at his office who had a last minute addition for the meeting. She told him she had sent it to his e-mail. There wasn't even time to change clothes.

Calvin brushed his teeth and washed his face before stuffing the paperwork in his briefcase and heading for the door. He was still in a daze. As he approached the elevator he remembered his encounter the morning before. Quickly he turned and walked down the hall toward the suite where he had reviewed Dr. King's speech. When he was several yards from the door of the suite it opened and a couple with two small children walked out. They were dressed for sightseeing and the kids were excitedly talking about going to the air and space museum. Calvin went back to the elevator and rode it down with the family. They were talking about all they had done the day before in the city. Clearly they had not just checked in.

Edward Chase saw Calvin get off the elevator and he made a move to intercept him before he left the building. He could tell from the look on the man's face that he was unsettled, but Calvin was so focused on getting outside that he didn't see the concierge coming toward him and didn't hear his name called. Chase thought it might be for the best. Calvin probably needed some time to himself to process everything he had seen. Chase would be waiting for him when he returned.

The meeting with the patent attorney went fine. The new information his assistant had sent helped fill in the gap that was holding up the patent and the attorneys felt certain everything would proceed normally. Calvin was happy to let his corporate counsel take the lead because his own mind was still spinning, but as the morning wore on he began to shake off the vivid dream he now believed he'd had.

After the meeting, he went for a walk on a street known for tourist shops. He had promised his son that football jersey and he liked to bring his daughters something from his travels as well, even though they acted like they were too old to care. He knew it was an act and that they'd be disappointed if he didn't bring them a trinket of some type.

At the fourth store he finally found the jersey. It had the number 10 with "Griffin III" on the back and it was so big he knew it would swallow his son whole. Will would probably lose interest in it before he outgrew it. Now Calvin could browse for trinkets for the girls. He found a miniature of the Alexander

Calder mobile from the National Gallery of Art. It was delicate and whimsical. Cecily would like this. She was fifteen now and consumed with all things art-related. She wanted to be a famous painter of watercolors.

Amanda would be harder to pin down with a tourist trinket. She was thirteen and believed her older sister to be terribly flighty and her little brother to be hopelessly sports-addled. Amanda fancied herself the intellectual of the group. She was the bookworm and told anyone who would listen that she was applying to one college and one only—Harvard. Her father knew most of the items in this store would fall flat with her so he continued walking. Eventually he stopped at the display of one of the ubiquitous street vendors who hawk their wares from sunup to sundown along the busiest sidewalks.

He doubted there would be anything there for her among the plastic snow globes and t-shirts with slogans like "Future President" and "You Don't Know Me: Property of Witness Protection", but something caught his eye. It looked like white plastic, but when he picked it up he found it was heavy and carved from stone. Emerging from the stone was a statue of Martin Luther King, Jr. Calvin remembered reading about the opening of the new memorial, but he had never seen it. This would mean something to Amanda so he paid for the statue and asked the vendor where the memorial could be found.

"Seriously, man? Where do you think it would be? It's down by the Lincoln Memorial," the vendor said.

"Of course," Calvin answered. He wasn't far from there and he started walking.

He couldn't explain why he felt apprehensive as he approached the memorial. There were quite a few people milling about, most in quiet reflection. Calvin noticed there were two large, stone sculptures with a walkway through the middle of them. Pushed further ahead, closer to the water of the Tidal Basin and with a magnificent view of the Jefferson Memorial, was a third stone that looked as though it had been hewn from the center of the larger ones. He picked up a brochure from an information box and learned that the split stone was called the "Mountain of Despair" and visitors passed through it to reach the forward stone, called "the Stone of Hope." As he made his way around the forward stone, he came to the larger-than-life statue of Dr. King. Calvin examined it and was astonished to see the likeness to the man in his dream. The sculptor had captured the look of determination in his eyes. On the sides of the memorial were walls inscribed with his famous quotations. Calvin walked around and read each one. There were quotes about freedom and justice. Others touched on war, poverty, and education. They were inspirational and aspirational words meant for all races and classes, not just the privileged. Calvin knew all this. He had studied the works of Dr. King in college and yet, in this setting and given the dream he'd had the previous night, he found himself profoundly moved by the words in a way he had never experienced. Just then he realized two older men were close by and they were having a conversation he had to hear. Both had been at the March on Washington in 1963. They talked of the crowd that day and the atmosphere of brotherhood that permeated the large gathering. They laughed as they remembered rushing ahead of the crowd as it left the Washington Monument because they wanted to get to the Lincoln Memorial first so they could get a good spot in front of the stage. One remarked how he thought about putting his feet in the reflecting pool to cool down from the August heat. The other remembered that some of the speeches went a little long for his taste, but they were all good in their own way. They both agreed none was better than the one by Dr. King and they were glad they had been there to hear it. Calvin didn't feel bad about eavesdropping because the two men sounded like they had told their stories a thousand times and enjoyed the reminiscing. They had been young men then, and now, in their old age, they had come to this place to relive a day that had meant so much to them. Calvin thought about introducing himself to them and joining in the conversation, but what would he say? *I was there too. It was some day, yep, sure was hot. I read that speech before he gave it that day. Oh yeah, and somebody shot me and I died there, but here I am and I haven't aged a day.* No, he wouldn't join the conversation. It had all been a dream and he knew that now, but he liked hearing the old men as they continued talking.

"I was so excited to hear Marian Anderson sing. She did a fine job."

"She did," the other man nodded. "Yes sir, she did. And when that Mahalia Jackson went to singin', Lord, you could have carried me on home!"

"I remember. That was a heavenly sound." The men were lost in thought for a moment.

"Wasn't that when it happened?" the first man asked.

"When what happened?"

"When that man got shot. Wasn't that when Mahalia was singing?"

"Yeah, I believe that was when it happened. We never did hear anything about that shooting so that ole' boy must have been alright. Might have just been a prank."

"Probably was. We were darn lucky nobody did try to hurt us that day. You know all the talk that was going on."

"Oh, I remember it well. It would scare me a lot more today if that was happening."

"We were young then. We weren't scared of anything."

"You're right. We thought we were as bulletproof as this stone statue!"

The old men laughed, unaware of the man on the other side of the statue who had steadied himself against the stone.

Calvin decided he wasn't up for the walk back. He got to the corner and hailed a cab to take him back to the Willard.

CHAPTER 78
OLIVIA FORDHAM
1913

After the parade, the crowd couldn't stop talking about the presentation at the Treasury Building. The finale had been everything the organizers hoped for. Also, as they had hoped, Victoria was among a growing number of young, well-to-do ladies who were ready and willing to join the effort that would bear fruit seven years later when the 19th Amendment was passed and ratified by the states. It wasn't full equality, but it was a critical step. Word around town was that when President-Elect Woodrow Wilson arrived in the city that day he asked where all the people were since there were so few to greet him at the train station. He was told they were attending a march for women's suffrage.

Olivia and James helped Victoria back to the Willard. She had turned her ankle in the collision, but aside from that the only damage she suffered was a dirty dress and a lifelong conviction that James was a menace on the road. They were happy to fill in the blanks for Olivia.

The night before, Victoria had struggled with whether or not to send a message to James. She ultimately decided she would try and find him in person and if she wasn't able to she would leave a note in care of his brother at the congressman's office. She spent hours on the note, searching for just the right tone. The next morning she went to Capitol Hill and found him working alongside his brother. When he saw her he was astonished. He had been struggling all night with his decision to go home that afternoon. Every time he thought he had made up his mind, he changed it and by morning he was still debating with himself. He'd even had a heated argument with his brother, ultimately telling him to butt out and that he thought the women who were planning to march were very brave. His brother told another staffer he'd never seen James look that way and thought Victoria must be something special to have him in such a tizzy.

When she walked in the office he knew with certainty he could never have boarded the train and she knew that no matter what nonsense he might spout today she was just going to have to work on him and eventually he'd come around. The eloquent words of her note were lost in a jumble of speech on both sides with each professing to be the fool in the situation.

Victoria had been asked the day before to ride on one of the floats and when the time came for her to leave he had promised to finish his work and catch up with her before the big finale. He thought he could get a car to take him there, but he hadn't counted on the traffic jams caused by the event. After hoofing it as quickly as possible he feared he was about to be late when he saw a carriage for hire on a back street and asked the driver to get him to the Treasury Building as quickly as possible. Apparently the noise of the parade excited the horses and their driver was unable to fully control them. In the end there were no serious injuries and the parade continued. It wouldn't warrant a footnote in the history books, but it was paramount to Olivia. It was the collision in the story of her grandparents' meeting that she'd always heard about.

She left the young people alone to spend some time together, but promised to meet them for an early dinner. Chase was relieved to see them and felt that everything would work out as it should.

❧

At six-thirty, Olivia went to the dining room to join James and Victoria as promised. They were chatting easily and laughing and anyone could see they were completely enamored with one another. They had a lovely dinner and both thanked Olivia for her kindness and for helping to bring them back together. Olivia had apologized to James for telling him to leave, but he wouldn't hear any apology from her. He told her she had been exactly right and that he was quite sorry to have been in such pitiable shape.

Olivia knew the time had come for her to leave them. She told them she was going back to New York the following morning, but before she took her leave she wanted to ask them one question.

"If you could see fifty years into the future, what do you hope it will look like?"

Victoria looked like she was going to answer, but James beat her to it.

"I don't care what it looks like, as long as I'm seeing it with Victoria."

Olivia knew what they didn't—that in four short years he would go to war and leave his youth on the battlefields of France. That their son, James Jr. would follow in his father's footsteps and become a lawyer and that his daughter, a dark-haired girl named Olivia, would one day do things her grandmother could only dream of, things Victoria had helped make possible. Olivia knew they wouldn't have fifty years together, but it wouldn't matter. They would make the most of every moment and she could leave them now knowing everything was as it should be.

She bid them goodbye and left the restaurant, but she couldn't resist just one look back. She felt a presence over her shoulder and knew he was watching too.

"They're exquisite, aren't they, Edward?"

"Indeed they are, as is their granddaughter."

He offered her his arm and walked her to the elevator.

"Will you sleep well tonight, Olivia?"

She smiled. "Yes. Tonight I believe I will sleep better than ever before."

"Very well. I'll see you in the morning."

"In the morning, Edward." And the elevator doors closed.

CHAPTER 79
CATHERINE PARKER
2016

It looked a bit different, but very familiar. People don't like change when it comes to historic places. The people in charge of Ford's Theatre recognize that and they've kept it as close as possible to the way it appeared on that night in 1865. Across the street, Catherine saw the sign outside the boarding house denoting it as the place Abraham Lincoln died.

The Petersen House. That's where they carried him.

Catherine went inside the theatre and walked around. The seats were different and there were modern lights, but everything else looked remarkably the same. She looked to the state box and saw its draped flag and portrait of George Washington. It looked very close to the way she remembered, but she could see subtle differences. She thought about going upstairs, but she couldn't bring herself to get any closer to the box than the spot where she sat in the audience that night. It just didn't feel right. It had been a dream and she didn't belong there. She felt that if she saw it for real she'd forget the way it looked in her dream. As terrible as it was, she wanted to remember the details she had dreamt. They were so vivid and complete. Looking in from behind glass wouldn't be the same. She went back to the lobby and proceeded down the stairs to the museum.

She was astonished at what she saw. There were artifacts that matched those in her dream exactly. She saw the president's clothing, stained with his blood. There was the playbill announcing his attendance and featuring in large, bold letters the name of the woman who befriended her in the dream. LAURA KEENE, it read. Even the original door to the state box was there, with the hole drilled in it so Booth could have looked inside before he entered. Catherine kept looking for one thing in particular until she found it. In a glass case not three feet in front of her was the boot of John Wilkes Booth. It had obviously been cut when Dr. Mudd removed it from the murderer's swollen leg. She remembered the way she had felt when Edward Chase told her she had been responsible for keeping history intact by causing Booth to fall and break his leg and here was the evidence of that fateful break. She knew it was just a dream, probably brought on by her excitement at the thought of making this city her home and her dreams of doing big things with her life. She thought about Edward Chase and wondered if he had just been a dream. She hoped not. He was an interesting man with a calming demeanor. She would like to be friends with him if she got the job and moved here. And Laura Keene, what an interesting person she must have been. Catherine wondered if she was really a nice person like she was in her dream or if she had been a diva like so many of the stars of today. She preferred to think of her as a nice lady.

As Catherine browsed the museum she saw a display about the conspirators including Mary Surratt. She thought about visiting her boarding house in the dream and about meeting her daughter, Anna. She wondered about Anna. Had she been there when they hung her mother from the gallows? Was Mary really part of the conspiracy or was she caught up in something she didn't fully understand? It was all so fascinating to think about and Catherine decided she'd visit the museum store on her way out and pick up a few books about the president, the assassination, and the conspiracy. There had to be much more than she had, literally, ever dreamed.

She took one more turn around the exhibits on her way to the store. She would only have a few minutes to choose her books before she'd have to find a cab and make her way back to Cameron, Hanson and Smith. They were kind enough to reschedule her appointment, but she had no intention of being late this afternoon. The dream was over and it was time to get the job—time to start making her own history.

She stopped one last time at the display of items that were found inside the state box after the assassination. That's when she saw it and her hand flew to her lapel. It was her grandmother's diamond brooch, on a gray velvet display pedestal under the lights. It was only inches away from the president's bloody shirt. She remembered pinning it to her good navy suit before she lay down for her nap, ensuring she'd have her grandmother with her in spirit for her interview. Then she remembered the lady's maid retrieving it from the rosewood box on her dresser and pinning it to her deep blue gown before she left for the theatre in her dream. She had wanted to feel like her grandmother was with her there, too. And now, as she looked down at the suit she was wearing, she could see it wasn't there. Somehow, someway, it had been found on the floor of the state box on the night of the assassination. It wasn't possible, yet there it was, her one-of-a-kind family heirloom with the distinctive design her grandfather had drawn for the jeweler. Under the brooch was a description card. It read:

Diamond Brooch
Owner Unknown
This diamond brooch was found on the floor of the state box after the assassination. It may have belonged to actress Laura Keene who rushed to the president's side after he was shot.

It wasn't possible, and yet it had happened. It wasn't a dream. Catherine stood there absorbing what that meant.

Across the room, a father was telling his little boy about the brave president who had given his life for his country. The boy thought it sounded awfully sad. All he could think about was the tall man in the stovepipe hat who had been killed, and how he'd had a little boy too. At that moment, he noticed the woman in the navy suit and high heels at the next display case. She seemed to be studying a beautiful, shiny piece of jewelry. Something about her struck him as odd. She had tears running down her face, but he realized she didn't look sad like he did. Whatever she saw in the case wasn't making her sad at all.

"Look, Daddy," the little boy said. "That lady is smiling."

CHAPTER 80
TOM KELLY
1962

For one hour, the man Tom knew as Anatoly Volkov told him a story he swore on the greatness of Mother Russia was true. His real name was Boris Bespalov and he wasn't the son of Tsar Nicholas' messenger at Tsarskoe Selo. He *was* the messenger. The tales he had spun about being the second generation of the organization were all part of his cover. After completing his formal education he had taken a job at the royal estate in the mews when he was thirty years old. He took care of the new motorcars and sometimes drove members of the family to various appointments in town if their normal driver was otherwise engaged. Since he had access to cars and was known to the guards he was able to come and go with ease, and he became the conduit between the imprisoned Tsar and his loyalist supporters. When the Romanovs were taken from Tsarskoe Selo, Boris was sent away with strict instructions to keep the lines of communication open among the loyalists. The organization grew from there and in 1920 he fled to New York with the secrets of the defeated regime in his possession. He had been in New York ever since. For ten years he operated in secret with the help of those still inside the old country. He cultivated a new identity as a Scottish-born professor of literature. High-level Russian contacts helped forge the necessary documentation and his inherent love of literature made his transition an easy one.

The Scottish accent was a bit harder to master, but his fair coloring and ability to charm his way through most situations helped immensely. He was living not a double life, but a triple life. He was Bespalov and McAdams and before long he added Volkov to the list. His Volkov persona would be his official "Russian" identity. For his safety and the safety of family still in the U.S.S.R., Bespalov no longer existed publicly.

Everything else he had told Tom about the founding of Back Channel was true. The organization Tom had infiltrated two years before would have been an invisible wall to anyone looking. Had it not been for his chance introduction to "Volkov" (in correspondence only, never in person) he would never have gotten into the pipeline. Volkov allowed it because he thought Tom could prove to be a useful resource at some future time. That time had come when the perfect storm presented itself. First, Castro made himself the number one target of the American government with his dedication to communism right in the backyard of democracy. Next, Khrushchev put his "secret" missiles in Cuba where they were discovered by the Americans. Finally, Tom had made the phone call on behalf of the American government to access Back Channel in an effort to avoid war. Though none of these things were set in motion by Back Channel, they worked perfectly to set up a scenario the group needed to make their final move, the one that had been in the works for more than forty years.

"You were going to burn it all down," Tom said.

"No, Thomas. *They* were going to burn it all down. When I left Moscow in 1920 we believed it was a matter of four or five years until we'd be able to get the bloody Bolsheviks out of power. I came here not to hide, but to give the organization a place from which we could rebuild a shadow government without interference from the secret police. First we had the iron-fisted Lenin, then when the puppet Rykov took power it looked like the perfect opportunity for retaking the government.

We put the wheels in motion, but before we could act Stalin assumed leadership and our plans fell apart. We regrouped and waited for a new opportunity to present itself, which happened when Malenkov assumed the top position and it was our best shot because he and Khrushchev fought each other for control, which made the government more vulnerable than it had been in years. The problem, Thomas, was that we couldn't pull it off. All along, Back Channel had believed itself to be stronger and better supported than it was. But when the time came, only the old-timers like me who had been around during the time of the Tsar were willing to lay our lives on the line for a new revolution. The others had lived so long under the iron fist of Communism that they didn't believe we could succeed and they feared being arrested as traitors. Ultimately, Khrushchev gained the upper hand and here we are, now more than forty years removed from the event that defined our purpose and we are nothing more than a small group of secret communicators. Our power has long been tapped. But then you came along two years ago and your interest in us and belief that we were larger and greater than we are reignited the fire that has driven our core members all these years. You gave an old boys club a new injection of purpose and it was like the old days. We've always had our ways of intercepting communications; I mean, we're not amateurs. But that's all we've been able to do. The foot soldiers have all died off or lost interest. Others will take the secrets to their graves, but in the interest of self-preservation they refuse to participate in further actions. We had become, in essence, a group of old men whose hobby was intercepting and decoding messages. We were watchers from the outside with no hope any longer of being the instruments of change. And then you called."

"I don't understand. If you're just a bunch of old guys longing for the glory days of the imperial realm what could a phone call from me do to change things? You just said you don't have any foot soldiers anymore," Tom asked.

"We have much more than foot soldiers now. The moment those missiles were discovered in Cuba and the battle lines were drawn, everything came down to the communication trail. War will begin or be avoided based on what happens with that communication. If we control the communication, if we can manipulate it to our advantage, then our 'foot soldiers' are the entire Soviet military. They will do the work for us. It's brilliant, really. The government we so hate will use its mighty forces to obliterate itself. All we have to do is a variation on what we've been doing for decades; intercept the messages and decode them. Only now, we inject our own messages to achieve the ends we desire," the old man said.

"You desire the destruction of the modern world?" Thomas nearly screamed. "You're not idealists for some lost, romantic view of the motherland. You're madmen, willing to kill millions of people because you couldn't have your own way. Is that it, Boris? You couldn't win any other way so you'll take the coward's way out and burn it all down?"

"Thomas, it's only cowardly if there is no greater purpose in the end. With a greater purpose it then becomes an act of self-sacrifice—of heroism. Russia is a big country and there are still loyalists ready to rebuild. As a matter of fact, there are a few thousand of them in a remote village in Siberia, a place your government would likely not bother targeting with its nuclear arsenal. Yes, Moscow and the other population centers would be gone, but in a hundred years the seeds of the motherland would be rooted deeply enough to bring forth the new Russia that resembles the old one, but with the principals of freedom and democracy that your country so enjoys."

Tom was sitting across from him with his head down. He looked completely defeated.

"Think about it, Thomas. Your citizens have been volunteering to die for your ideals for two hundred years. What makes this different? We will be our nation's George Washington and its Patrick Henry. 'Give me liberty or give me death', right Thomas?"

"And the American nation? You would wipe us out to save your Siberian remnant?" Thomas asked.

"Collateral damage, I'm afraid. Isn't that a term your government uses?"

Tom stood. He looked at his watch and saw that it was after 1 a.m. The thirteenth day.

"You didn't plan on one thing, Boris. You forgot that communication is a two-way street. In a few hours the world will wake up to learn that an agreement has been reached between the United States and the Soviet Union. Some of the details will remain secret, but the gist is your country will pack up its toys and get them the hell out of the Western hemisphere. I don't know what will happen to you, although I'm sure it won't be the glorious end you had hoped for."

"You can't stop it now, Thomas. The fuse has already been lit," the old man said.

"I didn't have to stop it. You stopped it yourself," Tom answered.

Bespalov looked confused and agitated. Tom realized the man had no idea his secret had been discovered.

"The teletype, my old friend. I found your machines in your apartment. Didn't you wonder how I found you here? I used your old machine, the one with the broken 'H' key, to send a new message through the pipeline. Your cover has been blown and you're exposed. Your plan is off and I imagine with the number of KGB spies in this country they're pretty hot on your trail by now, which means I really must be going."

As he stood to leave a thought crossed Tom's mind. "You know, you remind me of the *Wizard of Oz*."

The old man smirked. "How is that, Thomas?"

"When the curtain is pulled back you're just a little man making a lot of noise and frightening people with smoke and mirrors, but you have no real power."

Tom started for the door but turned back one last time to speak to the man he had thought was a friend. He saw that the old man had slumped in his chair and his face showed a look of total and complete defeat. Tom briefly wondered if he would avail himself of the cyanide hanging around his neck to avoid capture. Or maybe there was no such thing. It might have been a lie like so much of the story he had spun, or maybe just a spy game cliché. Tom felt nothing but disgust for him.

"You should have gone with the Tsar and his family when they were taken from Tsarskoe Selo. You could have died a noble death with them in that basement. Then you would have been heralded as a martyr. Now it won't matter what name you call yourself. Your countrymen will call you traitor."

CHAPTER 81
CALVIN WALKER
2016

Calvin walked into the Willard with purpose in his step. He saw Edward Chase approaching him from across the lobby, but he threw up his hand to wave him off and continued to the elevator. When he got to his room he began tearing his clothes off. Once he was down to his boxers and socks he stood in front of the full-length mirror and what he saw stunned him.

He ran his finger across the scar running from under his arm down and across his abdomen. Just below his right kneecap another one started and it snaked down his calf, sometimes as wide as an inch. The third scar was in the other leg. It was a huge, ugly mass concentrated in his thigh. It looked like a section of flesh and muscle had been blown away.

When Calvin was in fourth grade he had been roughhousing on the playground with some other boys when one of them dared the others to swing as high as possible and then jump off. The winner would be the one who could land the farthest from the swing set. When his turn came, Calvin pushed with all his might and soared higher and higher with each attempt. When he knew he could swing no higher, he closed his eyes and leapt from the swing. He landed outside of the mulch in the area that was covered with tiny gravel. He came down on his right elbow and slid nearly two feet, ripping the flesh from his arm. Until today, that was the only scar his body bore. But now he had hideous scars, marks that had been made as bullets tore through his body.

Calvin could feel himself starting to shiver but he wasn't cold. He grabbed a t-shirt and shorts from his suitcase to dress himself and sat down on the edge of the bed. Nothing made sense and he was beginning to feel like he was losing his grip on reality. He heard a knock at the door. When he answered it he found Edward Chase standing there.

"What happened to me?" Calvin asked without preamble.

"May I come in?" Calvin stepped aside to allow the concierge to pass then he repeated himself.

"What happened, Chase? Why can't I remember?"

"You do remember, Mr. Walker. You remember everything."

"That doesn't make any sense! And there's no way it could have happened!"

Chase could see that Calvin was coming unglued. He convinced him to sit down and he took the seat across from him.

"You did what you were sent to do, Mr. Walker. You stopped Kifo from detonating the bomb under the stage."

Calvin still wasn't speaking. He couldn't say what he was thinking so he let Chase continue his explanation.

"The duffel bag bombs were duds. The police found them last night at the apartment where you met Fish. They believe they were meant to create a panic only. It's possible the group couldn't afford multiple bombs so they settled for one carefully placed version where it could do maximum damage. This is just conjecture, of course, but I believe the investigation will bear it out. Police found the undetonated bomb under the stage and there were no injuries. In fact, the program wasn't even disrupted.

Fish did not fare very well in the end. It appears his compatriots did not take kindly to being abandoned. He was found with multiple gunshot wounds and the others have scattered to the winds. Thankfully it appears Fish was the only casualty in this unfortunate episode."

"You know that's not right," Calvin said softly. "If what you're telling me is true, then everything happened the way I remember it." He turned to look directly at Chase with a pained expression. As he continued to speak he became more emotional. "The pain was excruciating. I felt the blood draining from my body. I was getting weaker and weaker and I could hear the voices around me saying 'we're losing him.' I thought about my wife and kids and my parents and siblings. I won't say I saw my life flash before my eyes, but I was hyper aware of everything I was leaving behind. Then the voices around me seemed farther away and muffled and I couldn't understand them anymore. I started to feel really cold and my vision became like a tunnel and then went black completely. The last thing I remember hearing was the sound of Dr. King's voice as he was giving his speech. I don't know how I could hear that and nothing else, but that's what I heard just as clearly as I can hear my own voice right now. And then there was nothing. I was gone, Mr. Chase. Dead on the ground beside the Lincoln Memorial. And if that doesn't convince you then how do you explain this?"

He tossed a printout of an old newspaper page down on the table in front of Chase. On the way back to the hotel he had made a stop at a public library branch. He could have just looked it up online, but he wanted to see the actual microfilm newspaper from the day after the march. He found what he was looking for buried on the fourth page. It was the story of a man who had been shot at the march at the same time and in the same place as Calvin had been standing. The article went on to say the shooting appeared to be unrelated to the event and that no others were injured. The suspect had not been caught and there was no mention of the stage bomb or anything else. Either there was some bad reporting or someone had gone to great lengths to create distance between the shooting and the larger event itself. But none of that really mattered to Calvin. The only thing that he cared about was one line at the end of the second paragraph.

The unidentified victim was pronounced dead at the scene.

Chase read the article and considered how he would explain what happened to Calvin. In all his years as the concierge, he had helped shepherd people through historical events, but he had never lost a traveler before this. He had heard of other guides who had and how that turned out each and every time, but since he hadn't experienced it himself he was afraid to believe it could be true. He certainly didn't want to give any of his charges false hope.

"Mr. Walker, I have been doing this a long time, but there are others in the world who have much more experience than I. Stories have circulated and I had reason to believe it was possible, but I was never sure, until today."

"Sure of what?" Calvin asked.

"For whatever reason, everything you experienced while traveling really happened. All your actions, emotions, even the things you were able to taste and smell were all real. And yes, you did die on the ground beside the Lincoln Memorial. But from what I have been able to learn from others who do what I do, those who die while traveling return to their normal lives just as those who do not die during the experience. At least that's what I've been able to gather because it's an extremely rare occurrence."

Calvin was trying to let the idea sink in.

"So what you're telling me is that no matter what I did I was going to be safe the whole time? That I couldn't be killed?"

"I can't say that with certainty, Mr. Walker. There are many things I don't know and it's often very troubling to me, but I know that's no consolation for you. I'm not even sure there are any hard and fast rules for what we're doing here. Like you, and like everyone in your situation, I go forth on faith a good deal of the time. I'm very happy that you're here and safe. I just wish I could tell you more."

Both men sat in silence as Calvin tried to contemplate what that meant. Finally Chase spoke again. "It doesn't really matter what could have happened because you're here and you were able to right the wrongs. Kifo is not a household name now so they clearly didn't regroup. You put a stop to it. You met a man who had a tremendous impact on history and you had a tremendous impact as well although it will remain a secret. Since you fixed everything, that little news story about someone being shot will stay buried like a million other unsolved crimes in United States history. For all practical purposes, it never happened. And that means everything that *was* supposed to happen did happen. You can overthink it, but you'll never figure it all out. Trust me. I've had to accept that I'll never have all the answers either. Just know that you were here for a purpose and you fulfilled that purpose."

It wasn't everything either of them wanted to understand, but somehow it was enough.

Later that afternoon Calvin said goodbye to Chase and caught a flight back to Chattanooga. The kids were glad to see him, but his wife noticed he was strangely quiet. He'd been struggling all the way home with whether or not to tell her, or anyone, about what had happened to him. It was all just too much for the human mind to comprehend and he was already convincing himself it had been a misunderstanding of some sort. He just couldn't make two and two add up to ten.

After dinner when the kids could stand it no longer, he went upstairs and changed into his casual shorts and shirt before hauling his suitcase up onto the bed. He unpacked the football jersey, miniature mobile, and the King statue replica. He was getting ready to go back downstairs to bestow the loot upon the waiting kids when he saw something sticking out from under his gray suit. He reached in and pulled out several sheets of paper. They were the handwritten notes Dr. King had allowed him to keep. He reread them, taking in the prose with new eyes. Tears were welling up in his eyes when his wife walked into the room. He didn't care whether it had been real or not. Something profound had happened to him.

He wiped his eyes and stood to greet his wife. As he did he noticed the ugly scars on his legs. He realized his wife had no visible reaction to them. She acted like they had always been there. He had a thought.

"Babe, did I ever tell you how I got these scars?"

"Only about a thousand times. I will say the story has worked wonders at keeping Will from the edge of the rocks."

"How so?"

"*How so?* Calvin, the boy loves his daddy, but he doesn't want to walk around with scars the rest of his life like you have."

He needed her to fill in the blanks. "And how exactly have my scars kept Will safe?"

"Baby, those ugly scars taught our boy that climbing on the rocks at Lookout Mountain is dangerous! But don't you worry. I've always thought they made you seem a little dangerous, which every girl secretly wants of course."

She laughed over her shoulder and left the room. Somehow history had been rewritten, and yet everything that mattered had remained the same. Calvin gathered up the souvenirs and headed for the bedroom door. He could hear the girls teasing their brother that dad had probably forgotten the football jersey. He listened to them for a minute and then started down the stairs.

Yes, Calvin thought as the kids gathered around him to get their goodies. *Climbing Lookout Mountain can be dangerous. But the view from the top, not to mention the sound of freedom, is so worth it.*

CHAPTER 82
OLIVIA FORDHAM
2016

"Olivia. Olivia, it's time to wake up."

Olivia heard Jane's voice and felt her friend place her hand on her forehead as if to check for fever. She opened her eyes.

"What time is it, Jane?" Olivia asked as she sat up in bed.

"It's seven-thirty. Are you feeling alright?"

"Just a little groggy, that's all."

"I was so worried. When you didn't call last night I used my key and came to check on you. I've never known you to go to bed so early, but you were sleeping comfortably so I left you alone. Just to be safe I came back around ten o'clock and you were tossing and turning and calling out names I'm unfamiliar with."

"What names?"

"Victoria and James. And you kept talking to Edward so I went to find Mr. Chase, but he was not in the hotel overnight. I wasn't able to wake you so I called Dr. Goodwin in New York. He thought there was no cause for alarm. He said your body would be more tired and need more and more sleep as the tumor grows so he urged me to leave you be. I checked on you all during the night and you were at times peaceful and agitated. You seemed to be having very vivid dreams."

They just think they've had a dream or others assume they had too much wine with dinner or some bad fish. Wasn't that what Edward had said? But there was no way what had happened was just a dream. Olivia threw the covers back and hurried to the closet with Jane at her heels. The clothing hanging there was what her maid in New York had packed. There were no Edwardian dresses or elaborate hats. She walked to the bedroom window and looked out. The cars were normal, late model sedans and the ubiquitous taxis.

Jane knew all about the episodes Olivia had and she was accustomed to caring for her through them be it a few hours or several days. She could tell Jane what happened and she knew her friend would understand. But something held her back. This time had not been like the others and she wasn't sure she could explain it. She also wasn't sure she *wanted* to explain it. Unlike the other times, she didn't want this one to be explained away by her medical condition. It was too personal and too real.

"I was exhausted yesterday afternoon and decided to turn in early. I'm so sorry I worried you, Jane."

Jane wasn't convinced Olivia was telling her the whole story, but she was sensitive to her friend's feelings about what she was going through. Olivia had been a strong, independent woman for as long as Jane had known her and she knew these episodes and the life she was facing were hard for her to reconcile. She decided to let it go. Olivia looked none the worse for wear after her difficult night.

"I'm going to get dressed. What is the first item on our agenda today?"

"You have a meeting with the Smithsonian representatives here at nine o'clock and then a luncheon with the Juvenile Diabetes Research Foundation folks at noon."

"Wonderful. Please have coffee and tea service and pastries sent up for the morning meeting."

The meeting went according to plan and when the representatives from the Smithsonian left Olivia was satisfied that everything was on track for the upcoming announcement. She had just enough time to freshen her makeup and head over to the luncheon. Jane had talked with Mr. Chase and the car was waiting.

Olivia stared into the mirror, freshening her powder and lipstick without conscious thought. Her mind was miles away, years away in fact. She was walking the streets with Victoria and listening to James say things that would have been unheard of a hundred years later. She was listening to women argue for rights she herself had always enjoyed, and she was watching as her family history was being written. It couldn't have been a dream. She knew that it wasn't. Perhaps it was the tumor. She struggled with the possibilities, but knew she could never ask Edward Chase. The likelihood that the entire experience was yet another "episode" was too high and she didn't want him to think her mad. She ran a comb lightly over her silver hair and called out to Jane that she was ready to go.

As she crossed the lobby of the hotel she heard her name called and she saw that Edward was standing behind the concierge desk motioning for her to join him. She sent Jane ahead to the car and walked over to speak with him. He was helping another guest and she stood to the side waiting for him to finish.

While she waited, she looked around her at the furnishings and thought how different they looked now. Her eyes eventually settled on the wall of cubbies behind where Edward was standing. She glanced across them until something caught her eye. It wasn't obvious, just something that didn't seem to fit. It was a tiny cubby, unlike the others in that it was slim enough for just a single message to be held there. It was nearly invisible to the naked eye but Olivia had always had an eye for symmetry so she noticed the simple difference.

While she thought about what that could mean Edward finished with his guest and came to speak with her.

"Did you have a pleasant evening?" he asked.

She looked for anything in his expression that might indicate he knew about her experience, but there was nothing there besides his normal, professional demeanor.

"Yes. I was more tired than I realized and I slept soundly."

"That's excellent news. I trust you have a full day planned?"

"Very full. I'm on my way to a luncheon now."

"Yes, of course. I wanted to let you know I have a package here for you. Since you're going out I'll have it sent up to your room. One of the maids found it last night here in the lobby and recognized that it belonged to you. Would you like to see it before you leave?"

"Yes, please."

He reached under the desk and pulled out a large box. When he opened it Olivia pushed aside the tissue paper and what she saw took her breath away. It was the yellow silk hat she had worn the day of the march, the last time she had spent with Victoria and James. She looked up and saw that Edward knew exactly what it was. They exchanged a look that spoke volumes.

"Shall I send it up to your room?"

"Yes, Edward, please do. It is one of my greatest treasures."

CHAPTER 83
TOM KELLY
2016

Tom stood dripping on the bathmat in his suite at the Willard. After his return trip from New York he found that Ethan had removed all the communication equipment from the suite and left a note thanking him for all he had done to avert disaster. In the note he said he would come by to see Tom the next morning and urged him to get a good night's sleep. Tom did just that, and when he woke up the next morning it was to a wake-up call from Edward Chase telling him his reservations for lunch with his investors were all set and that he would have a bottle of champagne standing by for what he knew was bound to be a celebration. He was back to his normal life and everything that had happened over the past few days seemed to be only a dream. He couldn't even find the note Ethan had left. It was like none of it had ever happened. He decided to give the bath salts another try but vowed not to fall asleep this time.

During his long, lavender soak he thought about all that had happened. Anatoly/Hamish/Boris and the near-disaster of nuclear war. Ethan and his mother, an intern pouring through classified documents, and finding the lynchpin of the problem. The two Kennedys and their reliance on him during the crisis. The whole thing was crazy and by the time he was drying off to get ready for his meeting Tom decided it had all been a very elaborate dream. He wanted to sit down at his laptop and look up everything he could find on the crisis, but there was no time. He dressed in his best suit, which meant the one that was the least wrinkled from his travels, and went downstairs to meet his potential investors. The dog and pony show was on.

⌛

Chase had arranged for a private table in a corner of the restaurant and Tom met Scott Langdon there a few minutes before the others were scheduled to arrive. They caught up on everything Tom had uncovered on his scouting trip and Langdon was blown away by the photos from Abu Dhabi. He let Tom know that he would only have to impress one person today instead of two. One of the potential investors had told Langdon that he couldn't make the meeting, but that if he got a good report from the person coming today he would be in for $250,000. That meant Tom had to pull out all the stops to make this meeting go well.

Right on time a well-dressed woman in her thirties walked in trailed by a couple of men in suits. It was clear she was the one in charge. She had shoulder-length blonde hair and piercing eyes and when she smiled at him Tom thought he could feel a blush creeping into his cheeks.

Shit, he thought. *I was planning to pitch to an old crusty soldier-type.*

He knew he would have to get past his attraction to her and stay on script, although the script would have to be altered a bit. All he had been told about the investor was that he (Tom had *assumed* he'd be dealing with a man, mistake number one) represented a company that does business in both the public and private sector and has significant Defense Department contracts in play. Tom was pretty sure this woman wouldn't be as open to the boy's club way of thinking he was prepared for, given the three amigos who had recommended her company.

She accepted a warm hug from Langdon and stuck her hand out to introduce herself to Tom.

"Hello, I'm Emily Travers from PCS."

"Tom Kelly," he said as he shook her hand.

"I've heard a lot of good things about you from Uncle Scott," she said as she flashed that killer smile again.

Uncle Scott? Tom glanced at Langdon.

"I'm not really her uncle," Langdon said. "I was very close to her father and he made her call me "uncle" because I told him "Mr. Langdon" was too formal for such a little girl. Now she's not a little girl anymore, but she insists on calling me that." Langdon gave Emily a look like a father would give his daughter. Tom could see that they were close. "You should know she also has an Uncle Joe and an Uncle Marcus. All three of us knew her father well."

With the preliminaries out of the way Tom launched into his pitch. Even with her close connection to the three men it was clear right away that Emily Travers came to the meeting to be sold on the idea. She wasn't giving away money just because she liked the three men. Tom worked hard and showed her the script, the location photos, and the headshots and bios of the actors he had lined up. He showed her the projected cost versus three profit scenarios. Actually, only two made an actual profit, the other was a break-even scenario he felt duty-bound to include. He'd make sure she got her money back if he had to mortgage his arms and legs, but he couldn't promise her a profit and she seemed impressed that he was up front about it.

Finally, he ended with the importance of the story. He talked about the men and women in uniform, their sacrifices and what makes them the kind of people who are willing to give everything for a nation that seems to offer them comparatively little in return. He knew he had her with his closing. She was one of them—a true believer. She agreed to fund $1,000,000 on the spot. With the second investor's promise of $250,000, Tom had everything he needed to make the project happen. The light was officially green and Tom felt a lightness he hadn't in ages. He knew it would wear off and he'd start feeling the pressure of delivering on his promises, but for the moment he was enjoying the sensation.

As usual, Edward Chase seemed to know everything that happened in the hotel and he arrived with his bottle of champagne and filled everyone's glasses. They shared a toast and Emily's assistants excused themselves to deal with other business. As Tom lingered over the bubbly with Emily and Scott he asked about her company.

She told him the company had been founded by her father in 1970, five years before she was born. She had grown up learning from him and eventually working alongside him until his death two years ago in a skiing accident. PCS built communication platforms and had been integral in the early use of e-mail and improvement of fax technology. Today, they built multimillion-dollar secure systems that could encrypt messages that were sent from military bases to aircraft in theatres of war and to secure sites around the world. They were on the leading edge in both military hardened technology and consumer-protection data management.

It sounded like a big job and he was glad someone with her sensibilities was doing it. They moved on from business talk to how her father had become acquainted with his three veterans. Tom learned that her father had taken a leave of absence from college and joined the Army in 1965. He met Langdon and Green in Vietnam and became friendly with Chamberlain later. They had stayed in touch throughout their various careers and each served as consultants for the others' work.

The afternoon was getting late and Emily said she needed to get back to her office. PCS had a Washington field office, but their main facility was out of state. She walked with them to the hotel lobby and handed Tom her business card. It was heavy cream card stock with the PCS logo in bright orange with a palmetto tree and a crescent moon. The image seemed vaguely familiar and he realized he had never asked her what PCS stood for.

"It stands for Palmetto Communication Strategies. And if you're wondering about the odd orange logo you can thank my father for that. It's the state symbol for South Carolina, and of course, it's Clemson orange. My father was a diehard Clemson man. He even turned down a full scholarship to the University of Virginia in favor of Clemson and I'm not sure my grandmother ever got over the shock."

Tom felt a nagging feeling growing in the pit of his stomach. Emily Travers smiled at him again, shook his hand and left the Willard. Tom sat down hard in one of the French chairs.

"Are you okay, Tom?" Langdon asked. "You weren't expecting her to say yes were you?" He gave Tom two hard pats on the back. "You're in it now, kid. Time to make a movie."

"Her father. Tell me about him," Tom said.

Langdon thought Tom was looking a little green.

"He was a great man. Before college and before the war he had been an intern at the White House around the time of the missile crisis with Cuba. I don't know what he saw and he never talked about it, but it changed him. After that all he ever talked about was how we could fight the war with guns and tanks, but that the real war would be decided by communication between leaders. He was convinced a miscommunication at that level could prove disastrous on the battlefield. I didn't really get it, but he must have been onto something because he went home to South Carolina after the war and turned it into a booming business. I think half of that little town where he built it must work there."

"Fort Mill," Tom muttered.

"What? Yeah, that sounds right. I wish you could have met him, Tom. He would have liked you. But then again, I'm not sure Ethan York ever met a man he didn't like."

Tom stood up and bid Langdon goodbye. He gathered his bags and went to check out of the hotel. Edward Chase had asked him to stop by the concierge desk on his way out. After they said their goodbyes, Chase walked to the wall of cubbies and pulled out a folded piece of paper. Tom took it and slipped it into the outer pocket of his briefcase. At Chase's insistence he took the hotel car to the airport. This time it was a brand new Cadillac. Only the best from the Willard.

On the flight home he took the paper Chase had handed him from his briefcase. He unfolded it and found it was the note that Ethan had left him the night he removed all the phone equipment from his suite. He read the last lines the young man had written him. He hadn't noticed before the palmetto tree and crescent moon Ethan had drawn next to his signature.

If I don't see you in the morning I know our paths will cross again someday. Thank you for all you've done. I hope someday I can contribute to this country half as much as you have done these past days.

Sincerely,

Ethan York

Tom got off the plane, bought a bouquet of his mother's favorite lilies, and told the taxi driver to take him to Unity

Cemetery. He knelt by her grave and placed the flowers lovingly at the base of the headstone.

"Mom, I have something to tell you. I'm going to be a filmmaker."

Epilogue

Evening had fallen on Washington, D.C. and Edward Chase was eager to bring his day to a close. He went about his tasks as usual, but couldn't shake the feeling of melancholy that had plagued him for days. The year so far had been a difficult one, among the most difficult he had known. One of his travelers had died while traveling and he hadn't been sure whether or not the man would wake up in modern times. Another had a health problem he hadn't known about and he had nearly pushed her too far. More than ever before, he was struck with the knowledge that he was playing with people's lives. But he couldn't stop, for his hardest year by far had been the one where his traveler had failed the task she was given. The consequences had been terrible, although he and the woman were the only ones who knew for certain because they had been the only ones privy to both timelines. The woman had not been able to forgive herself and was currently confined to a mental hospital where she raved day after day about traveling back in time and how she had changed the course of history. Of course, no one believed her and Chase would never forgive himself for choosing her and ruining her life. Until that day he had naively thought success was guaranteed. Now he knew failure was possible and it haunted him each and every time he had to choose another traveler. But what was the alternative? He had chosen this life and he had no choice but to live it until such time as his work was finished. He knew that when that day came, he, like the librarian who had chosen him so many years before, would resume his normal, human life. He would resume aging and live out his days as any other man until he passed from this life. No one would know who he had been, just as no one knew of the others. The travelers would forget about him, attributing their experiences to dreams or sickness. Those who knew the truth guarded it for themselves. Only a few would seek further, as he had. Perhaps some would go far enough to take his place guiding travelers.

He knew some of them, his counterparts at the finest hotels in London, Dublin, Paris, and Rome. There were many more all over the world, likely in the United States as well, although he had never met them. Their stories of how they came to be were varied and secret. They were a society of shadow figures, appearing and disappearing as needed, giving up their own lives to serve history. Some were concierges like he was. Others were librarians, train conductors, tour guides. They were anything they needed to be for the portal they served. As he organized his work area for the night he asked himself a familiar question. *Knowing all that I know now, would I have chosen this life?*

As many times as he had asked himself that question he had never answered it and tonight would be no exception. A well-dressed gentleman had just entered the famed lobby and Chase recognized him at once. Duty called. He put aside his ruminations, straightened his jacket, and approached the man.

"Mr. Staynings?" Chase shook hands with the gentleman.

"Yes, I'm Eric Staynings."

"Mr. Staynings, my name is Edward Chase and I'm your concierge. Welcome to the Willard."

Acknowledgements

The first time I visited the Willard Hotel I was struck with a sense of awe by the history of the place and the feeling of gravity that permeates the space. I had reserved the Jefferson Suite as a location for shooting a series of interviews for a television show I was producing. While I was there I couldn't get over the feeling that I was standing in a special place—a place where the walls could tell stories featuring some of the most famous and infamous people and events of our nation's history. And since walls cannot talk, I was intrigued by the idea of being able to speak for them, with the added perspective of a fictional scenario that could be both fascinating and terrifying at the same time. I have taken artistic license with many historic moments and intermixed fact with fiction and have done so with the intention to preserve the spirit of the true event while giving the characters the freedom to interact in a meaningful way. Any historical inaccuracies are mine entirely.

So where does fact meet fiction in what you've just read? To begin, Chapter 2, "The Grande Dame" is completely accurate. Abraham Lincoln, Ulysses S. Grant, Mark Twain, Julia Ward Howe, and many more have all found a night's rest at the Willard during extraordinary times.

Martin Luther King, Jr. did, in fact, stay at the Willard the night before the March on Washington and legend has it that he finished his "I Have A Dream" speech there. However, history records that the portion of the speech we know so well, even the title itself, was likely an ad lib taken from an earlier speech Dr. King had given at another event. The day of the march there were several speakers and it may have been that by the time he spoke the crowd may not have been responding as fervently as he had hoped, which may have prompted him to add the extra content that went down in history as one of the greatest and most well-received speeches in American history.

One insider nod if you're into dates is the room numbers to which three of the guests are assigned. Catherine Parker is in room 414, a nod to the date President Lincoln was shot on April 14th. He died early the on the morning of the 15th. Tom Kelly's adventure begins in room 1022, referencing the October 22nd date of President Kennedy's televised speech to the nation about the nuclear threat. And Calvin Walker's room number, 828, is a nod to the date of the March on Washington, August 28th. Olivia Fordham is the exception to this pattern because she stays in the Jefferson Suite, which is also referred to as the Presidential Suite if you are planning to book a stay at the Willard and would like to experience all the comforts Olivia enjoys. The description of the layout of Jefferson Suite is entirely accurate. Ironically, the concierge desk itself has changed somewhat since the first time I was at the Willard. The desk is still in place, but it is now the reception desk and the concierge area has moved to another part of the lobby. I opted to put it back to the way it was when I saw it originally because I could picture Edward Chase there with a grand vantage point from which he could conduct his important work.

I must acknowledge friends and family from my childhood through the current day whose names I borrowed for various characters. My sons, Chase and Ethan, lend their names to main characters, as does my husband, Kelly. My niece, Catherine Jane, is the namesake for Catherine Parker, and though Laura Keene is an actual historical person, she shares the name

Laura with my sister and I like to think it is a nod to her as well. My mother, Jane, is the inspiration for the important, though briefly-seen character of Olivia's friend and caretaker. My mother has been taking care of people all her life and even when she's not in the room she is an important part of the lives she touches. Joe Chamberlain, the Navy SEAL takes his name from my father, Joe. Thanks also to Lisette Cameron, Lesley Hanson Mills, and LaDonna Smith Killebrew for the names of a high-profile law firm and to John Perry for a conscientious police captain who takes Calvin Walker's concerns seriously. Finally, thanks to my brother-in-law, Mark Staynings, for the character at the end who seems destined to take the next journey. Mark must wonder often if he's stumbling through some nutty history since joining our family. For those whose names I didn't use this time, keep an eye on future stories because I have a place for all of you. Some of the locations that do truly exist including Fort Mill/York County in South Carolina, Fort Mill High School, and Clemson University are used with my thanks. I'm a big fan of all three and as I sit here writing these acknowledgements I'm wearing my Clemson orange.

Special thanks to Barbara Bahny and the Willard Intercontinental Hotel for providing background information on the hotel itself and the important history that has taken place there, with additional gratitude to Colin Smith and to Willard Associates and Oliver T. Carr, Jr. for allowing me to use the name and image of the hotel to tell the story. From the beginning I wanted to use the real place; it just didn't seem right to make up a fictional name when the real thing is so magnificently rich with history. One of the hotel managers, Abdulla, gave me an extensive private tour and I apologize profusely for losing my notes that include his last name. It was an excellent tour and helped a great deal with the accuracy of my descriptions. The hotel has a history gallery that I recommend visiting if you are in the area. The Willard has played host to many more people and events than I have covered here. I also highly recommend taking a break from sightseeing in the nation's capital to sit for a moment in Peacock Alley and just soak in the atmosphere. You can almost imagine Mark Twain parading down from the back stairs. The Willard is known as the "Residence of the Presidents" because many of our nation's leaders have connections to the hotel, but it actually *was* the residence of the president for nearly a month in 1923 when Calvin Coolidge ran the country from the Willard after the sudden death of Warren Harding. Coolidge didn't want Mrs. Harding to be rushed out of the White House, so he conducted affairs of state from the hotel. The presidential flag flew over the hotel entrance during his residency. There are many fascinating facts waiting to be discovered in the Willard's halls.

I'm also very grateful to the National Park Service and to Ford's Theatre and William Cheek and Jeff Leary for hosting me for a private tour of the theatre and the Petersen House. Standing on the stage at Ford's and being able to get the complete perspective of the leap made by John Wilkes Booth and the proximity of the actors and the audience drives home the intimacy of the act and how truly surreal that moment must have been for those present. And standing in the Petersen House in the room where Abraham Lincoln died when the house is not open to the public is a sobering experience.

This book would not have arrived in your hands without the efforts of my editor, Laura Burnett Staynings, and my literary attorney, Amy Laughlin, who thankfully didn't set up a block against my e-mails when I would write every week to ask what was happening. And thanks to Peter and Caroline O'Connor for the beautiful cover. Your work perfectly captured both the mystery and grandeur I imagined for Edward Chase and his beloved hotel. I would also like to thank Bill O'Reilly for his amazing work, *Killing Lincoln*. Growing up a Kentucky girl, we studied a great deal about Abraham Lincoln and his ionnation, but O'Reilly's book went well beyond those widely-known facts and provided an excellent reference rich with detail about the entire environment surrounding the event. It is a must-read for fans of Lincoln history.

And finally, my most fervent thanks go to my husband and sons for their love and support and for understanding that writing all night and sleeping all day sometimes works for me better than the other way around. And thanks to Daddy, just because.

ABOUT THE AUTHOR

LeAnne Burnett Morse is a native of Kentucky and a graduate of Western Kentucky University. After more than 20 years writing and producing for television, she authored the non-fiction *Images of America: Fort Mill* and is currently writing a new historic fiction novel, *The Hunley Letters*. *The Willard* is her first novel. She and husband Kelly have two sons. They make their home in South Carolina.

32618753R00241

Made in the USA
Middletown, DE
11 June 2016